WHAT GOES AROUND

Amber Gray

To Anne,

my Norweigan friend at The keg. Thank you for welcoming me into your circle,

(June) Amber x

Copyright © 2023 Amber Gray

All rights reserved

The characters and events portrayed in this book are fictitious. Any similarity to real persons, living or dead, is coincidental and not intended by the author.

No part of this book may be reproduced, or stored in a retrieval system, or transmitted in any form or by any means, electronic, mechanical, photocopying, recording, or otherwise, without express written permission of the publisher.

Dedicated to Gemma, Verity and Emmi-Rayne

PART 1: KATHLEEN

1. Bird in a cage.
2. Enticement.
3. Snare.
4. Losing Freedom.
5. Ties.
6. Entrapment.
7. Prisoner.
8. Bonds.
9. Tethered.
10. Another Tie.
11. Dead End.
12. No Escape.

PART 2: MARIAN

1. Stepping Out.
2. Departure.
3. One More Step.
4. Road to Hell.
5. Crossroads.
6. Another Path.
7. Journey.
8. Crossing the Bridge.
9. New Horizons.
10. A New Beginning.
11. The Road to Madness.
12. Escape.
13. Fresh Start.
14. Diversion.
15. Bump in the Road.
16. Layby.
17. Back on the Road.
18. Where Paths Meet.
19. A Path Well Trodden.
20. Car Crash.
21. Driving Through Fog.
22. Pathway to Healing.

PART 3: SHAUNA

1. Greyness.
2. Light.
3. Outcast.
4. Madhouse.
5. Misery.
6. Vulnerable.
7. Psychotic.

PART 4: DOLORES

1. Setting Sail.
2. Jelly Fish.
3. Marooned.
4. Shipwrecked.
5. Floating.
6. Castaway.
7. Hook, Line and Sinker.
8. Driftwood.
9. Washed Up.
10. Raft.
11. The Deep Dark.
12. Sea Legs.
13. Seasick.
14. Lost at Sea.
15. Cave.
16. Swimming Against the Tide.
17. Murky Depths.
18. Hoorah, Up She Rises.
19. Waiting for the Tide to Come In.

PART 1

KATHLEEN

Dark, sticky blood pooled on the hearth, like red treacle; his tight sneer replaced by the slack mouth of a guppy. As his life drained away, she felt nothing.

CHAPTER 1

BIRD IN A CAGE

Manchester, 1940s.

The kitchen window was misted, so Kathleen gave it a quick wipe and peered out at the breaking day. A thick frost complimented the greyness of the morning, softened only by the amber halo around the streetlamp.

Kathleen tugged at the piece of fabric draped across the window to let in what little light there was, her mind on the morning chores before school.

The fire had been prepared, the last of her jobs before she climbed into bed the previous evening, exhausted. Before the war, it had been her father's task. Now, as the elder of the two girls, it was hers.

Crouching on the tiny rag rug, so grimy with

years of wear that it shone, she lit the screwed-up newspaper and watched with fascination as it caught fire. She took the tin shovel with its long wooden handle and propped it up on the grate; then she held a large piece of newspaper in front of the fire until it clung to the shovel, sucked in by the vacuum.

Her father had taught her the basics of housewifery, and she thought of him every time she set the fire, aching inside for his comfort. There was no time for sentiment now, though; her mother would be waiting for her tea.

Soon, the fire was roaring so she removed the shovel and hooked the kettle carefully in place, warming herself in the glow. It was the only part of the room with any life, the rest being starkly furnished with oddments picked up or inherited over the years; spindly wooden chairs, an old horsehair settee, and a few knick-knacks which sat on the dark iron mantelpiece. The smell of musty damp hung in the air and Kathleen rubbed her arms against the chill as she left the comfort of the fire.

She cut the bread into thick slabs, stabbed one onto a toasting fork and held it up to the heat. The bread took on the golden bloom of fresh toast and she salivated as she spread it with dripping from the pot. She loved this part of the day where she was alone, and her mother was quiet.

The kettle emitted its piercing whistle, so she unhooked it and placed it on the hearth. Clambering onto the wooden stool, she stretched up, only just managing to reach the tea caddy down from the shelf over the sink. The rickety stool wobbled – *oh my Lord, she'll have a dicky fit if I spill any!* – and the tin slipped from her hand, scattering loose tea onto the draining board. Trying to ignore her palpitations, she quickly scooped it up, thankful it was dry so she could put it straight back in the caddy. There would be hell to pay if her mother found out.

She put three scoops into the pot, poured on the scalding water and stirred. Then she replaced the lid and covered the pot with the grubby woollen tea cosy. She placed toast, tea and cutlery carefully on the tin tray, along with her mother's china cup, and started the slow climb up the narrow stairs to her parents' room.

'I've got your breakfast here, Mam,' she said as she approached the door.

'Look what the bloody cat's dragged in,' Mam cackled. 'You look like no one owns you. Where've you been, to India to pick the bloody tea?'

Good, it was the cackling today.

'I had to get the fire going, Mam. My dad used

to do that.'

'Watch your mouth, you cheeky little mare. Your father isn't here, is he?'

Kathleen dodged her mother's raised hand, and carefully set the tray down. She kept her head down, but her mother's attention was only on the food. She snatched the toast, chewed greedily, the dripping running down her chin, greasing her scowl, then she complained it was cold. Kathleen retreated silently, leaving her mother's bitter words hanging in the stale air.

She went into the bedroom she shared with her younger sister. Rosie was rolled up like a sausage in the eiderdown, her stockinged feet hanging out of the end.

'Rosie, it's time to get up, come on. The fire's going and there's bread and dripping today.'

Rosie muttered something while pulling at her bonnet, so Kathleen threw back the sheets and tickled her feet. Rosie squealed and sat upright, rubbing at her eyes.

'Come on, kid, we need to get dressed. I'll make the toast while you have a wash.'

'Toast? Have we got bread?'

'Yes, we have, and dripping too!'

Rosie squealed with delight and sprang out of bed, allowing Kathleen to whip away the filthy sheet, which she shook out of the window to dislodge the bugs. If it had been a better day, she would have scrubbed it and hung it out, but that would have to wait. Instead, she went back downstairs, taking advantage of the day they had bread. No doubt her mother would have something to say later but, for now, she gazed at the golden slice and inhaled the wonderful aroma.

Once they had eaten breakfast, put away the pots, stoked the fire, filled the coal scuttle, swept the floor and drawn the curtains, they shouted a quick 'Tar-ra, Mam!' and left for school. They pulled their tight woollen cardigans across their sunken chests, against the chill of a November wind.

'What mood do you think she'll be in when we get back, Kath?'

'I'm buggered if I know, but she's driving me half mad the way she flits from one to the other.'

'I know, and I think she's getting worse.'

'I think you're right, Rosie. She's either singing and waltzing round the kitchen, or else she's knocking seven shades of you know what out of us. From a cackle to a crack, I always think.'

'I prefer the waltzing,' Rosie giggled as they quickened their pace.

When they arrived home, freezing and hungry after a long day at school, they slid into the kitchen.

'About time an' all!' came the roar from above. Their mother was still in bed.

Kathleen went up, dreading what Mam would have to say.

'Where've you been til this time?' she demanded.

'Walking home, Mam. It's freezing out there, so we didn't dilly dally, just came straight home.'

'Aye, well I'm starving here. Bring me something up, will yer?'

'Right, Mam, but there's not much in, only bread, dripping and a few spuds.'

'What do you expect, eh?'

'I'll see…'

Before Kathleen had chance to finish her sentence, her mother had knocked her to the floor. She slumped out of the room, tears stinging. By the time she got back down to the kitchen, Rosie was toasting the bread at the fire.

'You're a good girl, you are, Rosie,' she sniffed.

'Are you alright, Kath?'

'Yes, but no waltzing today.'

It must have been about a year after her father had left for war before the first visitor came. The girls had been sent out to play, but it was a freezing February day, and they could no longer feel their fingers and toes. They plucked up the courage to tap on the door, but it was no use. The neighbour's net curtain moved aside, then was quickly straightened. Kathleen hopped up and down, rubbing her sister's hands, trying to stop her shivering and sobbing.

'Why won't she let us in? We'll be good,' Rosie whimpered.

'Because she's wicked, that's why. If our Dad finds out, he'll have a dicky fit, then she'll be sorry.'

Emboldened, Kathleen banged on the front door, shouting to be let in, complaining of the cold and the hunger.

The door opened a crack and her mother appeared, half-dressed, clutching a flimsy robe to her chest. 'Get gone, you ungrateful little mares,' she seethed.

The girls flinched as the door slammed and they scampered to the end of the street. They tried to keep warm by playing hopscotch, hoping Mam would relent soon. Finally, they heard the latch go and the door opened. A young man slipped out. He smiled warmly, then walked off at quite a pace.

The neighbour's curtain twitched again, and the girls edged into their home, quietly, in shock. They could hear Mam humming upstairs, lumbering about. When she finally appeared, she looked at them with such contempt they shrunk even further into themselves.

'Don't you ever dare tell your father any of this,' she said, scowling. 'Cos if you do, your lives won't be worth living.'

She finished by slapping each of them around their heads. They crept upstairs, rubbing their burning ears as they went.

Later, they were called down for tea.

'There's crumpets and jam there for you,' Mam declared, wearing a strange smirk.

'Is this a trick?' whispered Rosie.

'Shh.'

The girls ate quickly and quietly. After mopping up the last traces, they cleared the plates and washed up, wondering what they had done to deserve this rare treat.

As well as her mother's moods, Kathleen had to cope alone with her own bodily changes. The monthlies had started, and she needed to talk to Mam about sanitary protection. Of course, she mocked her.

'Sanitary protection?' she howled, her laughter bringing tears to her eyes. 'Sanitary protection is a rag in your bloomers which you'll change and wash as you need to.'

What else did Kathleen expect? Like all the other challenges, she'd have to get on with it as best she could.

The war was dragging on. She didn't know when, if ever, her life would change, when her father would return to soften the edges. Her one consolation was the letters which arrived, albeit sporadically, from wherever he was posted.

> *My Dearest Girls,*
>
> *I hope you are both well and being good for your mother. It won't be long before I'm back in Longsight and we can be a family again. Meanwhile, you must help as best you can with the chores.*
>
> *It doesn't seem right, me being out here having all these adventures, while my family is suffering hardships, as I know you all are. But keep going, girls. I'll be back when this war ends, and remember I'm saving all my kisses for you.*
>
> *I'm doing alright, so don't worry about me, keep your heads down and try hard at school.*
>
> *Looking forward to the day when I come back home, and I can see my girls again.*
>
> *Your loving father xxxx*

When the war eventually ended, and her father returned, Kathleen was happy beyond belief. His warmth was like treacle. Her mother was less than happy, and she made no attempt to hide her disdain.

Life returned to a different normality. The nation's food supply was patchy, and money was tight, so feeding the family was still a struggle.

Although her father was happy to be home, he seemed to wear a tiredness which wasn't there before. It may have been the war taking its toll, it may have been that he was a few years older, or it could have been that his wife was more demanding than ever. Whatever it was, her father looked beaten.

Kathleen didn't understand much of what was happening in the lives of her parents. She only knew that her father was weary and her mother's moods were unbearable.

It was difficult to avoid the odd clip around the ear, even more difficult to avoid the hurtful comments which came in a constant stream: 'You're bloody useless, get out of my sight, you useless bugger, I couldn't care less if you're dead on your feet, get that floor scrubbed, get that grate cleaned, set the fire, be quick, you feckless git.'

If it wasn't for her father sticking up for her, or her sister wrapping her little arms around her, Kathleen didn't know what she would have done.

CHAPTER 2

ENTICEMENT

A stunner looked back from the mirror, but eighteen-year-old Kathleen couldn't marry this image with her own sense of self. *If only I could be as lovely as I look.*

She reached for her lip liner and glided it skilfully around the outline of her mouth, forming a cupid's bow at the top. She filled in the outline with the red lipstick she had bought yesterday. She pouted at her reflection and hoped she didn't look like too much of a floozy with the red lips, not least to keep her mother from calling her brazen.

It was Saturday, the big dance night in Manchester. A knock at the door made her start. With one last glance, even she could see she looked good. Her pencil skirt clung tightly to her slim thighs and showed off the curve of her bottom perfectly. The fitted jacket flattered her figure; showed off the roundness of her bosom, the breadth of her shoulders and her narrow waist. She twisted round once more to check the seams of her stockings, then she grabbed her handbag and went downstairs. She didn't want to risk facing her mother's disapproving looks, so she headed straight for the front door.

'Tar-ra Mam, Dad,' she shouted down the lobby where she waited for the backlash. She heard no response, so she slipped quietly out of the house, closing the door gently and turning around to greet her friend.

'God Joan, you don't know how good it feels to be out. I've had the day from hell and me mam's proper getting on me nerves. She never has a nice word to say and the house stinks like shite. Me poor father to be stuck in there with that mare of a woman, God help him.'

'Come on, it can't be that bad,' said Joan. 'But it doesn't matter now. We're free, if only for a night, and I'm going to dance until I drop.'

'Me, too. I can't wait to dance this week away. Who knows, I might even meet a handsome stranger and get whisked away to Wonderland.'

'The nearest we'll get to Wonderland is soddin' Woolworths!'

They laughed and trotted along the street towards the bus stop, linking arms and swapping tales, giggling like schoolgirls trading secrets. The toils and frustrations of the week slowly waned as they looked forward to an evening of freedom.

They arrived at the dance hall, joined the queue and chatted while they waited to get in. Too vain to wear thick winter coats, they shivered as the November chill hung around them and stung their work-worn hands. Their short jackets may have accentuated their trim waists, but they were no contest for the biting wind. They clung to each other for warmth and support, vowing to wear their big coats next time.

After a long, cold wait, they made their way through to the main bar and dance floor, holding on to each other for reassurance. It was dim but they could see some people were up already, gliding, gyrating and twirling to the music while the band belted out Glen Miller's *In the Mood*. Some girls, braver than Kathleen, were dancing alone; others danced with partners.

'Look how happy everyone looks,' Kathleen said. 'When will I feel happy like them?'

'Oh my, we are feeling sorry for ourselves tonight, aren't we? Come on, let's find a table,' suggested Joan.

As they approached the seating area, they heard a commotion at the entrance, and they looked to see what the fuss was about. A group of men had arrived by coach, spilling noisily onto the car park. Kathleen squinted, as if this would help her get a better look. She stopped and gripped Joan's arm as one of the men caught her eye. He was tall and stocky, smartly dressed and had a distinct cleft down the centre of his chin. His hair was black with a quiff Brylcreemed to perfection and: *Oh Lord, a smile that would stop clocks and hearts.*

There was no doubt he was handsome but, despite being in the company of others, he looked a bit self-conscious the way he kept casting his gaze down to the ground. *Hey up lad, there's nowt to see down there, look at me!* He gave her a half-smile as he caught her staring, and her stomach flipped like her mother's dolly tub on wash day.

'I thought you were going to pass out then, for a minute. Who were you looking at?' asked Joan.

'What do you mean, who was I looking at? Did you not see him, the one with the Kirk Douglas chin?'

'All I saw was a bunch of fools falling off a coach.'

'They may be fools, Joan, but they're handsome fools. Don't make it obvious, but he's on the other side of the bar.'

'That's where he can stay an' all, for all I care,' said Joan.

Kathleen watched as he got himself a pint and chatted to his mates. He looked more confident now, yet somehow vulnerable, and she couldn't believe it when he started to walk over to where they were sitting. *Please let it be me.* He approached the table and placed his pint in front of them.

He wore pleated trousers, cinched in at the waist with a black leather belt. His shirt was crisp and white, but it was that charming smile that out-dazzled everything else.

'Nice to meet you,' he said as he shook Kathleen's hand. 'I'm Cyril.'

'Kathleen, and this is Joan.'

'Nice to meet you, Kathleen and Joan.'

Kathleen blushed and giggled, nudging Joan's arm to say, here he is, that handsome stranger, but Joan didn't look happy at all.

'What do you for a living, Cyril, apart from fall out of coaches with your mates?' asked Joan.

'I'm a butcher.'

'Ha, I knew it!' said Joan.

'We're machinists,' said Kathleen. 'We're the ones that make the shirts you wear when you go out to woo the ladies.'

'Ha,' said Cyril. 'Chance would be a fine thing.'

Kathleen laughed, but Joan remained stony-faced. He took Kathleen's hand and kissed it, standing back to admire her.

'Come on, let's have a dance,' he said as he led

the way to the floor.

He was a good mover, easy and natural but with a manly, strong grip.

'You've a neat little figure on you,' he said as he twirled her once, twice. He guided her round for a third time then held her securely round the waist.

'Thanks,' said Kathleen, not really knowing what else to say, being unaccustomed to compliments.

They danced some more until, exhausted with the moves and first-meeting nerves, they slumped into the chairs lining the side of the dance floor. Kathleen spotted Joan looking over at them with an expression which she couldn't fathom. Whatever it was, it wasn't friendly warmth. *Just like the Mona bleeding Lisa.* Kathleen lifted her hand in a wave and smiled, beckoning her to join them, but Joan looked straight through her.

'She doesn't look right pleased with me,' Kathleen commented to Cyril.

'Aye, well she knows what a catch you've got,' said Cyril, winking, his eyes twinkling in the light. 'Listen, I should go and be with my mates, but I've really enjoyed the dancing tonight.'

'Me too,' said Kathleen, feeling uncertain of what she should do next.

As she stood looking to the floor awkwardly and straightening her skirt, Cyril gently lifted her chin. 'Will I see you again?'

Kathleen froze and bit on her lip, trying to stop the blush that was rising from her neck.

'Yes, if you want,' she said, 'but it's a long way to come from Bolton, isn't it?'

'Aye well, there's always the train,' said Cyril. 'What about I meet you next Saturday in Manchester, about twelve o'clock?'

'Yes, why not? We could meet outside Woolworths; you can't miss it.'

'Grand,' said Cyril 'See you outside Woolies at twelve then.'

She looked up and smiled nervously. 'Grand, it's a date.'

Then he gave her a quick peck on the cheek and headed back towards the main entrance where she'd first caught sight of him. She saw Joan standing alone by the bar and she made her way over, hoping the backlash wouldn't be too bad. When she was sure he was out of view she did an excited little jig and gripped Joan's hand.

'Well, are you seeing him again?' asked Joan.

'He's meeting me in town next Saturday. Isn't he just a dream?'

'Yeah, he's alright.'

'I think he's the most handsome man I've ever seen,' Kathleen replied dreamily. But, from the look on Joan's face, she could see that she didn't agree.

CHAPTER 3

SNARE

For the following week, Kathleen was distracted and could think of nothing else but meeting Cyril. She didn't tell her mam for fear she'd try somehow to jeopardise her happiness. She could predict how her mother would react to the news that she'd met someone: 'Did he have a white stick? Does he know you can't cook?'

Predictably, her dad had looked happy when she told him, although she thought she could also detect a glimmer of disappointment, just for a second. Then it was gone, and he beamed his lovely smile and said how glad he was she had a young man who could take her out.

'Cyril might, just might, be my saviour, Dad, to take me off into the sunset to start a new life beyond the factories and the muck.'

'Can I come with you, then?' he'd asked jokingly.

But, as he cast his eyes up to the ceiling, she sensed desperation in him.

Saturday came and Kathleen's hand shook as she tried to put on mascara. Today, of all days, she seemed to notice every blemish, every imperfection. She got out her powder compact for the second time and patted away. Once again, the cupid's bow was formed, the same words going through her head: *do I look like a floozy?* She looked long and hard at herself in the mirror and hoped she'd done a good enough job. *That's if he turns up*, she thought, as she gathered her coat and handbag, looking back to see if her skirt was straight. She caught sight of her sister peeping around the door.

'Hey up, our kid, do I look alright?'

'You look lovely, as usual,' she replied.

'Aye, well I'm on a date with my very own Prince Charming, but don't tell Mam else she'll have a fit.'

Rosie looked her up and down, 'If he doesn't fall for you looking like that, he wants his head testing. You're the best-looking girl in Longsight.'

'Aw, thanks, Rosie. Here, have this for some sweets, but don't let Mam know, else she'll have it off you more than likely.'

'Thank you! I better go to the shop before it shuts for dinner.'

'Hurry up before she knows what you're up to. You can come out with me and sneak back in once you've been.'

'I'm going now, Mam,' said Kathleen as she stepped around the kitchen door.

'Where are you off to dressed like a prize tart?' came the response.

'I'm going to meet Joan' she said through gritted teeth. 'I'll see you later. I won't need any tea; I'll get something in town.'

'The only thing you'll get in town, lady, is a nasty disease, looking like you do, and make no mistake.'

She stepped out of the kitchen, raised her eyebrows at her sister and did a little jig at the door, the first two fingers of each hand raised in the ultimate insult. She grabbed Rosie's hand and, stifling their giggles, they slipped out into the light.

Kathleen felt unsteady as she stepped off the bus at Piccadilly, lost her balance slightly and stumbled a little sideways on the pavement. *Christ, anyone'd think I've been on the sherry.* She tried to compose herself, but her mind raced. She stopped by Woolworth's window and squinted, tried to see if she still looked half decent. Then she felt a tap – more like a dig – on her shoulder and she spun round to see Cyril smiling down at her like one of those cherubs you see on the walls in churches.

'Oh, you made me jump,' she said, as she tried to regain control of her quivering lips.

'You look lovely,' said Cyril. 'I thought we might go to the flicks if you want.'

'Yes, that'd be nice,' said Kathleen, trying to keep calm.

They talked about the kind of week they'd had, Kathleen looking up at him, taking in his features, especially that wave of black hair arranged so perfectly down to one side. She couldn't believe she was stepping out with such a good-looking man.

'Do you have brothers and sisters at home?' she managed to ask, thinking, too late, how uninventive the question was.

'Yeah, just the two. A brother, eighteen, and a sister, fifteen.'

'There's only two of us, me and my sister. She's sixteen.'

'Right,' he said, looking uninterested.

Then he turned to look at her, flashed that crooked smile and she was trapped in his gaze.

There was an awkward moment as they arrived at the picture house; she wasn't used to stepping out with a man. She started to rummage in her handbag, but Cyril put his hand firmly on hers.

'I'll pay for this,' he said as he squeezed her tiny fist.

'Oh right, thanks,' Kathleen stuttered.

Tickets and sweets were bought, and she followed Cyril into the darkness of the cinema. She let him choose where to sit, didn't want him to think her too forward for choosing the back row. They climbed the central stairs right to the top and he winked as he edged his way into the middle of the very back seats. He chose a double Pullman and they settled down against the velvet, Cyril arranging his arm around her shoulder. She felt warm and wanted, and it felt good. That was when Cyril moved in for the first kiss. It wasn't tender, as she'd expected, but urgent and rough. It hurt and she pulled away. His eyes were black and unreadable, so she stared straight ahead at the screen, fearful that she might cry and spoil everything. Cyril put his hand on her knee, then took her hand, this time more gently, and they settled in to watch the film.

The rest of the date was uneventful. They arranged to meet again the following week, then she waved him off at the station and made her way home.

On the second date, after a few drinks in the pub and before he got the train home, Cyril suggested they walk through the park. It was dark and the park gates were closed, but they found a gap and squeezed through. She giggled, but when she looked at Cyril he wasn't smiling, only staring intently at her. He took her hand roughly and led her into a grassed area behind the bushes. He sat on the ground and pulled her down next to him where she landed with a thud. It was frosty and she shrieked with the shock of the cold.

'Hush,' he said. 'Someone might hear and tell us to clear off.'

Then he straddled her, kissing her hard on the lips, pushing her breast with one hand and trying to part her thighs with the other. She was terrified, unable to move or speak, only just managing to breathe between each assault on her mouth. Her skirt was tight, and he used both hands to yank it up to her waist, ripping the seams, and all without looking at her, without speaking. All she could do was freeze into the already frozen ground and hold her breath to stop the tears. He grabbed roughly at her underwear, ripping her nylons. He pulled her knickers down over her knees. She was terrified as he overpowered her and, when he unbuttoned himself, she couldn't help but let out a gasp.

'That's right, you want it too, don't you?'

But she didn't, and nothing could prepare her for the searing pain as he entered her. She groaned. He covered her mouth as he gyrated and pushed and pushed, only stopping when he had spurted into her. He let out a grunt then rolled off her and leaned back on his elbows. He turned and winked at her, then bent down to retrieve his underwear. Now it was his turn to gasp.

'Shite, Kathleen, you didn't tell me you were on.'

'I'm not. What do you mean?'

She sat up and looked down at the bloody mess, ashamed of what she'd done. She found a hankie in her handbag and quickly wiped herself, wincing as she did. She was cut and bruised; this was not how she had imagined it. She sobbed and pulled on her underwear, trying to hide her mood from him. Her nylons were unsalvageable, so she rolled them into a ball and threw them under the hedge. She hoped her mother would be in bed when she got home. Thankfully, her skirt was around her waist, so it hadn't been bloodied. She pulled it down. It was crumpled and torn, like her: nothing like it had been at the beginning of the night.

'I'm sorry,' he said, not looking her in the eye. 'I didn't know, like. Didn't think anyone your age was still, you know, a virgin.'

'Aye, well I'm not now, am I? Anyway, it doesn't matter. It had to happen sooner or later, didn't it?'

'I would have been more careful if I'd have known.'

'Yeah, I know.'

But she didn't know. She didn't know anything about life, about men, about how you were supposed to behave. She had only really known one man and that was her father. Was *he* like this? Is this what it was like for them? She couldn't imagine it. She stood up and glanced back at her outline in the frost: it looked like a murder scene.

'I'll walk you home before I get my train.' He grabbed her hand and walked beside her, out of the park, down the back streets and to her door where he kissed her briefly, said a quick 'Goodnight,' and disappeared into the evening fog.

Kathleen mouthed a quick prayer, her hand shaking as she tried to engage her key in the lock. Just as she managed to, her father pulled the door open, and she fell into him. She held him and cried for a long time, her body convulsing with sobs until she was spent. He stepped back and, when she dared to look up, she saw a single tear escape down his cheek. That's when she knew that all men were not the same.

'Is that Kathleen?' her mother roared from on high.

'Yes, she's in now. She's going to bed.'

For a time, Kathleen sat on a towel on the edge of her bed, as frozen as she was earlier. Gingerly, she used a warm flannel to clean her stinging parts. She pulled on her nightdress, crawled into bed, and hugged her knees. After a couple of hours of fitful tossing and turning, she cried herself to sleep, her head aching as if it were in the grip of a vice.

Despite the pain and confusion of their first intimacy, Kathleen decided to go on the next date, telling herself it wasn't his fault she was so naïve. She would talk to him about taking it more slowly the next time.

She needn't have worried though, for on the next date he was sweetness itself, holding her hand, guiding her forward with a hand on her back, treating her like a treasure. She was so relieved she could have cried.

After that, she saw him most weekends and, as they got to know each other more, their lovemaking became more of a shared experience, much to Kathleen's relief.

Meeting him was the highlight of her week and her thoughts revolved around what to wear and where they'd go. Afterwards, she'd analyse each word and look, questioning what each meant, then telling herself not to be daft.

At work, she would drift into daydreams

about what lay ahead for her and Cyril. *We could get married soon, get a little house. I wonder how he'd feel about that. I wonder how he'd feel about having a baby, or two, or three. I wonder when he wants children, if he wants to wait, or if he wants them young. I wonder what we'll call them.*

Inevitably, one of her colleagues would nudge her and remind her that she was on piece time, then Kathleen would jump into action, guiding the garments through the machine as quickly as she possibly could, smiling to herself.

Eventually, she had to confess to her mother that she was courting, and this provoked endless questions, endless comments, none of them good.

Kathleen was accustomed to her mother's ways, but she wished, just for once, Mam could be happy for her.

Instead, she said, 'You'll be getting yourself knocked up next, mark my words. And don't come crying to me when he buggers off. What do you think he sees in you anyway?'

CHAPTER 4

LOSING FREEDOM

The next few months went by in a blur of meetings with Cyril, trying to ignore her mother's insults, and working at the factory. As Kathleen became more engrossed in her relationship with Cyril, her friendship with Joan weakened.

She'd noticed Joan had become quite sullen and seemed to completely switch off when Cyril was mentioned. On one occasion, when she was telling her about a date they'd been on, Joan asked, 'What are you bothering with him for? Anyone can see he's not good for you.' Kathleen asked what she meant, but Joan shook her head and gave her a look of pity. Kathleen put it all down to jealousy, especially as Joan hadn't met anyone yet. They still went out occasionally, but Joan kept saying it wasn't the same now Kathleen was mooning around like a lovesick fool.

Now, she stood on Joan's doorstep, her heart

heavy with fear, regret and apprehension, and her mind full of scenarios waiting to be aired and ironed out. She lifted the brass knocker and rapped a couple of times half-heartedly, as if she wasn't sure she wanted Joan to appear.

She could hear footsteps coming down the hall, bare floorboards allowing the sound to filter through the barrier of the door. She straightened herself and drew a deep breath. The sound of the latch being lifted and the clunk as its mechanism released and allowed the door to be pulled slightly open jolted Kathleen further from her daydreams. Joan's face appeared through the gap like a luminous moon, gliding ominously from the cover of cloud.

'Hiya kid,' Kathleen said, in a futile attempt to keep the tone light.

'I was just making myself some tea,' said Joan, even though Kathleen could see that she wasn't, as she was wearing her pill box hat perched on one side of her head.

'I need to talk about something,' said Kathleen. 'It's important.'

'Right, well you'd better come in for a minute,' said Joan, opening the door slowly as Kathleen stepped into the breach. She followed Joan up the stairs, careful not to slip on the threadbare runner.

As Joan slowly pushed open the door to her

bedroom, she suddenly spun round and faced Kathleen with a contemptuous look laden with something bordering on hatred.

'Don't tell me, please, for the love of God, don't tell me you're pregnant.'

The tears fell now, and Kathleen felt stupid.

'It's not what you think, Joan, we were careful!'

'Careful? You don't get pregnant by being careful, Kathleen.'

She followed Joan and plonked herself on the edge of the bed.

Joan paced the room, impatient to be somewhere else. 'I've not got long. I'm going out in a minute.'

'I thought you might be. I didn't know who else I could talk to, Joan. You know what my mam's like'.

'You're going to have to tell her sooner or later.'

'I know, but I wanted to work things out first, before I go blurting it out to my mam and dad.' Kathleen waited for Joan's response, but she just stood there looking at her in disbelief.

'I want to see what Cyril thinks first, before I tell anyone else.'

'What Cyril thinks? I can tell you what Cyril thinks. That he's sorry he ever met you, getting into trouble like this. I can bet he isn't the settling down type.'

'You don't know him, Joan. He treats me right, you know.'

'Well, evidently he doesn't, or else you wouldn't be in this mess.'

Kathleen realised the futility of the visit. She wasn't going to get any reassurance from Joan. If anything, she felt worse than ever. 'I'd better go. I hope you have a nice night out.'

'Thanks. I hope you sort it out.'

Joan pushed open the bedroom door and followed Kathleen down the stairs. Kathleen waited at the bottom, but when Joan reached her, she walked past and opened the front door, holding it so that Kathleen could go out first.

Kathleen lifted her hand in a half-hearted wave and walked away. When she looked back, Joan was half-running in the opposite direction. *How did we get to this?* Later, she realised Joan hadn't smiled once during the whole conversation.

Kathleen put off going to the doctor for a while, and when the time came, she sat nervously at the end of a row of chairs, hoping nobody would see her.

'Kathleen Atkins', she heard through the buzz of her thoughts and it made her jump. *Shine a light, here we go.*

She pushed the door and edged her way into the consulting room, her heart racing. She sat down and clung onto her handbag as if he wasn't a doctor at all, but a bandit waiting to rob her of all she possessed.

Doctor Fraser looked at her with that same unreadable expression he always wore and asked, 'What brings you here today, young lady?'

'I think I'm pregnant,' she replied, bowing her head and trying to look sombre, but not quite managing to stop the corners of her mouth turning upwards slightly.

He looked at her intently and said, 'Remind me of your age.'

'I'm eighteen,' she said, fumbling with the edge of her jacket.

'And the father, is he around? Do you intend to get married?'

'Oh, yes, he is and yes we do,' she replied, crossing her fingers behind her back.

'I suppose congratulations are in order then, young miss. Take this bottle and bring us a sample of urine. We'll do the test and see you in two weeks.'

Kathleen took the container, her hand shaking as she did so. She slipped it into her bag, got up and said 'Thank you' as she left the room. The visit to the doctor's made everything real, and she walked home in a daze. She slipped her hand through the gap between the buttons on her coat and rested it lightly on her stomach.

What if Cyril wants nothing to do with the baby?

She could only hope that her fears were unfounded, because the alternative was too much to bear.

She arrived home and walked through to the kitchen where her mother was perched on a wooden stool by the fire.

'What are you looking so pleased about? And where've you been til this time? Your tea's been ready nearly half an hour.'

'Nowhere,' replied Kathleen. 'I called in at Joan's for a brew after work. Sorry Mam, I didn't think.'

'No, you never think, do you? That's why you're going to spend the rest of your days in that factory til you get yourself knocked up by some poor sod too blind to see how useless you are.'

Kathleen flinched. Her mother always seemed to know. She hung her head, shuffled to the stove, took the warm plates out of the oven and carried them over to the table.

'Thanks for tea, Mam,' she said, trying to conceal her hurt. She lifted the top plate off to reveal a dried-up portion of shepherd's pie.

'It's your father you've to thank. He's the one daft enough to cook for a little mare who doesn't deserve it. And what's this letter on the mantelpiece, from Bolton, eh?'

Kathleen ate slowly, nearly choking on the meal and the atmosphere. She gazed sideways at the letter and speculated about its content.

She finished eating, washed up under the oppressive glare of her mother and took the letter up to her room, cherishing the feel of it. She slumped on the bed and slipped off her shoes, then rolled her stockings down and removed them carefully. Her hand settled on her stomach as she tried to steady her breathing. She picked up the envelope, studied the writing and the post mark, then slipped her thumb along the gummed flap that sealed his words:

Dear Kathleen,
I am having to sort out some problems at home, so I won't be able to see you for a couple of weeks.
It's my mam. She's not very well, no thanks to my dad, and I've to look after the others til she gets better.
Cyril.

No kiss at the end. Kathleen sobbed with disappointment, her hand dropped limply to the bed and the letter crumpled under it. She thought about the brevity of the note, the lack of feeling. She felt guilty for thinking what bad timing it was; now she'd have to keep her news of the baby buried until she saw him again, *if* she saw him again. *I bloody hate life!* She cried big, heavy tears which plopped onto the crumpled letter, and her frame convulsed with pathetic sobs.

When the tears finally stopped, she felt numb. Then she remembered the baby. *Pull yourself together, you daft cow.* She unfolded herself slowly and looked at her image in the dressing table mirror. *What a mess, what a bloody rotten mess.*

CHAPTER 5

TIES

For the following weeks, Kathleen's emotions soared and dipped and never seemed to settle into any semblance of calm.

She finally met up with Cyril again after three agonising weeks. They were sitting in a little back-street café near Oxford Road Station in Manchester, waiting for their food. Trying to gauge his mood, she reached for his hand over the table, but he wasn't giving much away. He seemed a bit sullen, if truth be told, and Kathleen tried to convince herself this had nothing to do with her, more to do with his mother.

'So, how've you been? How are things at home? How's your mum?' she asked, holding on to his fingers and trying to stroke him back to her.

'Oh, alright, you know. She's alright,' he replied, withdrawing his hand and staring moodily out of the window.

Kathleen tried to keep her thoughts rational.

'Good, I'm glad things are better,' she managed, withdrawing her own hand now and looking down into her lap so he might not see the tears.

'What's up now?' he asked, with such a lack of feeling that Kathleen finally broke and allowed her words to tumble:

'What's up now? I'm going to have a baby, if you must know, and it's been so bloody awful these last few weeks, not being able to tell anyone, waiting to tell you, then getting your letter and now, *now*, you don't even look pleased to see me! God, what a bloody stupid rotten mess.' She slumped and gave in to the despair.

There was a long pause.

'Aren't you going to say something?' she said through sobs which made her gasp for breath.

'Jesus, Kathleen,' he said at last. 'What do you want me to say? Do you think I came here today expecting this? My mind's buggered up enough as it is, with what's happened at home, without having to deal with this as well.'

'Well, you better bloody had deal with it,' she blurted, as two plates were put down between them, causing them both to sit up as they tried to pull themselves back to normality.

'My mum's in a bad way, battered half to

death by my dad, if you must know. She lost the baby; we didn't even know she was pregnant,' said Cyril, picking up his cutlery and looking down at the plate in front of him. 'Now, if it's all the same to you, I'm eating this before it goes cold.'

Kathleen was shocked. 'How on earth can you think about sodding egg and chips after what you've just told me?'

'Because I'm starving, that's how. I haven't eaten since breakfast, so you can please yourself, but I'm having mine.' He speared the first chip and thrust it down into the egg, breaking its membrane.

Kathleen didn't think she'd ever felt so wretched. She watched as Cyril ate ravenously, apparently oblivious. After what seemed like a lifetime, he cleaned his plate with the last of the bread, then wiped his mouth with the back of his hand.

'So, what do we do now?' he asked, his voice shaking. 'I hardly know you, and now this, as if I haven't enough to think about.'

Kathleen's throat was so thick, she doubted she could get any words out.

'No child of mine is going to be raised without a father,' he eventually offered. 'I'll have to look for work here in Manchester, and we'll have to get married,' he said, spitting out the last word.

She managed to look at him and hope he

wasn't repulsed by what he saw, the state of her.

'I'm sorry,' she whispered. 'I didn't want it to be like this.'

'We'll just have to make the most of it, won't we,' he said.

'We'll be alright,' she said shakily, unsure of who she was trying to convince.

CHAPTER 6

ENTRAPMENT

The wedding was a small affair with a reception held in the back room of a Longsight pub. Sandwiches, pork pies, port and lemon, brown ale, and each family weighing up the other.

If you looked at social bearing, neither family was in the gutter; nor had they reached the heady heights of being middle-class. They worked hard in menial jobs, trying to feed their families and getting by with a 'make do and mend' philosophy. Their neighbours played an important, supportive role in times of need. They looked out for one another, minded one another's children, gave loans of bread, sugar, butter, whatever was short until pay day. They handed down clothes, gave advice and listened to troubles. The only thing they couldn't give was money.

Kathleen sat in a dark corner of the snug and looked around at the happy scene of the two families sharing food, drink, jokes and anecdotes. The strain of the last couple of months had taken its toll and, although she was over the initial bouts of morning sickness, she still felt weary. The wedding had been a rush to organise but had served as a tool with which to appease her mother after the news of the baby. Kathleen had braced herself through the *I told you so, it's your bed, lie in it, stupid girl* talks. Eventually, her mother resigned herself to the news and even helped to arrange the registry office, flowers and cake.

Kathleen wasn't sure what lay ahead but was certain it could only be an improvement on what went before. No more of her mother's disapproving looks and put-downs. No more sneaking around and worrying about what her mother would say when she got in. She was looking forward to starting married life with Cyril in the house they'd managed to rent. He'd found work in Longsight, which meant she didn't have to relocate. She didn't know if that was a blessing or a curse.

Her mother, still stern even on her daughter's wedding day, sat resolute in her martyrdom and misery: 'I thought your wedding day were supposed to be the happiest day of your life. You look like you've lost a pound and found thruppence.'

'I am happy, Mam. I was just thinking, that's

all.'

'Aye well, thinking won't put clothes on the back of the child, will it?'

'No Mam, I don't suppose it will, but at least I can sew. I can make a lot of my own clothes and I'm sure I'll be able to knock up a few baby clothes when the time comes.'

Her mother gave her a contemptuous look. 'Putting clothes on the baby's back is a saying. It means earning enough to keep your family! How do you think the pair of you are going to do that, eh? God knows *we* struggle, and your father's twice the man Cyril will ever be.'

Kathleen wondered why her mother couldn't let her be happy for once. 'We can only try our best, can't we? And that's what we'll do, our best.'

Kathleen walked over to Cyril and caught the tail-end of a taunt from one of his friends about an end to his womanising days. This didn't help Kathleen's state of mind at all. She pursed her lips as she tried to smile and stem tears at the same time. She knew she had to stop being so sensitive; maybe it was the pregnancy, or maybe she was starting with mood swings, like her mother.

'We were just telling Cyril how lucky he is to have such a beautiful woman for a wife,' said the one who had taunted.

Kathleen smiled tightly and held Cyril's hand,

looking forward to when they could escape the party and be alone. She felt him stumble slightly and realised he must have had a few pints. *Oh well, it is our wedding day.*

She stood a while longer, but she slipped away when the harmless banter deteriorated into smutty jokes and tales of past conquests. She found her sister perched on a barstool.

'Hey up, our kid, what's up? Has no one asked you to dance yet?' she asked as she took hold of her sister's hands and pulled her gently down from the stool. 'Come on, let's have our last dance before I leave you to go and live in me little house. You'll have to buy your own lipsticks now, won't you? Or nick 'em from Woolies, more like.'

This made Rosie smile, and Kathleen's heart lurched: 'You know you can always talk to me, don't you? You can come to tea, even stay over sometimes if you want, and you can help me look after the baby when it comes.'

'I'm going to miss you, Kathleen. I don't know how I'll go on with Mam on my own. She's bound to pick on me now.'

Kathleen took Rosie's hand, 'That's what I've just said, haven't I? I might not be in the same house, but you know you can come around any time you like.'

'I know, but you don't want me there all the time. You've just got married, you don't want your little sister spoiling it by turning up on your doorstep.'

Kathleen knew her sister was right. She also knew Cyril would not approve of Rosie spending too much time with them.

'Don't worry, our kid. It will all turn out good in the end.'

She kissed Rosie's cheek and led her over to Aunty Betty, where she left her being fussed over.

It was almost midnight before the last of the revellers left. She found Cyril at the bar and slipped her hand into his. He snatched it away with such force, it stung. Then he was looming over her, his face almost puce with an expression of pure hatred.

'Don't you come here trying to work your way around me,' he spluttered, slurring his words and spitting. 'Don't think I didn't notice you sneaking off to dance with your sister, and all the men staring at you.'

Kathleen was taken aback, but she managed to speak. 'I was only trying to cheer her up because she's going to be left on her own with Mam, and you know what *she's* like.'

'You didn't have to do it in the middle of the pub, did you? You didn't have to dance around like a pair of tarts with all eyes on you. You'd already shown me up when you walked off in front of me mates.'

Now Kathleen was confused; she'd thought she wasn't welcome, that he wouldn't mind her slipping away. She'd never seen him this angry before and it scared her.

'Can we go now? I'm really tired.'

She was relieved when Cyril's tight expression seemed to relax a little and he replied, 'Yeah, we might as well as there's no one left. I've had enough now, anyway.'

He took her hand roughly and led her around the room to say goodbye to the few remaining guests. She tried not to show her hurt, and she was thankful when they were on their way home. Neither of them said a word, and Kathleen felt she should break the silence as they reached their front door.

'Sorry if you felt shown up. I thought you wanted me to leave you to enjoy the banter with your mates.'

'Listen, you're married to me now, and I'm not having you flirting like some cheap floozy,' he said, his face red and contorted.

Kathleen knew he was drunk, that it was no use trying to reason. She put the key in the door and entered the two-up-two-down, the little haven they'd rented near her parents. Cyril stumbled in after her, pushed her aside and headed upstairs. She locked up and followed him to the bedroom. There he lay, stupefied. She let out a frustrated sigh and started to undress, reluctantly peeling each garment away. She had wanted *him* to remove her wedding attire, wanted him to gasp at her bosom, to be overcome with love and lust when her demure underskirts revealed the stockings beneath. She had never felt so lonely and, as she snuggled into him, he turned his back on her, making her feel thoroughly wretched.

The night passed slowly, graced by fitfulness, disturbing thoughts and Cyril's snoring. When her body finally surrendered to something resembling sleep, she was nudged sharply in the ribs; not by the child within, but the one without: Cyril demanding tea.

As she awoke, images of her so-called wedding night presented themselves and she groaned. The thought that it shouldn't be tea he was asking for didn't escape her, but she knew better than to risk reaching out to him, as another rejection would bring her to tears.

She swallowed down the hurt. 'Cup o' tea, then.'

He mumbled something and she trudged slowly down the narrow stairs. At the bottom, she stopped for a moment to contemplate. She had no choice but to try and appease Cyril somehow, and hope this black mood passed quickly.

It was a nostalgic climb back up the wooden stairs. She used to take tea up to her mother with the same heavy heart and sense of dread.

'I've brought your tea,' she said as she edged her way on to the bed.

'Thanks, love.' He reached out for her hand. 'Look, I'm sorry about last night. I'm an awkward sod when I've had a drink, and it's been a tough time, what with me mam and everything.'

The grin across Kathleen's face clearly displayed her relief. 'I know. Let's just forget last night. Give us kiss and I'll forgive you.'

Cyril leant up on one elbow, his face still crumpled from sleep on one side, his hair tousled, eyes red and puffy. She kissed him, smoothing back his hair and feeling light. *Thank God*, she thought, as the focus at last shifted from needing tea to wanting each other. They drew into a hug and laughed as the lump got in the way.

'How's our little Eric, anyway?' asked Cyril, as he rested his hand on the ever-increasing mound.

'She's fine, thanks,' said Kathleen.

They continued with their banter, and one thing led to another.

They finally emerged from the marital bed about midday, dressed, then strolled back to the pub to collect the wedding presents. The landlord raised an eyebrow to them.

'Alright this evening, are we?' he asked, directing his gaze at Cyril.

'It's barely twelve o'clock, and we're right as rain, thanks,' said Kathleen quickly, sensing Cyril's unease.

'Pint o' bitter for me and – what are you having, love?'

'I thought we were just collecting presents,' she said, and noticed how Cyril's face dropped.

'No harm in having a pint to celebrate your first day of married life, though, is there?'

Kathleen smiled. 'Just an orange juice for me. I'll take these home while you drink that.'

She started towards the table in the corner, piled high with gifts and cards, their shiny presence a welcome oasis in the gloom of the bar's lounge.

Cyril stepped forward, took her arm and pulled her sharply back to him. 'There's no rush, is there?'

'No, I don't suppose there is,' she said, shrinking from the force with which he pulled her.

It's like being on the bleeding big dipper.

One pint turned into three, and Kathleen tried to feel a part of this world, but the truth was she wasn't comfortable watching Cyril slowly get drunk again. He was at the merry stage now, but she knew that could change.

'Do you think we should go and get some lunch?' she asked as Cyril lifted his glass to drain the last inch of bitter.

He glanced at her sideways, slammed his pot down and shouted over for another pint. Humiliated, Kathleen bit her lip and looked down to the floor.

'I'll take the presents home now,' she suggested.

He agreed.

She lifted a card from the pile; *The Happy Couple*, it read. She didn't know whether to laugh or cry. As she struggled to get through the door, trying to balance packages on top of her pregnant stomach, she cast a glance to the bar and saw Cyril laughing, his face flushed. He was oblivious and she should have been angry, but all she felt was hurt.

Her mother's words came back to haunt her: 'You've only known him two minutes. You don't know anything about him.'

Although it pained Kathleen to admit it, her mother had been right.

CHAPTER 7

PRISONER

The first time he struck her, it hurt more inside than out. Kathleen had given up work in preparation for the imminent birth, and money was tight. Cyril had taken to going for a pint most evenings after work with his boss from the butcher's, which didn't help matters at all.

It wasn't every night, but it was enough to drain the finances to the point where sometimes they'd go without a decent meal. Pressure was bearing down from all angles. When money was tight and food sparse, Kathleen worried about her own health and that of her unborn child. What if it was born deformed because she didn't have the right food to eat? What if she didn't have the strength to cope with carrying the child, giving birth or feeding?

Cyril's moods had become increasingly unpredictable which meant she never knew which face he would present when he arrived home. If he'd only had a couple, he could be the warmest, most affectionate husband she could wish for. A couple more and he'd be quiet and often morose, sinking into his own miserable world and not wanting to talk, not wanting her near him.

The real concern for Kathleen was when a couple of pints turned to seven. Seven or eight pints, and Cyril went from being reticent and deep to openly abusive and aggressive. He'd come home wanting to pick an argument and it could be triggered by anything and everything. Kathleen found it impossible to avoid such conflicts. Try as she might to make sure everything was as good as it could be, there was always something he found lacking, and it could be the smallest, most insignificant thing imaginable.

That's how it had been that first time. She had taken half an hour out from the household chores to put her feet up and eat. There was half a tin of beans in the fridge, and she decided to have them with some toast. As she buttered the toast, she salivated, she was so hungry. She ate like she'd never been fed, savouring every mouthful. When she'd finished, she made sure to clear away the dishes. She sat back in her armchair and took another look around the living room which, as usual, was clean and tidy.

Cyril arrived home at about eight thirty to find Kathleen snoozing in the chair. She opened one eye and struggled up, reading the expression on his face. She went to greet him, not wanting him to think she was lazy for staying in the chair. He stood stock-still in front of her with beery, bloodshot eyes.

Then he walked over and opened the fridge door.

'What's for tea?' he snapped.

Kathleen bit her lip. As she stepped forward to appease him with suggestions, he spun around and struck her with such force that he knocked her backwards. She slumped, dazed, against the wall. She raised a hand to her stinging cheek, trying to fathom who this stranger was. Her stomach had jarred awkwardly against her ribs, making it difficult to breathe. Too numb to cry, and too shocked to move, she sat frozen.

Cyril stood before her, and they locked eyes for a moment, like a pair of alien species, each trying to make sense of the other. Then, slowly and painfully, Kathleen managed to stand and catch the breath which had eluded her for the past minute.

'I wanted those bloody beans!' he shrieked, and she watched in disbelief as he turned his back on her and rummaged through cupboards in search of food.

She sat at the kitchen table, head in hands, and wept. Once again, her husband gave no indication at all that he cared in the least for the pain she was in. She had got used to the verbal abuse, the odd little shove, but this was the first time he had really hit her and, even though there were plenty of warning signs, she hadn't seen it coming. She should have known that his increasingly dark moods would lead to something bad.

A snippet of a conversation she had overheard on the factory floor came to mind: 'It'll only get worse from now on', the woman had said to her friend whose husband had struck her.

Her spirits sank further.

She sat there for a while longer, knowing anything she said would make matters worse. Finally, she went to bed. The more she thought about what had happened, the worse the palpitations became, until she thought her heart would give way. With morbid thoughts of who would miss her if she died, and what would happen to the baby, Kathleen eventually succumbed to sleep.

CHAPTER 8

BONDS

For the next few days Cyril was notably subdued; so much so that Kathleen thought an apology was imminent, but it didn't come. This lowered her mood even further and she went from being edgy and trying to please, to being sullen, dejected and apathetic. She no longer cared about the house being spotless and had even left dirty dishes in the sink from breakfast time, not having the energy to fret about what Cyril would say. Cyril said nothing, an indication to Kathleen that he must have felt something resembling remorse.

She was now very near to her due date and the physical and mental implications of the baby's arrival bore down on her. She knew this lull in Cyril's aggression wouldn't last forever and her thoughts were dominated by what would happen once the baby was born.

An extra mouth to feed would mean further strain on the household finances and more pressure. More reason for Cyril to drink, increasing the likelihood of more violence. She somehow had to try and keep him calm, but how? Everything she tried had failed; making sure his tea was ready, his clothes clean, the house tidy, and the pots washed. Before, when she'd heard stories of girls who had violent husbands, she had thought them stupid for getting themselves into such a fix. Now here she was enduring the same predicament as those feckless wretches.

As if her life wasn't bad enough, she bumped into Joan purely by chance as she stepped off the bus in Longsight on one of her dutiful visits to her mother and father. Kathleen felt a fierce blush rising from her chest until it burned her whole face. As she pulled herself together enough to say hello, Joan gave the smuggest sneer, which quickly evolved into a short, mocking laugh.

'By heck, you chose a right one there, didn't you? Bet you wish we'd never stepped foot in that dancehall, don't you?'

'What do you mean?' asked Kathleen, dreading the response.

'Oh, come on, you must know. If you don't, you're the only one that doesn't.'

'Know? Know what?' Kathleen whispered.

'That your husband's knocking about with some little tart.'

Kathleen stumbled back, reaching out for something to steady her. The pain she felt now was worse, by far, than that she felt when Cyril struck her. She had a burning impulse to tear this child from her and run, but she found herself rooted to the spot.

Joan prattled on regardless: 'I saw them in town, bold as brass the pair of them, strutting down the street like they've a right. Aye, and don't say you weren't warned. I knew he were trouble from the start and tried to tell you as much, more than once.'

She spun on her heel and headed off in the direction of home, stopping briefly to glance back at Kathleen, with a softer look now, more of pity than disdain. This tipped Kathleen over the edge and she sobbed bitterly. She paced the back streets aimlessly until she stopped crying and, limp with despair, she made her way back home. Once there, she crawled into bed without undressing, without eating, pulling the covers up tightly around her head which seemed about to explode.

Kathleen woke when a new pain seared across her back. She rolled slowly onto her side and sat semi-upright, trying to breathe through what she now assumed to be the first contraction.

The subsequent, unrelenting pains of labour relegated any thoughts of Cyril to a recess in her befuddled mind. Her body had the strength to take on only this new challenge, to get through this agony and produce her first-born. She managed one thought though: how fitting it was that Cyril wasn't here to support her.

Is there anything right, anything good about this marriage?

She managed to get herself up, and she stumbled awkwardly, slowly down the stairs. She rested at the bottom, then slid her shoes on and shuffled next door.

'Hey up Kathleen, whatever's the matter?' was the greeting, as Mrs Barker opened the front door to see her neighbour almost crouching in agony on her step.

'It's coming, the baby,' Kathleen whispered as she grabbed the door jamb for support.

'Oh, of course, the baby, of course it is. Now you come in and I'll send for Mrs Brown. Don't you worry about a thing; it'll be over in no time, love. Where's your Cyril?'

'*My* Cyril is at work, or at least I think he is, although he could be anywhere, with anyone, who knows?'

'Ee, you're not making much sense, love; come in now and we'll get you comfortable. Frank, Frank! Be a love and get Mrs Brown to come. Quick sharp now, Frank. Hurry up!'

Frank appeared in the doorway from the kitchen, clutching his newspaper and looking somewhat bewildered and bedraggled, as if he'd been roused from a deep sleep. When he saw Kathleen, so fully pregnant and in pain, he leaped into action, as if he'd sat inadvertently in the embers of the fire. Despite the warmth in the room, Kathleen wanted to be home, wanted to crawl into her own bed and stay there for as long as she possibly could.

'Would you mind helping me back home? Only I'd rather be there, you know.'

'Course I will love,' and with that, Mrs Barker, a woman of slight proportions, hooked Kathleen's arm around her shoulder and took her weight as well as she could. She beckoned for her husband to do the same and together they shuffled next door so that Kathleen could have her wish.

It was a struggle to get upstairs, but they eventually managed, and she was settled into bed and made as comfortable as she could be. Within the hour, Mrs Brown, the local midwife, arrived on her bicycle, equipped with a leather bag containing all the things she would need to assist the birth.

For Kathleen, there was less breathing space now between pains which were increasingly intense and almost unbearably long. She had never been so glad to see the reassuringly stout figure of the woman who had guided her through this pregnancy. As the midwife strode across the bedroom with an air of ownership, Kathleen knew she was in safe hands. She smiled weakly as Mrs Barker held her hand and Mrs Brown busied herself with preparations. Frank made his excuses and left Kathleen in capable hands.

Cyril arrived home some time later to find the front door ajar, and a bicycle propped up against the wall. He immediately recognised it as belonging to the lady he'd often seen cycling determinedly through neighbouring streets, the baby lady. All previous thoughts and actions seemingly erased from his mind, he pushed open the door and flew upstairs to the source of the gentle voices of women intent on seeing a task through.

When he crouched beside her, Kathleen wanted desperately to hurt him, but only had the strength to look sideways at him, hoping he could read the despair in her eyes. Wanting to punish him but wanting more for him to hold her through this agony, she reached for his hand. Taking this as permission, he held hers so tightly it hurt. They locked eyes for a moment, Kathleen searching for goodness in his. She was sure she saw a glimmer of something – love, regret, remorse, she wasn't sure – and, for the first time, they worked as a team. Cyril held her hands as she pushed for all she was worth, the midwife offering words of encouragement and advice. At the end of their efforts the child was born, and Kathleen leaned forward.

'A bouncing baby girl,' said Mrs Brown. 'What will you call her?'

They hadn't had the inclination to sit down and talk baby names in the days preceding this one.

'Sylvia,' said Kathleen, for it seemed only fair and fitting that she named her after the midwife who had shown compassion and care in her hour of need.

With a look of pride, Sylvia held the baby up by the feet until she let out her first cry. She was bloody and slimy and beautiful. Kathleen forgot the pain and held out her arms so that she could receive her daughter. As she cradled her, Cyril looked on. Kathleen didn't know if the look on his face was wonder or fear, but she didn't care. Little Sylvia seemed perfect in every way, from the shock of black hair to her tiny waxy feet, and Kathleen wondered how something so beautiful could have been born from such dire circumstances.

She wondered how she could ever have thought about ridding herself of this little bundle of sweet charm. She shuddered at the thought of wanting to rip this baby physically from her.

I must have been in a right state, and we all

know who was to thank for that.

But if anyone had walked in on the scene, they would have thought Cyril the epitome of a proud new dad, for he held the baby so tenderly in his strong arms, he looked like the vision of a great protector.

For a few days, Kathleen's priority was to establish herself as a new mum, to be good at it, to do a better job than her own mother had. She knew, as she nursed her child, that she had never experienced love before, because this love had a whole new dimension to it. This child had taken over her whole being and had given her life a new meaning and purpose. The joy she felt when those bleary little eyes tried to focus on her face was like no other. For a while, at least, her life took a turn for the better and she concentrated her energies on tending to her newborn.

Cyril was like a different person, possibly because his trips to the pub, apart from wetting the baby's head, had now reduced significantly. Kathleen relaxed into this new way of being, and hoped they'd turned a corner.

A couple of months after the birth, galvanised by Cyril's displays of affection, she found the courage to confront him. She hadn't forgotten her encounter with Joan and the news she shared. Or was it merely gossip?

'Right, I'm not going to beat about the bush,' she said one night after supper, when she sensed Cyril was restless and fidgety. 'You've been spotted, stepping out with some young girl, making a fool of me, as if I wasn't fool enough already.'

'What?' Cyril asked. He turned to face his wife, to face the inevitable showdown, the big truth, the payback for all his reckless, thoughtless actions. 'What do you mean, I've been spotted? Who's told you that?'

'Never mind who told me. Is it true?'

'It was that interfering cow Joan, wasn't it? Best thing you ever did was break ties with her. She comes back on the scene and there's trouble straight away.'

Kathleen stood resolute and faced her husband square-on. 'I want the truth, Cyril,' she said wearily. 'Are you seeing another woman behind my back? Because if you are, be man enough to admit it.'

'Man enough? I'll tell you what I'm man enough to do!'

The blow knocked Kathleen back into the armchair, which toppled. She landed in a heap against the wall. Catching the blood from her nose, she looked in disbelief at her husband.

That Brylcreemed quiff that she loved so much hung down now and covered half of Cyril's reddened face. He flicked it sharply to one side in the heat of his anger, and she came to her senses, back to red alert. She had to take the heat out of the situation before he exploded again and frightened the baby.

Cyril turned his back and strode away, his trousers hanging from his thin backside. He seemed to have shrunk. He slipped on his jacket and, without a word, he went out, slamming the door with such force the window shook in its frame.

Exasperated, Kathleen collapsed into the armchair. She cradled her daughter and wondered what would come next for them.

CHAPTER 9

TETHERED

One afternoon, a few years and two more children later, there was a loud knock at the door. Kathleen could see the outline of a stout shadow and for once it wasn't Cyril. She knew this to be so; it stood stock-still for a start, and surely after five hours on the ale, he'd be rocking by now. Why was she instilled with the same sense of dread then, as if it *was* him? She unlatched the door and slowly pulled it open. It was then that the dread really took hold. The sight of the uniform hit her with the same wallop as Cyril's fists. She feared something had happened to one of the kids.

'Mrs Benson?'

'Yes.'

'Is Cyril Benson your husband?'

'Yes, he is.'

'I'm afraid I've some really bad news.'

Let him be dead.

'He's been involved in a bad accident. He's in Manchester Royal Infirmary. If you want to get a few things together, we can take you there now.'

'I'll have to ask the neighbour to look after the kids. Come in, I won't be long.'

Kathleen took off her apron and tried to wear a look of concern. She busied herself putting away baking equipment, secretly planning her life without him.

'I'm afraid you'll have to leave that, Mrs Benson. We need to go soon.'

'Why? Is he that bad?'

'We don't know, but we do need to get you there.'

She tried to hide her disappointment. So, he wasn't on his deathbed, after all. She grabbed her cardigan and the youngest and walked around to her neighbour's house. She knocked on the back door, peering through the window as she did so. Margaret opened the door and asked her what was wrong.

'It's Cyril, he's had an accident,' she said.

Although she had often confided in Margaret, she didn't want her to think she was heartless by adding, *pity it wasn't worse.*

'Can you mind our Frank and baby Gail, by any chance, and get Sylvia from school at half past? I don't know how long I'll be.'

'Course I can, love. Leave them here and I'll pick Sylvia up later and give them all something to eat, so don't worry. I'll see you when you get back. I hope he's alright, love.'

Kathleen smiled weakly, pushing down the *I don't* that threatened to escape.

In the car on the way to hospital, the officer explained that Cyril had been crossing the road when he was struck by a van. He had broken legs and other injuries, the severity of which was uncertain.

That's all I need, a crippled husband, as if he wasn't bad enough before.

If Kathleen looked miserable on the journey to see him, it wasn't because she was worried about his health, but because her chances of escape had just narrowed to zero.

When she finally arrived at the ward, Kathleen was shown to Cyril's bed. She only knew it was him by that damned quiff flopping out of the bandages around his head. His face was purple, not with anger, but with bruising. He was comatose and helpless. One leg was suspended in the air on traction, the spindly form of the other outlined beneath the counterpane.

What would other wives do? Weep and howl and wish him better?

She felt nothing. Now that the police officers had gone, she couldn't even bring herself to hold his hand, couldn't be bothered to keep up the pretence.

You selfish bastard of a husband.

She sat down beside the bed and stared at the mess before her, the mess she had once idolised and now feared. His mouth hung open, dry spittle and blood congealed in each corner. His thin arms flopped limply at his sides and his chest had sunk like a failed sponge cake. How had this man exerted such power over her?

After an unsuccessful operation to repair his broken bones, and subsequent episodes of infection, Cyril was discharged from hospital. He was by no means healed and the infections had left him in pain. But he still managed to hobble to the pub most evenings. Kathleen's situation was even worse than it had been as his moods became darker and less predictable. He lashed out in anger at whoever was nearest, whether that was Kathleen or one of the kids.

Today it was Sylvia's turn.

'Pass me those pills, will you?'

'Which ones, Dad?'

'What do you mean, which ones? The ones I take every bleeding day, that's which ones!'

Sylvia handed over the bottle and was felled by a blow to the head, uncalled for and unexpected. She crouched, holding her head in her hands, unable to move with the effort of trying to stem the tears.

'Get up, you soft shite, or I'll give you something to cry about! Tell your mother I want my tea. *Now!*'

Sylvia scuttled off to the kitchen, still nursing her head.

'What's up, has he hit you? I've told you to keep away from him when he's in this mood. Go and play out. I'll shout you in when tea's ready.'

'Kathleen! Come and help me with this shoelace, will you?'

Kathleen tensed. 'I'm doing the tea. I can't be everywhere.'

Cyril flashed up again, 'Is there anyone in this bleeding house who has a clue what to do? You're bleeding useless, the lot of you!'

Since she'd seen him so helpless in his hospital bed, Kathleen had become less fearful of her husband, and more intolerant. She had become almost immune to his outbursts, but she knew if she left him any longer he would deteriorate into a raging ogre and somebody would get hurt. She put down the potato peeler and went to him.

She knelt and tied his shoelace, resentment churning in her stomach. As she was about to get up, he brought his foot up sharply and kicked her in the face. She crouched for a moment too long and he pushed her face into the carpet. She could feel his breath on her ear.

'Next time, you'd better come quicker', he whispered, shoving her head along the floor.

She struggled up and back into the kitchen where she bathed her face and returned to her chores.

Sylvia opened the back door a little, 'What's for tea, Mam?'

'Shit with sugar on,' she called back, as she wiped away a tear.

CHAPTER 10

ANOTHER TIE

It was 1960, a new decade. Kathleen held the child in her arms. It was her fourth, another daughter. She could hear children outside: it must be the end of school. The midwife finished washing her hands and came over to the bed.

'That was a tough delivery, Kathleen, not only because the baby's big, but because you're worn out. The doctor was right; you need to stop at this one. They advised you after the third not to have any more. Your body's not up to it love, as young as you are.'

Kathleen's expression didn't give much away. She was tired, *fatigued*, and her body throbbed with pain.

'I know what you're saying, Sylvia, but you try and push a sixteen-stone man off you when he wants his way. You try and explain the basics of family planning when he's had nine pints. You try and tell him another child might be the difference between eating and not.'

She wept then, inconsolable. The midwife took the baby and placed her in the makeshift cot, a drawer at the bottom of the bedroom chest.

'I'm sorry, love. I wasn't trying to make you feel bad, but I care about your health. Has Cyril thought about using the withdrawal method?'

'Don't make me laugh.'

The midwife smiled. They talked about how Kathleen would cope with the children, how she'd feed them, clothe them and get them to school on time. Frank, only five, didn't know a nappy from a hankie, but Sylvia, at eleven, had a bit more of a clue. Gail was only two, still a baby herself. It was all down to Kathleen. Not only had she to cope with four kids, but with the biggest, most selfish child of them all, Cyril. She could have done a better job without him there, but she was stuck. Even though he always complained about how useless she was, he showed no signs of leaving.

The midwife cleaned up and had one last peep at the sleeping baby.

'What are you going to call her?'

'Marian, after a lady who used to live on our street when I was a kid. She used to give me bread and butter when me mam wouldn't let me in. I think she felt sorry for me. She'd turn in her grave if she could see me now, what I've become.'

'Come on, love, it's not that bad. You've got four healthy kids, good neighbours and you can always talk to me, you know that.'

Kathleen smiled and nodded, 'I know, but it's hard, Sylvia, and I'm tired.'

'I know you are, love, but you're a trooper and you'll get through like you always have.'

She promised Kathleen she'd call tomorrow and left as Cyril arrived home, swaying slightly and filling the doorway with the sheer size of him.

'You've got another girl,' she called as she rode off, unwilling to hear the drivel that would emanate from his drunken mouth.

Cyril staggered in, hardly registering that there was another addition to his growing brood. He was more concerned about finding food than he was about Kathleen or the baby.

'It's a girl, Dad,' said Sylvia.

'Another one?' he replied and carried on with his search.

Sylvia scuttled upstairs and sat around her mother's bed with the others, fussing over the new baby.

'Where's your father?' asked Kathleen.

'He's in the kitchen looking for food.'

'He'll be lucky.' She flopped back onto the pillow and closed her weary eyes.

CHAPTER 11

DEAD END

Kathleen sat down on the hard vinyl settee, weary from the morning's chores. She looked at the threadbare rug in front of the hearth and the faded lino around its edges. *When did I stop caring?*

She was certainly finding it difficult to cope with four kids, especially with Cyril the way he was. His constant criticism was getting to her. *Maybe I am a useless wife, a rubbish mother, just like mine was.*

The kids had noticed a change in her, were always asking her what was wrong, why wasn't she dressed, did she want some breakfast?

Although Marian was a placid baby who slept well, her birth had somehow managed to tip Kathleen over the edge. She knocked on Margaret's door for the third time this week and it was only Tuesday.

'Hello love, come in,' said Margaret with a smile.

'I can't do it anymore,' said Kathleen, handing over baby Marian as if she was a loaf of bread.

'It's difficult love, having a newborn, but you'll get there. You always have before.'

'I know, Margaret, but it's him, he's getting worse.'

'What do you mean?'

'His temper, his anger, his bitterness, it's getting worse.'

'What can we do? You know I'm always here to listen, but I don't know what else I can do for you, love.'

'You are, Margaret, and thank God for that. If it wasn't for you, my head would have been in that gas oven years ago.'

'Oh, don't talk like that, love,' said Margaret, squeezing Kathleen's hand whilst trying to hold the baby over her shoulder.

'I mean it. I think I'm going mad like my mother. I feel like I'm turning into her with her mood swings and all. But what worries me the most is I seem to have lost interest in everything, even the kids. Sometimes, it takes all my strength just to get out of bed, never mind have a wash and get dressed.'

'It sounds like you're a bit depressed, love, and that's no surprise with a husband like Cyril and four kids to tend to.'

'A bit depressed? I'm flipping doolally!'

Kathleen let out an involuntary laugh. 'See, I even have my mam's cackle.' She cackled louder.

'Oh love, you are funny,' said Margaret, laughing too, but Kathleen's laughter had turned to tears. In fact, she was sobbing heartily.

Margaret laid the now sleeping baby on the settee and went to comfort her. 'By the way, love, where's little Gail?'

'She was still in bed,' said Kathleen, without feeling.

'Kathleen, you can't leave a two-year-old in the house on her own. Anything could happen.'

'Aye, well I'm past caring.'

Margaret was shocked. 'Come on, let's go to yours. I'll help you with the kids.'

'The house is a shit hole,' said Kathleen.

Kathleen felt increasingly useless. She went to the doctor, who prescribed medication. Kathleen wasn't sure the pills were helping with her mood; they made her feel as if she wasn't quite there.

The kids had said a few things: 'You're always tired, Mam'; 'Did you hear what I said, Mam?'

Then there was Cyril who wasn't so subtle: 'Wake up! It's like talking to that sack of spuds in the kitchen!'

His drinking had become steadily heavier, his moods even darker and less predictable. He was lashing out at the kids more, but Kathleen felt nothing.

Sylvia was taking on more and more of the chores and childcare, while Kathleen lay in bed late, or sat in the armchair, with that dead look in her eyes. She had started to reminisce about her time at home with her parents before she married. Compared to her life now, it didn't seem that bad at all. Why had she married the first man that came along? Why couldn't she have been like Rosie? Rosie had waited a bit longer and had met the loveliest bloke you could wish to meet.

Kathleen looked at the bottle of pills.

How easy it would be to take myself out of this.

CHAPTER 12

NO ESCAPE

Kathleen could hear the commotion downstairs but could not bring herself to move. Cyril snored loudly and the stench of stale beer hung in the air. She mustered enough energy to open the window and took a deep breath. The mangle stood in the narrow yard, a bucket beside it. In the bucket were snotty hankies, shitty underwear, vomit-stained vests.

Dear God, what is this life I have?

She shuffled into the front bedroom to see if she could get five minutes' peace. The room was a mess and she tried to ignore the piles of dirty socks, knickers, crumpled school shirts and nighties. The joy of having three girls sharing one room.

Sylvia's bed was the worst, being a teenager, but that's where Kathleen chose to sit.

Smoothing the bed covers, she sat for a moment with her feet on the bed. She was weary; not only in her body, but her head felt like it was being squeezed. She didn't know how much longer she could cope.

Pulling back the sleeve of her dressing gown, she winced at all the scars and bruises, and wondered how much longer it would be before his rage really got the better of him. He no longer seemed to feel remorse after the beatings. In fact, she wondered if he felt anything at all.

In the early days, the moments of tenderness, the regret after each loss of control, had kept her going and kept her with him. Now, what kept her here were her circumstances. How could she survive on her own? She had nowhere to go, and Cyril was going nowhere. She was stuck.

The door swung open, and she almost jumped out of her skin. Cyril towered over her, his face red with rage. She didn't have time to move before he launched at her with his fists, pummelling her body, spouting words of hatred: 'Lazy, useless, idle bitch!'

She tried to protect herself, but it was no good. When anger consumed him, he had the strength of ten men.

By the time the kids came flying upstairs, she was a sorry mess and he'd staggered back to their bedroom. She was guided downstairs by Sylvia who soothed the others while boiling water to bathe her mother's wounds.

'It looks like your nose might be broken, Mam', she said as she wiped it gently, her mother sobbing with the shock. Perhaps it was the lack of warning, or the timing. It certainly wasn't the actual beating that was a surprise. Kathleen's eye was swollen and already beginning to bruise.

'I hate him! I wish he was dead,' said Sylvia, stifling sobs, trying to be brave.

'So do I, but we're stuck with him.'

When Sylvia had finished tending her mother, she made sure the others were fed and got them off to school. Then she sat with Kathleen, despite her assurances that she'd be alright.

After a short period of the house being unusually and eerily quiet, they heard Cyril thumping about upstairs. They instinctively clung to each other, then broke away and made themselves busy with chores.

He staggered downstairs some time later, cleanly shaven and smartly dressed. Sneering at them as he passed, he made his way to the kitchen to prepare his breakfast.

There was cheese and bacon set aside for him, and woe betide anyone who dared to touch it. Sylvia was ravenous by now, Kathleen not so much, but they didn't dare go into the kitchen. So they sat and waited, the aromas of melting cheese and bacon driving Sylvia mad with hunger.

Cyril left the house at eleven, almost slamming the door off its hinges. As soon as he left, Sylvia hurried to work, concocting a story for her absence as she walked.

Kathleen called at Margaret's and was greeted with, 'Oh, my goodness, Kathleen, whatever's happened?'

'What do you think?'

Kathleen stayed there for the best part of the day, only moving when she heard the kids coming home from school. Cyril didn't arrive home at four o'clock, as he normally would.

Kathleen was on edge all evening, waiting for him to stagger in, wondering what state he'd be in. She was just about at breaking point when the younger ones went up to bed, leaving her and Sylvia to gather their thoughts.

'You look done in, Mam.'

'I am done in. I've had enough of the lot of you and of him.'

'We're not that bad.'

'Wait til you've got kids, Sylvia. You'll see.'

'From what I've seen so far, it's not for me.'

'We'll see about that an' all. Anyway, I'm going up in a minute and you need some sleep if you're to get up for work. You've already had time off.'

'Yeah, you're right, I'm going up now. Night, Mam.'

Kathleen sat for a while enjoying the silence, then, just as she'd decided to move, she heard the key in the door. She gripped the arms of the chair and waited for the entrance.

Cyril stumbled in, his red face set in a drunken grin.

'What you still doing up?' he managed to mumble.

'Why shouldn't I be up? I live here an' all, you know.'

'Yeah, well it's my name on the rent book and don't you forget it.'

'As if I could.' She stood up.

Cyril grabbed her and pressed his face into hers: 'Where do you think you're going?'

Kathleen tried to pull herself away, but it was no use. 'To bed. I need some sleep.'

'It's not sleep you need,' he said.

He hit her and she dropped to the floor.

She lay for a moment, her head spinning, not so much with the force of the blow, but with the accumulation of feelings: anger, regret, frustration, shame. Everything leading up to this point was gathering momentum inside her. She grabbed his leg. He stumbled, and caught his head with a sickening thud on the edge of the hearth as he fell.

Despite all the hatred she felt for him, Kathleen's heart was beating wildly, and she began to shake uncontrollably. She didn't know where the fear was coming from or who it was for, but she struggled to breathe, and her chest tightened as she knelt beside him. He mumbled something. She went closer, moved his hair away from his face. His eyes rolled back, and his tongue lolled. He made a feeble attempt to raise his head, but he was either too drunk or too weak. A pool of blood was spreading around his head and she watched with grim fascination as it seeped into the rug and radiated out across the room. It was as if another person was in her place.

There was movement upstairs.

'It's alright, your father's drunk,' she shouted.

Someone grunted, and she heard them walk back into the bedroom and close the door.

Kathleen stared at the distorted face of her husband. She watched as blood oozed from the wound. She stood up, went into the kitchen and scrubbed her hands thoroughly.

For once, it wasn't her own blood she was washing away, but Cyril's.

PART 2

MARIAN

Frozen rigid, she squeezed her eyes shut and wished herself away. A song played on a continuous loop inside her head until the nightmare was finally over.

CHAPTER 1

STEPPING OUT

Manchester, 1960s.

Marian squeezed her tiny frame behind the bookshelf. If she was quiet, they might forget her.

The teacher followed her. 'What are you doing behind there? It's Marian, isn't it?'

Marian was scared, but she answered nervously, 'Nothing. I wanted to be quiet. I don't know anyone.'

Mrs Harvey knelt, her perfume hanging in the air like roses. Her pale blue jumper was clean and soft. She took Marian's hand and pulled her up. 'Come on, pet. I'll introduce you to some of the others. Let's see if we can get to know someone.'

She took her to a table where other children were playing with bricks. 'Mary, Richard, this is Marian. She's a bit shy, so play nicely, won't you?'

Marian didn't feel comfortable; she wanted to crawl back to her corner like she did at home. She sat and watched quietly, hoping they wouldn't bother her.

At story time, she sat engrossed as Mrs Harvey told the tale of *Hansel and Gretel*. She ached inside as she heard about the little boy and girl who didn't have enough to eat, about the stepmother who didn't like them. All the other children gasped when the wife told her husband to leave the children in the forest, but Marian didn't. She wished she could go to the forest with them.

After school, she looked for her mother in the crowd. She noticed how pleased the other mothers appeared as their children ran towards them. She spotted Mam gazing into space, Gail by her side.

'Mam, I've painted a picture for you,' said Marian.

Kathleen looked at her through dull eyes, grabbed Gail's hand and moved off. Marian grabbed hold of her other hand and skipped to keep up.

'I heard a nice story today, Mam.'

Her mother stared blankly ahead.

'Mrs Harvey says I'm a clever little girl,' said Marian, squinting up at her mother.

'Does she now?'

A few days later, Marian's mother failed to turn up at all. Marian waited for Gail to come out, then they ran all the way home, but Mam wasn't there, either. They searched every room, but there was no sign of her.

Frank came home from school. 'What are you two doing on your own? Where's me mam?'

'I don't know. She wasn't at school, so we came home, and there was nobody here.'

'What's there to eat?' asked Frank.

'Nothing,' Marian replied.

They heard the back-door latch being lifted, then the neighbour came in with their mother. Mam's face was red and puffy. She saw the kids and tried to go back out of the house.

'Come on, Kathleen, the kids are home. They want their tea, love,' said Mrs Barker, but their mother hung her head and sobbed.

'I'm going to bed,' Mam said. 'Frank, you'll have to sort the tea out.'

She snatched herself away from Mrs Barker's support.

'But Mam, there's nowt –'

Before he could protest about the lack of food, the kitchen door slammed in his face.

The following week, Marian was reading

behind the settee when she heard the front door open. Her father's heavy footsteps sounded down the hallway.

Here we go. I wonder what mood he'll be in today.

She shuffled into the corner and hid behind the armchair, but her father caught sight of her backside and grabbed her by her flimsy dress. It ripped, and she landed on the rug with a thump.

'I'm sorry, Dad," she whimpered, unable to look him in the eye. "I was looking for the cat.'

'Get in that kitchen and put the kettle on,' he shouted.

Marian quickly scuttled away before he had chance to lash out with his fists.

I hate this house. I hate him!

She held the kettle under the tap, the water splashing everywhere, she was shaking so much. She couldn't think straight and had to pause for a moment to gather her senses. Once she had finished making the tea, she handed it to her father, praying it wouldn't spill on him, then she snuck upstairs.

A little later, her mother's screams rang through the house. Marian's instinct kicked in. She clattered downstairs and flung open the lounge door to see her father with his hands around her mother's throat.

'You're a lazy, fit-for-nothing whore!' he

snarled.

'Please, Dad, leave her alone!' said Marian, spurred on by a gust of bravery. She pulled at her father's leg, but he batted her away.

Her mother took the opportunity to escape his grasp.

'When do I have time to be a whore?' she shrieked, tears streaming.

Marian ran to the door, crept out, and sat on the bottom stair.

He's going to kill her!

But her mother came flying out of the door after her and nearly stood on Marian in her haste to escape. Marian went to see if she was alright, but her mother knocked her away. She followed her to the bathroom anyway.

'Are you alright, Mam?' she asked, noticing the thick splodges of blood in the sink.

'Sod off!' her mother screamed back.

Marian gently closed the door. She was too scared to go downstairs and find a cloth; she'd tell Sylvia about it later.

Her father sat upright in the armchair by the fire. His face was grey, not puce, not filled with violent rage but simmering with quiet contempt and disgust. Marian could hear her mother's pathetic sobs.

'Can I let her in now, Dad?' she pleaded.

'No, leave her there where she belongs', he said.

When Marian had emptied the bin earlier, there was a layer of furry frost on the top of the lid. The cold made clouds of her breath in the air and she'd almost slipped on the ice around the grid as she ran in. It was a bitter cold winter's night and her mother had been locked out for more time than Marian could stand.

She tried again, 'Please, Dad, can she come in? It's freezing out there.'

'No, she bleeding can't,' roared her father. 'She can stay out where she belongs, in the bastard gutter like a dog.'

Marian flinched and went to comfort Gail who had crept downstairs to see what the fuss was about.

Sylvia took each of the girls' hands, 'Come on, it's time for bed, you two. You've got school in the morning.'

'I wish he was dead!' said Marian as she climbed into bed and pulled the counterpane up to her chin.

'So do I, but we're stuck with him,' said Sylvia.

Her tears plopped onto Marian's arm.

CHAPTER 2

DEPARTURE

Marian awoke to the sound of sirens. Warily, she made her way downstairs and into the lounge. A policeman was sitting in her father's chair. He was writing in a small book, but he paused to smile at Marian.

'What's your name, young lady?' he asked, smiling warmly.

'I'm Marian.'

'Hello Marian, I'm PC Carter. Do you mind if I ask you a couple of questions?'

Marian looked to her mother for reassurance, but her mother only looked scared.

'Did you hear anything last night Marian, any noises?'

Again, Marian looked at her mother, 'No, I was asleep.'

'Do you know what time you went to bed?'

'Sylvia took us up.'

'Do you remember the time, sweetheart? Was

it dark? Was your dad home?'

'It was dark, but my dad wasn't home.'

Marian looked around and noticed the red gloop on the rug. 'What's happened? What's that?' she asked, standing over the treacly substance.

'It's nothing,' said her mother. 'Go and get your breakfast.'

Marian did as she was told.

Later that day, Marian was met from school by Mrs Barker.

'Hello love,' she said as she gestured for Marian to take her hand.

'Where's me mam?' asked Marian. 'Is she poorly again?'

'You'll see, love, when you get home. How about something from the ice cream van?'

Marian's eyes lit up, 'Yes please!'

When Marian arrived home, Sylvia was sobbing in the kitchen. She had never seen Sylvia in such a state.

'What's wrong? Where's my dad? When will he come home from the hospital?'

'He's not coming home, Marian. He fell and banged his head on the hearth last night and, well, he lost a lot of blood and they couldn't save him.'

Marian felt frisson of glee, but she frowned to match Sylvia's grief. 'Don't cry, Sylvia, it'll be alright,' she said, wondering whatever could happen next. 'Where's Mam?'

'She's in bed, sleeping. I'll be looking after us for a while until she feels better.'

'Don't worry, we'll manage,' Marian said to her big sister.

Sylvia blew noisily into her hankie. She looked wretched. 'We'll have to manage! What else can we do?'

They hugged once more and set about the task of preparing tea for when the others arrived.

Marian didn't see much of her mum after that. She wasn't up when Marian and the others went to school, and she was either out when they got home or she'd put herself to bed and wasn't to be disturbed.

As time moved on, Sylvia became less of a sister to Marian and more of a mother.

After her father's death, visits from the police were replaced by visits from social workers who asked questions about her mother. Sylvia had told her to say nothing.

Marian's life was better in some ways, in some ways worse. She didn't have the spectre of her father hanging over her, waiting to pounce, but times were tough in other ways. Sylvia had to take weekend work, as well as doing her regular job. Mam had been using the family allowance to buy drink and go out instead of paying the bills, so Sylvia had to work extra hard to make sure the rent got paid and there was food. Marian was not allowed to talk about this to Social Services, or else they could all be put in a home.

This carried on for a couple of years, the visits from Social Services eventually dwindling away when they were satisfied the children were being fed.

From then on, Marian noticed a change in her mother. Her evenings out became more frequent, and she started to bring a man home who she introduced as Brian. He seemed alright, but sometimes he would snap at Marian or one of the others to *be quiet!*

About two years after her father's death, Marian was eating breakfast when her mother struggled into the kitchen dragging two suitcases.

Marian stopped eating. 'Where are you going, Mam?'

'I'm going to live with Brian,' she said, not looking Marian in the eye.

Sylvia followed her mother into the kitchen, her eyes red and puffy.

A horn beeped, they all jumped, and their mother slid out of their lives without looking back.

It was a whole year before Kathleen finally allowed Marian and the others to visit her in Stockport where she now lived. They would get the bus from Longsight after school on a Monday.

Sylvia couldn't go with them as she was working, but she always asked Marian how she'd got on. The story was always the same: she'd been made to sit quietly and not disturb Brian. And her mother acted strangely, slurring her words, laughing at nothing.

CHAPTER 3

ONE MORE STEP

Life continued to be difficult for Marian and the other girls. Since their mother left, they had become the targets of Frank's angry outbursts. He was only sixteen, but he seemed to be happy to step into his father's shoes.

Marian, who had always been a timid child, withdrew into her books, escaping on adventures and learning of other worlds.

Then one day, Sylvia pulled her to one side. 'You've passed your eleven-plus. I always knew you were a clever bugger.'

Marian was stunned. She couldn't wait to go back to school the next day, knowing her teacher would be so proud.

'You'll be too good for us soon, won't be talking to us,' Sylvia said as she combed Marian's hair that night, but Marian could see the pride in her eyes. 'You've done well, our kid. I'm only teasing you.'

'I'm a bit scared of going to Grammar.'

'Why?' asked Sylvia.

'Because they'll all be posh, and I won't. I've got nothing to wear.'

'Oh, don't you worry about that, our kid. We'll sort all that out nearer the time. You'll be fine. You're dead clever, you are.'

Marian looked her sister square in the eye. 'I'm going to get a good job. I don't want to end up like me mam.'

It was her first day at Grammar School and Marian was dressed from head to toe in new clothes. She slipped on the shiny black shoes, free from the Co-op, and walked around the rug. They were stiff and made her feet feel like wood.

'Do I look stupid, Sylvia? I feel like I can't walk in these shoes.'

'Don't be daft, it's only because they're new. We're not used to having new shoes, are we? They'll be alright when you've worn them in.'

Sylvia straightened Marian's tie. 'You look great, our kid. Come on, I'll show you.'

She led Marian upstairs to the main bedroom where a mahogany chest of drawers stood with a central mirror just low enough to get a full-length view. Marian stood in front of it.

'That's not me!' she said.

'It is,' said Sylvia. 'Now stand proud and hold your head up, because you were meant to go to Grammar. You have as much right to be there as anyone else, and don't you forget it.'

Marian tried to believe, but inside she still felt like a misfit.

She was nervous as she walked up the path to the school. She climbed the stone steps and went through the big wooden door, where she was met by a teacher.

'Good morning, and welcome,' said the woman. 'Can I take your name?'

'Marian Benson.'

'Ah Marian,' she said as she scanned her list. 'Here you are. You need to go to Room 21 on the right side of the hall, just through those doors.'

'Thank you,' said Marian.

She found the room, a classroom of single wooden desks with inkwells, all facing the blackboard at the front. There was a scent in the air like shoe polish and she guessed it must be from the battered but gleaming wooden floor.

She felt slightly better now that she was in a smaller space. She looked round the room, feeling the familiar twinge of inferiority, but Sylvia's words came to her and she sat up straight.

She was embarrassed, though, when they

went to line up for dinner tickets. The queue moved on and it was her turn.

'I'm free dinners,' she managed to mumble, knowing they were all looking. The lady asked for her name and ticked it off the list. She handed her a strip of five tickets, each with *FREE DINNER* written across it. Even though her clothes were new, Marian felt like a tramp.

Marian was twelve when Sylvia dashed straight home one day, after a phone call at work. She looked very solemn and gathered the others to tell them the news.

'I don't know how to say this,' she said between sobs. 'But today… today –' Sylvia broke down and sobbed into her hands.

'What is it, Sylvia? Just tell us,' said Frank, now a bold eighteen-year-old.

'My mam died today,' she said, putting her arms around Gail and Marian.

'What?' said Gail. 'What do you mean? We only saw her last week.'

'Yes, and you said she looked very thin and tired, didn't you?' said Sylvia, rubbing Marian's back.

'She did,' said Marian, sobbing. 'But she's looked like that for ages.'

'I know she has, she's been poorly,' said Sylvia, looking at her and Gail with pity. Frank had sloped off.

'What was it? What did she die of?' asked Gail.

'It was cancer, Gail. Have you heard that word?' asked Sylvia.

'I have,' sobbed Marian. 'And it's not good.'

'No, it isn't, not good at all,' said Sylvia.

Marian knew her big sister felt the full burden of motherhood, and she sensed that, soon, Sylvia too would leave them.

CHAPTER 4

ROAD TO HELL

Marian jumped at the sound of the front door slamming shut. Although her father was long gone, his power over her wasn't. She realised it must be Frank coming home from his night shift. He was on ten–six this week, which meant he would be in bed by the time she got up for school. She was thankful for that.

Sylvia had left home a couple of years ago, and she had a child of her own with another on the way. Since she'd left, it had been carte blanche for Frank to throw his weight around even more than he had before.

Marian turned over, trying to get comfortable in the lower bunk. A searing pain in her side took her breath away. She sat up as an overwhelming urge to empty her bowels came over her. Fortunately, the house had been fitted with an inside toilet a couple of years before.

Crawling back into bed, she felt another wave of nausea and had to visit the bathroom again.

By the time her alarm went off at seven thirty, she felt shocking. Drained of energy, she padded down to the kitchen, but had to sit down before she passed out.

'Jesus, Marian, you look like a ghost. What's up?' asked Gail, seventeen now and working as a cashier at the local Co-op.

'I don't know. I've been sick and, you know, the other one. I feel shocking.'

'You look it an' all. You'd better stay off.'

'I know, I've already decided that. My first ever day off, but I can't go in like this. Can you phone in for me, Gail?'

'Course I can. Go back to bed and I'll bring you a cup of tea up.'

'Oh, thanks, that would be great. I'm parched.'

Marian slept for a while, then ventured downstairs to look for a suitable snack. She felt much better now, just weak.

Her peace was shattered by an almighty bang, followed by another and another.

Bloody Frank. Banging on the bloody floor, just like my dad. No doubt he wants a cup of tea.

She put the kettle on and was looking for a clean cup when he banged again.

'Get up here now!' he shouted.

Marian dropped the cup she was drying, and it shattered in bits on the lino. She left it glistening on the cold floor and rushed upstairs, arriving out of breath by her father's bed, where she stood with her head down, trying to recover.

'What are you doing home, waking me up?'

'I'm not well,' said Marian, not meeting his gaze.

'What's up with you? You look alright to me,' he sneered, looking her up and down.

Marian wrung her hands together, still looking at the floor, 'I'm not well, I've been sick this morning and I couldn't face going.'

'Couldn't face going?' he mimicked.

Marian was terrified, made sure she kept a step away from him in case he lashed out. But, suddenly, his mood changed, and he reached for her hand. 'Why don't you get in bed with me, get warm?' he said, pulling her to him.

Marian took a step back, but he yanked her forward. His expression changed into an angry snarl and he pulled her again, making her fall onto the bed.

'I should go and make some tea,' she whimpered.

'You'll lie in this bed and do as you're told,' he said. 'Or else, God help me, I'll wring your skinny neck.'

Dread washed over Marian like a death shroud. She slipped under the covers, staying as far from her brother as she possibly could.

'I want you to do to me what you do to all those boys at school,' he said, grabbing her hand and thrusting it down his grubby underpants.

Marian gasped. 'I don't know what you mean, Frank. I don't do anything with any boys,' she sobbed.

That was when he slapped her. She sat bolt upright and put her hand to her cheekbone.

'Like hell you don't know what to do, you little whore,' he snarled, pinning her down with one hand and grabbing her breast roughly with the other.

Shock and pain rendered her mute and immobile. A song, which came from nowhere, started to play in her head, taking her away from the horror of the moment: *'This could be the last time, this could be the last time, maybe the last time, I don't know...'*

The ordeal lasted no more than ten minutes, but to Marian it was a lifetime. She limped back to her own bed where she sobbed until she was empty.

Her brother's demands became regular, but no less traumatic. Each time, Marian would shut her eyes tight, and the song would play on a loop in her head until it was over. She was trapped into silence by her brother's threats:

tell anyone and you're dead. No one will believe you anyway, and if they do, you'll be taken away and put in a home where terrible things will happen to you.

Marian put all her efforts into her schoolwork to keep her mind off what was happening at home. Gail called her boring, but she had to keep busy. Besides, if she did well, she had more chance of escaping.

She was nearly at the end of her final year at secondary school when Frank took her to Ireland to solve a family problem which she had to swear, on threat of her life, to keep a secret.

CHAPTER 5

CROSSROADS

Marian had started as a hairdresser's apprentice shortly after leaving school, a job she grew into after an initial struggle with confidence. Despite it not being her first choice, she enjoyed listening to everyone's chatter, even joined in sometimes. She was offered a place at college, on day release, which she had taken willingly. Now, she was a fully qualified stylist. Mrs Robinson, her mentor at school, would be mortified: *'That's no job for a Grammar School girl.'*

But Marian loved her job; she loved the chats with clients and their interest in her and her life. It was physically hard though, being on her feet all day, making small talk. At least Frank had left home and she didn't have to face him anymore. She and Gail could afford the rent and life was getting better. However, Marian suffered bouts of depression which would descend without warning, enveloping her in a black blanket of doom. On days like those, she would hardly speak, then she'd crawl into bed after tea, thinking how futile her life was and how she'd be better off dead. Most times, she'd feel better after a few days, then she'd wonder how she could have felt so awful just the day before.

It was one of those cool spring evenings when the brightness of green gives way to a gentle dusk. Marian and Gail were getting ready to go out. Marian finished off her make-up with another layer of mascara and admired her work. She knew her eyes were her best feature; she felt there was nothing else about her that was interesting. She stood up and checked her profile, smoothing her stomach.

'Are you nearly ready?' she called to Gail.

'Two shakes of a donkey's tail.'

Marian smiled: another one of Gail's quirky sayings.

'Come on, let's go. The love of your life might be waiting in the pub.'

'Yeah, like hell. More like the son of Frankenstein.'

Finally, they left the house and walked into town, both holding their heads rigid so as not to spoil their perms which were held in place by copious amounts of lacquer.

'Where first?' asked Marian.

'*Oddfellows?*'

'Great stuff, our kid.'

They had their first half of lager and black, savouring the sweet liquid which felt like a great reward after a long week. They chatted with people who had become familiar faces, then moved on to the next pub. There were a few pubs in Longsight, but they had their favourites. They were getting to know the regulars and it was nice to have a bit of banter with them.

Marian still had that thing about not wanting to talk sometimes, couldn't quite believe anyone would want to listen to her. Gail more than made up for it, though. She always started the chat, which probably led Marian to meet more people.

They were back in the *Oddfellows* now, and Gail was laughing at the bar with some young lad.

'Cheer up love, it might never happen,' the person next to Marian said.

She looked up to see the face of an unfamiliar lad. She blushed and wished Gail would hurry back. Finally, she did return, and Marian took her drink before Gail had chance to put it down on the table.

'Bloody hell, love, you were desperate for that, weren't you?' said the man.

Marian blushed, embarrassed that the focus

was on her. More people came to sit in the corner seat. They all squeezed up, so that the lad who had made Marian blush ended up sitting right next to her.

'I know this is corny,' he said. 'But I'm sure I've seen you before.'

'Probably, yeah. We come down here nearly every week, so there's a good chance.'

'I'm James, by the way.'

'Marian.'

James looked nervous, twisting his hands, 'Look, before you go, can I ask you out for a drink sometime?'

Marian didn't really know what to say but she quickly wrote down her number and handed it to him, conscious of Gail wanting to move on.

'Thanks,' he said. 'I'll call next week.'

For the rest of the evening, Marian couldn't get James out of her mind. He'd had such kind eyes, but she wasn't sure she wanted a relationship. She wondered if he would call and what she would say if he did. Gail asked her, on more than one occasion, what was wrong, but Marian told her: 'Nothing.'

When they finally staggered home, later that evening, Gail told Marian that she'd also given her number out. They talked about how exciting it would be if they both got a boyfriend.

'They've got to call us yet,' Marian reminded Gail.

'I'm not that bothered anyway,' said Gail. 'They weren't that good-looking.'

Marian laughed. She was secretly pleased to have caught someone's attention, and was hoping, against the odds, that he would call her.

The call finally came on the Tuesday night, after three days of wondering if he meant what he had said and if he liked her at all. They arranged to meet the following night and she managed to borrow a decent outfit to wear, having worn her 'best' one at the weekend.

Once she got dressed, the nerves kicked in and the self-doubt started.

What if he only found me attractive because he'd had a few drinks? What if he doesn't turn up? What if he walks away when he sees me? I bet he'll be disappointed when he sees the size of my chest and how thin I am. I don't care what they say about Twiggy, men seem to want curvy girls and I've got a lot of growing to do.

Her thoughts were interrupted by the beeping of a horn. She grabbed her coat and handbag and opened the front door.

His car looked reasonably new, and she let herself in the passenger side.

'Hiya, how are you?' said James, that warming smile melting her doubts.

'I'm alright, thanks,' she said. 'I like your car.'

'Oh thanks,' he said. 'I've only had it a couple of years. It costs a lot to run, but I kind of need it for work.'

'Where do you work?'

'I'm a banker, work for *TSB* in Stockport.'

'Oh right, *Trustees Savings Bank*.'

'That's the one. Well done for knowing what it means. Most people don't.'

'Yeah, well my brother told me,' said Marian, suddenly nauseated.

'Are you alright?' asked James. 'You're shaking.'

Tell anyone and you're dead.

'I'm fine,' said Marian, gaining her composure. 'Where shall we go, then?'

'*Oddfellows*?'

'Yeah,' said Marian. 'That sounds good to me.'

Inevitably, the conversation turned to family.

'Do you have any brothers and sisters?' asked James.

Marian laughed nervously, 'Two sisters and a brother, but there's only me and our Gail at home now.'

'Is she the one you were with when I met you?'

'Yeah, that's the one. She's two years older than me.'

'What about your mum and dad? Are they around?'

Marian went quiet: she had been dreading this moment.

'I don't mean to pry, just making small talk.'

She tried to think of the best way to say it. 'My dad, he died when I was little.'

'I'm really sorry to hear that,' said James.

'Don't be. He was a drunken bully who made our lives a misery.'

'It's a good job he's dead, then. I'd want to knock his lights out,' said James, visibly angry.

'He honestly wouldn't be worth it.'

'Maybe. What about your mum?'

'She left us, then she died,' said Marian, looking down.

'What, as in walked out on you?'

'Yep, a couple of years after my dad died. My sister, our Sylvia, brought me up. She's got her own family now.'

'God, I can't imagine what that was like,' said James, looking at Marian in disbelief.

'We managed,' she said.

'What did she die of, if you don't mind me asking?'

'Cancer.'

CHAPTER 6

ANOTHER PATH

James was late for their second date.

I bet he's not coming.

Finally there was a knock on the door, and she sprang up. Opening the front door, she was dazzled by that glorious smile, and all was forgiven.

'I'm sorry I'm late, the traffic was awful.'

'It's alright,' said Marian, trying to disguise the tremor in her voice.

'Your carriage awaits, my lady,' said James.

This time, they decided to venture out to Worsley, where James lived. They settled on the *Bridgewater Hotel*, a traditional-looking pub in the village itself. Marian felt out of her depth, as if everyone was looking at her, judging her.

'It's posh in here, isn't it?' she said.

'Maybe, compared to Longsight, but not really,' said James.

'I didn't realise you lived here. What were you

doing in Longsight that night?'

'A few drinks after work with a colleague who lives near there. I needed a change and, well, the rest's history, as they say.'

'I can't imagine anyone wanting to come to Longsight when this is the other option.'

Marian didn't think he realised how uncomfortable she was. Everyone appeared to be so confident, smug even. And some of the girls were stunning.

I bet he wishes he'd come on his own now.

To make matters worse, she thought she saw him eyeing one of them up. This didn't help her mood at all and there was an awkward silence.

'What's wrong, Marian? You seem quiet all of a sudden.'

'I saw you.'

'Saw me what?' he laughed.

'Looking at that girl with the blonde hair.'

'Oh, come on! Do you never look at men?' He seemed incredulous, affronted even.

He would deny it, wouldn't he?

The whole scenario built up into a bit of a nightmare and she suddenly wanted to go home.

'Come on, do you think I'd have asked you out if I wanted to chat up other girls?'

Maybe she was allowing her insecurities to ruin their first date. 'Good point. I'm sorry. I have this thing about trusting people.'

'Give it a chance, Marian. Get to know me a little. I'm not a womaniser, but I am human.'

'I know. I blame the parents. Let's just say they were far from perfect, but that's for another time. I do apologise. I don't want it to spoil the night.'

'Forgotten already,' said James, grinning.

Over the next few months, they became physically and emotionally close and, before long, they began to talk about the future. It was an exciting time, but very unsettling for Marian as she swung between being completely sure of his love to doubting it.

This roller coaster of emotions was hard to deal with, but it was worth it to have someone who cared about her, who loved her. She'd hardly experienced being loved before, and maybe that's why it was difficult for her to get to grips with.

It reminded her of the time she went to a friend's house and her mum went to hug her.

You're as stiff as an ironing board, I won't bite.

She didn't bite, but Marian remembered feeling very awkward and not knowing what to do. Maybe there was an art to accepting love and hugs that she hadn't yet learned?

As if building a relationship with James wasn't difficult enough, she also had to spend time with his parents, which she found uncomfortable. They were nice enough, but she got the feeling she wasn't good enough for them.

James was from a very different family background, and this added to her feeling of being inferior. It was little things, like the way they looked at her and spoke to her as if she was stupid:

'What's that you've got on, Marian? What *do* you look like?'

Sometimes she wanted the ground to swallow her up. *Can they not see how much it hurts; how much it embarrasses me?*

She had to keep reminding herself that she was as good as anyone else, but it was difficult. She supposed they wanted what was best for their son, but so did she.

On one occasion, she was feeling down, and his mum asked what was wrong. Marian told her she was a bit depressed, and his mum laughed, asked what she could possibly have to be depressed about. Marian didn't know; she was as confused as anyone else as to why this black cloud would descend from nowhere, for no apparent reason, and follow her around for a while.

She kept telling herself she'd done well to come through her childhood without resorting to drink or drugs. She felt the need to pat herself on the back, because no one else would.

James said he loved her, and she believed him, most of the time anyway. It was when the black cloud came that she doubted everything, not just James. She would convince herself she was worthless, that she'd never amount to anything, never get over the shyness, the lack of confidence, the blushing and reluctance to speak.

When the cloud lifted though, it was as if she'd been reborn. She would feel lighter of spirit and able to get on with things, to go to work willingly, clean the house, shop and cook, without feeling like she was battling.

When James picked her up this particular evening around a year into their relationship, he was wearing smart clothes and a strange smile.

'What's up with you? You look happy about something.'

'Nothing's up, I'm just happy to see you, as always.'

Marian slipped into the passenger seat.

'Are you ready to knock everyone dead with your knowledge?' she asked.

'I thought we could go for a meal tonight for a change. The quiz is great, but I fancy an Indian.'

'What about the others? They'll be expecting

us on the team, won't they?'

'No, I rang Dave before I left, and I've booked us in at the *Shere Khan* for eight.'

He looked nervous, loosening his tie.

When does he ever wear a tie?

Then the penny dropped, and Marian had to sit on her hands to stop them shaking. It was too soon: she hadn't been able to tell him about her trip to Ireland, and wondered if she ever could.

'We'd better get a move on then,' she said. 'Or else we'll be late.'

She didn't say another word until they parked up and walked towards the restaurant. 'Do I look alright, James?'

'Course you do. As gorgeous as ever.'

Marian had acted out this scenario many times – where he would do it, what he would say – but she didn't expect it so soon into their relationship.

They were greeted at the front desk and shown to their seats.

'It's nice to be taken for a meal, especially when I didn't expect it,' said Marian, noticing that James was nervous, positively shaking.

'That's what I thought,' he said, trying to act casual, but fumbling with his serviette.

'Are we having the works?' asked Marian.

'The works?'

'Yeah, you know; poppadoms, starters, mains, desserts.'

'Most definitely.'

The waiter took their orders and returned almost immediately with a plate of poppadoms, warm and greasy. They tucked in, glad of a distraction from their nervous chatter.

They'd relaxed a little by the time the mains arrived and they'd both enjoyed a glass of wine. Marian hadn't commented on James' insistence on ordering a posh red instead of the usual pint and a half of lager; she wanted to feign surprise if her instinct turned out to be right.

Finally, they got on to desserts and James fumbled around. Next minute, he was down on one knee and a knowing murmur was circulating around the restaurant.

'Will you marry me, Marian?' A simple question. No build up.

'Yes, I'd love to.'

They hugged and cried, and people whooped and cheered.

In the commotion, he almost forgot the ring. 'Oh, you might want this.' The solitaire slipped easily onto her finger. 'Do you like it?'

'Do I like it? I love it!'

Marian skipped into work on Monday morning, eager to tell her colleagues the news and show off her ring. There were gasps of appreciation and admiring inspections. She held it up to the light so it would sparkle, but a couple of her workmates were not smiling, and Marian wondered why.

Could be they're envious of the ring, or they think I'm too young?

But Marian knew what she was doing, and nothing was going to burst her bubble. The only thing that would destroy her was if he left her. She had thought about this often, maybe too often, but she couldn't help it. Now though, she could look at her ring and know he would be with her forever.

CHAPTER 7

JOURNEY

It was the morning of the wedding and Marian was dwelling on her past, her regret at not being completely open with James. Her hand instinctively rested on her tummy. She'd have to tell him soon; she should have told him before now.

She thought ahead to the walk down the aisle. No father to give her away, no mother of the bride. It would be awkward. She could imagine his family judging her or pitying her; she wanted neither.

To say that she and her mother had not been close was an understatement. Marian had never felt Kathleen was a real mother, and when she left them, the chasm had widened.

When Mam first left, Marian and her siblings would catch the bus to her new house in Stockport. But she had never made them feel welcome there. Their mother was always on edge, waiting for them to go. She would be critical of them and dismissive if they tried to discuss their home life.

After a while, Sylvia had stopped going with them to Stockport, then Frank, until it was just Marian and Gail. Then one day Gail confronted Mam about leaving her children. The exchange became heated, their mother screaming at them, and Marian was taken right back to when their father was alive. She stood up, walked out and didn't visit her mother again. Soon after that came the news that she had died.

Marian could feel herself going down a rabbit hole of sadness. She needed to get a grip. She walked over to the mirror and, for once, she knew she looked beautiful. She even *felt* beautiful. Her hair and make-up were just right, the dress fitted and flattered her figure perfectly. She took a deep breath and told herself she *was* good enough.

There was a tap on the door, then Frank came in. He had insisted on giving her away.

He who took it away is giving me away.

'We're ready to go, kid,' he said, holding out his arm.

She was shaking inside her perfect dress, still scared of him, stomach churning, hands sweating. She slipped her hand through his arm and felt like his little whore, like she was his property and he still had control.

Don't you dare tell anyone. Who'd believe a little

slut like you, anyway?

That song was there again. Song on a loop in her head and the world in front of her spinning.

'What's the matter, Marian?' she heard Sylvia say, as they stepped into the lounge.

'Nothing, I'm just nervous.'

They walked out into the street where a few neighbours had gathered. There was squealing and sighing, and *doesn't she look lovely*, but Marian moved through the confetti as if it were treacle.

She put her head down and climbed quickly into the car. She had wanted to look perfect, but she felt dirty. She needed to pull herself together before she got to the church, so she thought about the smiling faces that would greet her there. She thought about her sisters and her friends, then she took a few deep breaths and stared out of the car window at the streets, the traffic, the grime of the place, and wished for better things.

By the time she reached the church, she had calmed down and she walked down the aisle with confidence. She looked straight ahead, to where James was standing. He turned and smiled, and she swam in that moment of love. It swept her forward to her rightful place, next to the man she loved.

She cried at her own wedding, at the words of the vows.

To love and honour, until death us do part.

Those words made her feel safe, like nothing could hurt her.

Someone is going to look after me, someone who loves me more than anything, and it feels good.

She looked at her now husband and it didn't matter that his mother was looking down her nose at her and her family. It didn't matter because he'd done it, he'd married her, Marian, the common girl, the one from Longsight with a mother who left her and a father who drank himself to death.

She would show them.

I'm a nice person and I'm worth as much as anyone else because I have a good heart.

This was her mantra, the words she needed to repeat whenever she had doubts, whenever she was in that pit of depression feeling sorry for herself. Sometimes, she'd felt it would be better to die than battle with her bleak thoughts every day. But today was a good day.

After the wedding breakfast, she was reluctant to circulate around the 'other' side. Her own family presented enough of a challenge as far as personalities were concerned, but at least she knew them, knew they were on the same level. The 'others' were a different matter. She thought of them as way above her, even though she knew that it was only money that set them apart. Or was it?

They seemed to have neat little families who stayed together and cared about each other. When she looked at the sea of faces on the other side of the room, she saw smiles, easy chatter and loving glances. She saw them as a different breed, and she looked on them with envy. It struck her how different their lives had been.

But why should I feel inferior when none of it was my fault?

She knew she was being irrational: everyone was born the same, on the same planet, made of the same stuff. But she still couldn't shake that feeling of being the scruffy little kid with the seedy secret.

'Hello Marian, you look miles away there.'

It was James's mother, Connie, looking down her elegant nose, her beautiful chiffon attire seeming to mock Marian's sub-standard dress, bought from a department store sale not a select boutique. Even on her wedding day, when she knew she looked good, on the inside she felt like second-hand goods.

'Oh, you made me jump. I was just thinking how nice everyone looks.'

Why do I always feel like what I'm saying is inane and pointless? Why does she make me nervous?

'Yes, we scrub up well, don't we? You look lovely, by the way.'

'Thank you,' said Marian, blushing furiously.

Then off she went, back to her ladies who lunch.

Connie's sharp departure somehow served to deflate Marian, but she was determined not to be sad on this of all days, so she sought out her husband who was standing near the bar with a couple of his mates. As she approached, they were laughing out loud and she was sure she heard them mention a girl's name, someone James used to see before he met her, but they fell silent when they saw her.

'Here she comes, the beautiful bride,' one of them said, and she smiled, but she felt like sliding away.

'Which one of you is going to buy me a drink?' she said, hoping they didn't think she was being forward.

'Are you not looking after your missus, James? Get her a drink, lad, and get me one while you're there.'

James looked at her in a puzzled way. Wondering, no doubt, why she was desperate for a drink so early in the day. She followed him to the bar, stood next to him, and slipped her hand into his just as he pulled it up to attract the attention of the barmaid. She felt stupid, but she gulped down the tears and hoped he hadn't noticed.

'It's alright, I've still got some Cava left on the

table. I'll go and see if I can find it.'

James gave a quick nod to let her know he'd heard and carried on with his drinks order. She felt lower than ever, so she returned to the table, found the Cava and drank it fast to get a quick buzz.

'Bloody hell, our kid, you knocked that back, didn't you?' Sylvia said.

And suddenly she was back to what she knew, where she felt comfortable on an equal footing.

'Yes, I needed that. Are you enjoying yourself?'

'Course I am. How could I not? It was a great meal and it's a lovely place. They're a bit posh, his family, aren't they?'

'Yeah, a bit posh for the likes of us. But never mind, it's not them I've married, it's James and he's not posh at all.'

'Don't you be too sure, our kid. They're all posh and they all stick together. I've seen the way they look at us, like we're tramps.'

'Don't be daft, we're all the same, we all come from the same place,' Marian said, but her sister was right, and she knew she'd have to fight for her place. She'd have to stand her ground in this new territory. She'd have to prove herself worthy.

CHAPTER 8

CROSSING THE BRIDGE

In the months following the wedding, Marian and James busied themselves with decorating their home. They had bought a small terrace in Swinton where James had been transferred with work. They couldn't afford Worsley prices, and Marian was glad.

I'd stand out like a sore thumb there.

Once the house was finished, Marian became consumed by the need to have a baby. It governed her every thought and deed. Sensible people told her to wait, to enjoy the time they had together, but it was all she could think of and she felt ready.

Sometimes, she'd pretend she was pregnant, cradling an imaginary lump, hoping it would happen easily. This fantasy carried on for almost a year, until James made it clear he didn't want children any time soon. He thought they were too young. Marian tried to dispute this, but it was no use. She wondered how he would feel if she were to get pregnant by mistake. Would he accept it? She didn't want to take that chance though, as she knew only too well how it felt to be unwanted.

Despite still obsessing about having a child, Marian stopped raising the possibility with James. He was right: they were young, and they were having fun, building their lives and making their home comfortable and secure.

After a couple of years, though, Marian thought she would go crazy with the endless daydreams and fantasies about becoming a mother.

James came home from work one day and bounded into the living room with his usual big smile. He hadn't even taken off his coat before she spoke.

'Can I talk to you about something?' she said, patting the space next to her on the fabric settee.

'Course you can. Anything.'

'I want a baby, James.'

His face dropped. He took off his coat, hung it in the hallway, then shuffled back in.

'We've been through this, Marian. You know how I feel. It's too soon, and we can't afford it.'

'We can! I've worked it out, look.'

She thrust the piece of paper in front of him and he laughed.

'Is this how you spend your time?'

She felt deflated, but she wanted this so much.

'I did a bit of working out, that's all. Look: incoming and outgoing. There's still a bit left at the end of the week when we've paid all the bills.'

He looked at the paper and laughed again. 'What about all the costs of having a baby? The pram, clothes, food? You haven't written that down.'

'We know a couple of people who've had kids, we could get the pram cheap, or your parents might help us out.'

He made his way to the kitchen. 'How long has tea been on? It'll ruin if we leave it much longer,' he called.

She shouted back, 'Don't you *want* a baby? I thought you did!' She was trying to hold it together but failing.

He walked back in and she slouched on the settee, holding her piece of paper like it was the answer to everything. He sat next to her, took the paper and held her hand.

'I do want a baby, Marian, but it's got to be when the time is right.'

She started to cry. 'Ann at work says the time is never right, that no one would ever have kids if they waited for the right time.'

'There will be a right time, but it isn't now. We need to save, so we can have enough for a good start.'

Marian knew he was right, but her body was screaming.

CHAPTER 9

NEW HORIZONS

Marian had waited for this moment for what seemed like forever. The surgery was busy, and she fidgeted with the hem of her skirt.

'Marian Walsh?'

She jumped at her name being called and stood up abruptly, knocking her handbag to the floor.

'Ah, Mrs Walsh, do come in,' said Doctor Marsh. 'I'm very pleased to tell you that your result is positive.'

Marian released the breath she had been holding, and tears of relief spilled onto her cheeks.

'Here you are,' said the doctor as he passed her a tissue. 'I hope those are tears of joy?'

'Oh, they are,' replied Marian. 'I've waited a long time for this.'

'There's no reason at all why you shouldn't have a healthy pregnancy. You're fit and active, so I wouldn't worry too much about approaching thirty. Although, you probably know that early twenties are considered to be the optimum time to have your first.'

For a moment, Marian faltered under the weight of a flashback to her time in Ireland: being made to feel like a dirty whore; pain, confusion, and the emptiness and guilt she'd felt on the ferry home. *James needs to know.*

'My husband took some persuading.'

The doctor smiled and reassured her that her husband would be bowled over when the baby was born. 'They turn our worlds upside down, but we wouldn't have it any other way, would we?'

'No, I can't imagine going through life without a child,' said Marian. 'I'm so lucky.'

She floated out of the surgery and went straight home, where she sat for ages thinking about what to say to James.

Finally, she heard his car pull up and she went to greet him at the door. It took him a while to gather his things from the passenger seat as his lunch box had fallen into the footwell. She strode over and opened the car door.

He seemed flustered: it wasn't the right moment.

'You're home early,' he said. 'I didn't think you'd be in yet.'

'I had a bit of time owing me and I was tired,

so I came home at three.'

He seemed so miserable, she was deflated. She made her way back into the house, through to the kitchen to put the kettle on. 'Do you want one?' she asked as he hung up his coat.

'Yes, please. I'm parched.'

She placed the steaming mug on the tiny dining table and pulled out her chair. James sat opposite her. 'What are you smiling at?' he said, smiling himself.

Relieved his mood wasn't so bad after all, Marian said, 'I've got something to tell you.'

'You're not–?'

'Pregnant! Yes!' she said, grinning widely.

James' face dropped, just a touch, 'Are you kidding?'

'No! I didn't really have time owing. I went to the doctor's. I'm nine weeks.'

James leapt up and hugged her. They stood in the middle of the kitchen, holding each other, before James broke their silence.

'We've only just started trying. I thought it would take ages.'

'I know, but I'm glad it didn't.'

'Who have you told?' asked James.

'No one. I wanted to tell you first.'

'Shall we go and tell my mum and dad?' asked James. 'I can't wait to see their faces.'

'Yeah, shall we?' asked Marian, wondering

how they'd respond. 'I'm too excited to eat tea yet, anyway.'

She didn't have the heart now to tell her husband what he had a right to know.

Marian felt the usual trepidation as she walked through to the lounge at her in-laws. She'd never been comfortable here, always felt inferior, but she was sure they'd welcome the news.

'We've got something to tell you,' said James.

'Oh, you're not pregnant, are you?' asked his mother.

Marian's heart sank and she slumped into the easy chair. 'Yep, nine weeks,' she said. 'Due next April.'

James's dad came over to Marian and hugged her lightly. 'Congratulations, love,' he said.

'I thought we'd escaped the grandparent thing,' Connie said.

'Come on, Connie,' said his dad. 'You know it's what you want, really.'

'We'll see,' she said. 'But don't be asking us to mind it. We're too old.'

Marian tried to hide the hurt, but James had picked up on it. He'd edged onto the arm of the chair and slipped his hand in hers. She squeezed it and willed away the tears. All was smoothed over with tea and cakes and the promise of a chip shop tea to celebrate.

Despite the lack of enthusiasm from her mother-in-law, Marian was able for the most part to enjoy her pregnancy; the physical aspect, at least. Marian loved being pregnant. It gave her a sense of purpose, of belonging. Although she was nervous about the birth and about being a good mum, she was sure she could do a better job than her own.

Mentally, she didn't feel as prepared. She would worry about the baby's development, whether it would be normal, how she would cope if it wasn't, how she would cope if it was. However, she tried to prepare herself for the imminent birth as much as possible.

Having given up work six weeks before the due date, she spent her afternoons daydreaming whilst stroking her growing bump and watching in wonder as the baby moved around and her stomach morphed into all sorts of wonderful shapes.

She would spend hours sorting out the layette of essentials, rubbing soft knitted cardigans between her finger and thumb and smelling their newness, smoothing out tiny vests and baby-gros, trying to imagine her child filling them.

James, thankfully, had fully come round to the idea of being a parent, and was probably as excited as she was. Sure, he talked about the sacrifices they would have to make, the ones they were already making, but he seemed happy, and Marian was relieved.

She just wished she could shake off these awful feelings of dread and guilt.

CHAPTER 10

A NEW BEGINNING

Marian was engrossed in her chores one afternoon when she felt a sudden pain across her back. She unplugged the iron and sat down, thinking she'd been standing for too long. As she was about to get up, the pain came again, stronger this time. *This is it!* As agreed, she waited until the contractions were well established before she rang James at work. He couldn't afford to have more time off than necessary.

'The baby's coming! Can you come home as quick as you can without killing yourself?'

'I'll be there in about twenty minutes. Stay where you are, don't move. I'll sort everything out when I get there.'

Marian thought James had sounded panicked. She hoped he was being careful on the roads. Her mind started to wonder how awful it would be if he got hurt. But the contractions brought her back to the present.

True to his word, James arrived almost exactly twenty minutes later. He burst into the room, quickly assessed Marian, then grabbed the hold-all which had sat in the corner of the lounge for a couple of weeks. Marian was beyond excited, even though the pains took her breath away.

An hour later, they were well-established in the maternity wing of Hope Hospital, and the staff nurse finally arrived.

'Hello love. I believe it's your first child?' she said, looking Marian up and down.

'Yes, it is. I'm getting contractions about every two minutes.'

'You don't look as if you are,' the nurse responded, and Marian wondered what she should have looked like.

'We'll examine you, but I think we'll be sending you home.'

Marian lay back: she must have got it wrong.

'Blooming heck, you're halfway there. Are you *sure* it's your first?' asked the nurse, looking doubtful, feeling the top of the bump and frowning.

Now Marian felt faint. She had dreaded this moment for so very long. She quickly glanced at James, tried to read his face for any sign that he understood, but all she could see was joy.

The nurse saw something was wrong, even if James didn't. 'Stay there, love. I'll get you some water.'

Marian took a small sip, glad that her pallor had saved her from further questions.

James held her hand, and the whole process began. They were moved to the labour ward and assigned a midwife who carried out more checks. Marian was offered gas-and-air, which she accepted gratefully, declining the other options. By the time the pains became more intense, she regretted not taking something stronger, but it was too late. After five painful hours, on the final push the baby arrived.

The midwife whisked the child away and there was an awful moment when the room fell silent Marian and James held their breath.

Then they heard the unmistakable cry of a newborn and they both cried.

'It's a girl,' said the midwife as she placed the slimy bundle on Marian's chest.

'She's perfect,' said Marian, in awe of this creature she had created.

She had a tiny button nose, matted blonde hair, pink cheeks and a rosebud mouth. Her fingers were long and waxy. They curled around Marian's, and she was overcome with love. She could not take her eyes off this beautiful creature. She was in a state of euphoria and thought she would burst with love.

'Put that child down,' her mother-in-law ordered on her first visit.

Marian didn't respond. *I will hold my child all I want. When I hold my baby, I feel like I can take on anything.*

'You'll spoil her,' she said.

Why can't she be happy for us? It's not as if we've asked her for anything.

'She looks just like you, James, when you were born. The same little nose,' Connie said.

James grinned that wide grin, and he looked like the happiest dad on earth.

After three days, they had taken Dolores home. Marian noticed the smell of *Shake n Vac* as soon as she entered the lounge. There were still traces of the white powder scattered on the brown carpet. Marian smiled, remembering their excitement when they'd chosen that carpet with its deep pile. The orange and brown patterned corner suite matched perfectly and now she sank into it, exhausted.

James carefully placed the carrycot next to Marian, then crouched down and lit the gas fire.

'Do you want a brew, Mummy?' he asked, and Marian glowed.

The waft of toast reached her, and she was suddenly ravenous.

Thank God for James. He knows just what I need.

They worked together on night feeds, changing nappies, soothing and comforting, learning as they went. There were difficult moments when Marian would cry and snap at James, but he seemed to take it in his stride, and Marian adapted easily to motherhood for the first few months.

But then things started to change. The criticisms were getting to her. It was either James wondering what she did all day, or his mother wondering how on earth Marian had the time to feel 'down'.

She started to doubt her ability as a mother, felt that everyone was against her. She tried going to mother and toddler groups, but the things the mums talked about didn't interest her. She didn't want to spend an hour talking about cooking batches of food and labelling them for the freezer. She didn't want to see how happy the others were and how well they were coping. She would come away feeling more lonely, isolated and doubtful than ever.

Every day was the same. She got up, fed the baby, got dressed, went out for a walk with the pram. Same place, same shops, then back home. Most days, she merely went through the motions.

I don't understand what's happening. I wanted

this baby so much and now I'm miserable.

Every day she told herself she'd feel better after a good sleep, but she never did. Sometimes her own thoughts were the only words she heard. She felt like she was living inside her head. She tortured herself thinking about what James was up to at work, how many young girls worked there, and whether he talked to them. When he came home it was always the same: he'd ask about her day, she'd tell him the same list of routines, they'd eat tea, then the evening would be taken up with the baby, bathing and feeding and hushing and shushing and leaving and checking, then sleeping. The same old cycle every day until she thought she'd go mad.

And the passion, their desire for each other had gone. When it did happen, it was a chore, for Marian at least. She wanted it to be over with quickly so she could go to sleep.

When Dolores was one, Marian suggested she look for a job, go back to work part-time, James was not pleased, and neither was his mother. They both believed a mother should be with her child and, as Marian had wanted this baby so badly, she should be happy in the role. They said it should be enough for her. But she was ashamed to say it wasn't, and she felt like she was losing her sanity.

She was a monochrome version of her former

self; dull, lifeless and tired. The tears came randomly: when she was feeding the baby, cooking, walking, or simply sitting and staring. Always the tears. She wiped them away, but they kept coming. The tears, and the cotton-wool head, and that song going around and around in a loop.

It got so bad she no longer wanted to play with her child, didn't even want to talk to her. She pushed her along in her pram, hoping the fresh air would awaken something in her, but she was just as miserable when she got back home.

Four o'clock was kids' TV time. Dolores would jiggle about to the theme tunes, but they made Marian die a little. Every day the same. Every day she felt a few more cells in her miserable body give up the ghost. Every night she told herself it would be better tomorrow, but tomorrow came and she felt the same. The same effort to get dressed, the same irritation, the same black pit. The same dead limbs and dull mind. The same her. She wished she could morph into someone else, wished she could take out her brain and put it in a glass next to her bed, like people do with teeth.

CHAPTER 11

THE ROAD TO MADNESS

Marian was in the living room, waiting for James to return from work. There was a gnawing ache in her belly. The key rattled in the door, and her stomach flipped. He entered with a grin as wide as the Mersey.

'I need to go back to work, James.'

'Whoa, let me get in the door first.'

He slung his jacket and bag down and looked at her with scorn.

'I can't do this anymore, James. I think I'm going mad.'

His look was pure hatred, or so it seemed to Marian.

'I'll tell you what *I* can't do, Marian. All this drama, all this bloody misery. Anyone would think you have the worst life in the world, but you don't, do you? You just *think* you do.'

'I've thought about all this, how lucky I am. I know all that, but I'm still miserable. I'm not doing this on purpose to make everyone around me suffer. I want to change the way we are, the way *I* am, but I can't do that by staying at home.'

James slumped into the chair and took a deep breath. 'This,' he said, wiping his forehead, 'is what we agreed. You couldn't wait to finish work and become a mother. I thought you were made for it, but I was wrong, wasn't I? Sometimes I think you hate it. Poor Dolores to have a mother who can't wait to get away from her.'

'That's not true!'

He'd hit a nerve.

'It is, and you know it. Every day I get home from work hoping you'll have snapped out of this depression, only to find you looking more miserable than ever. Honestly Marian, you need to look at yourself, because I am finding it very hard to come home to this night after night.'

He held his head in his hands.

'That's exactly what I've done. I've done nothing but look at myself and think about what's happening to me. I need to go to work to save my sanity. I'm not being dramatic. If I do this for much longer, I really think I'll go mad.'

'I can't agree to it. The deal was you look after Dolores until she goes to school. That's why I agreed to have a child. I want my child to have the best start in life, and that means having a mother who is there, not rushing off to work.'

'I want that too, but I just can't do it.'

'Well poor you! It's all about you, isn't it? Not a thought for how I feel, or how Dolores would cope. I don't want to talk about it anymore. What's for tea? I'm starving.'

So that was it, Marian's attempt to discuss with her husband a return to work. She'd known how it would go, but she'd had to try.

The only thing I can do now is carry on, see how I go.

The endless days turned into endless evenings. She couldn't find the joy in life anymore. Dolores was getting increasingly demanding and Marian more tired than ever. James tried to keep life on an even keel, to suggest 'fun' things they used to do, like eating out and going to parties, but the lack of support with childcare made going out difficult.

Things bobbed along, but her anxiety, insecurity and boredom built up and her moods began to swing wildly.

She didn't understand why one minute she could be dancing around the living room, full of joy, and the next, collapsed on the settee convinced life was shit. And James certainly didn't understand. It felt to Marian as if their lives were being pulled in different directions.

Increasingly, she felt like a shadow of who she used to be. The pressure of being responsible for a little human who was completely dependent on her was too much to bear. She didn't wish Dolores had never been born, but sometimes she wished she wasn't there, so she could be herself again, not merely Dolores' mum or James' wife. Sometimes she wanted to stay in bed, so she didn't have to face another day. Trying to make her child feed when she didn't want to, changing nappies, getting sore hands from all the washing and cleaning, walking to the same old shops and back along the same streets was mind-numbing for her, and she didn't know how much longer she could stand it. This was the nineties after all, she thought, surely times have moved on?

James kept reminding her how lucky she was. On the surface, she had everything she wanted, a house, a husband and a baby. Underneath, she died a little more each day.

CHAPTER 12

ESCAPE

She pulled the duvet tightly around her ears to block out the sounds of a household carrying on without her. She was cocooned in her nest of oblivion. If she couldn't hear them, they couldn't see her. She knew she had a child to tend to, but she couldn't muster the strength to get up.

What if I don't get up? I'm rubbish at being a mum and I've let everyone down.

Her head felt like it was splitting in two and was stuck to the pillow like a magnet.

I can't face another day, can't face pretending to be happy and normal when I know everyone is talking about me. He thinks I'm a failure. So does his precious mother, and who can blame them?

The door opened and her stomach flipped. She didn't want to speak to anyone. She wanted to be left alone.

'You'd better get up, Marian. We're going to

Mum's in a bit. Come on, you can't expect me to do everything when I've been at work all week.'

She wanted to answer, to make everything better, but she couldn't. Tears flowed and her throat constricted. The vice around her head tightened. She could hear James muttering something about doctors, but she couldn't move so she lay there and cried.

He'll do a better job than me anyway. I might as well stay here.

She pulled the cover up over her head and held it tightly, willing him to go away, and he did.

When she woke up it was dark. She could hear pots being put away. Her head was still splitting but she managed to get out of bed. Her legs wobbled, so she sat on the bed until she felt steady enough to stand. She edged down the stairs like an old woman.

'I'm sorry,' she whispered.

Feeling judged and owned and controlled and useless, she stood there like a child in her own house. The tears came again.

'You look awful,' he said.

I already knew that. 'I'm sorry,' she said again.

'You're in at the doctor's tomorrow, ten o'clock.'

She slumped in a chair, didn't know what to say. 'Where's Dolores?'

'Where do you think she is? She's in bed, it's nine o'clock. Mum wasn't happy when you didn't come. Says she can't understand it. I told her, that makes two of us. It's not like it's the baby blues, is it? She's nearly three, for God's sake. You sit there, or lie there, without saying a word, just crying. God knows what you've got to cry about. You've got the house, me; you wanted us, now you've got us and all you can do is cry. I don't know how much more of this crap I can take.'

She saw how his face was changing. The anger was coming.

If I say I'm sorry again, he'll say he's sick of hearing sorry. If I don't say anything, he'll get frustrated.

So, she sat and hung her head. Damned if she did, damned if she didn't. Her head felt thick again and she let James drag her back upstairs and plonk her onto the bed. She let him do it because she didn't know what else she could do.

The doctor looked up and swivelled round in his chair.

'How can I help you today?'

She'd lost her voice again. The tears came.

'Oh dear. What do you think is making you feel like this?'

She shrugged. He asked a few questions about housework, interests, sex life. All she could muster was 'I don't really know.'

Then he asked about her relationship with her parents.

'I don't have one,' she said.

'Relationship or parent?' he asked with a smile.

The floodgates opened, and she couldn't stop sobbing and shaking. The doctor looked shocked. He mentioned something about in-patient care. She just wanted to go back to bed.

She got her wish. The bed was high and hard with a metal headboard. She felt detached from her body, which was stuck to the mattress like a big sack of potatoes that ache and are as lazy as you like.

Strangely, she felt at peace. She didn't have anyone telling her to get up, didn't feel guilty for not tending to Dolores. Dolores wasn't there, so she couldn't do anything about it. She could hear distant, incoherent voices which rose and fell and dipped in and out of her consciousness.

Next to her bed was a wooden locker on top of which sat a small plastic cup and a plastic jug of water. She was thirsty, but her arms felt like iron and she didn't think she had the strength to reach over. Tears seeped out. The voices disappeared, replaced by a loud hum, and she drifted off.

Her slumber was disturbed by someone shaking her.

'Can you sit up for me, Marian?' A nurse loomed over her with a kindly look, but spoke to her like she was two, or maybe ninety-two.

She sat up without meeting the nurse's gaze. The nurse plumped up the pillows.

That settles it. I must be ninety-two.

'We've got an appointment for you later with a lovely lady who's going to talk things through with you and make a plan.'

'Great.'

'Take these, then we'll get you up and dressed.'

The nurse handed some pills to Marian, and she knocked them back obligingly with tepid water. But they stuck in her throat, along with all the words she meant to say but couldn't. Eventually she swallowed them, then threw back the covers and swung her legs around to one side of the bed.

'Steady, young lady, you'll come to grief doing that. Take it easy.'

But before Marian had computed the words, she was up on her feet, legs wobbling and vision blurred; until she stumbled, and accepted help to get back onto the bed, like an old person whose life was all but done. She was frustrated beyond belief, but other emotions were there too: gratitude that her child was being looked after properly, and relief that she didn't have to do it.

She was thankful Dolores no longer had to look at a useless mother every day, taunted by her presence yet not benefitting from any love. She was grateful Dolores could have the chance of a life without her.

And that's when she decided: *As soon as I get out of here, I'm leaving. It's the best thing I can do for everyone.*

She would go away, as far as she could. She would leave her husband and child to get on with their lives without the burden of this useless 'ghost-being' gliding around the house unable to participate. The irony that she was following the same path as her own mother, who had so spectacularly messed up, was not lost on her, but she didn't have the energy to resist it.

The 'lovely lady' came to see her the next day, as promised.

'I'm going away,' Marian told her.

'Going away?'

'Yes, I've decided it's no use pretending. I'm a crap mother and everyone will get along so much better without me. I can't see an end to all this, so *I* need to end it.'

'Is that how you really feel, Marian? That everyone would be better off without you?'

'Yes. I bring everyone down. I can't help it.'

'That's why we're here: to help.'

'By giving me pills? No thanks. I'd rather get away, make a new start where I'm not somebody's crap mother or useless wife.'

'The treatment we offer is designed to get you through this hopelessness you feel until you can manage without pills. There's no shame in it.'

'There's no shame in taking pills, but my shame comes from knowing everyone is looking at me and thinking what a rubbish mother I am, what a terrible wife. My husband thinks I'm dull and I might as well not be here at all for all the good I do my child.'

She knows I'm right. She's looking at me, trying to think what to say next, but she knows I'm right.

Marian felt slightly better.

'When you came into hospital you agreed to treatment which would involve both drug therapy and the help of a psychologist. The combination of these two could make a massive difference to the way you are looking at life.'

'Maybe they could, but they're not going to change who I am. I'm a fucking mess. Nobody ever wanted me. I should never have had a child of my own. I'm not even capable of looking after myself.'

'What's the thing you're most proud of?'

'I would say giving birth, but that's caused too much grief, so I suppose it's passing my eleven-plus.'

'How did it feel?'

'I don't know, I never really thought about it. It just happened. I took the exam and I passed. Then someone mentioned I was in the top five percent in the country, and I thought "*wow*", because I never thought I was clever.'

'Why do you think that was?'

'Because everyone was better than me. I always felt different.'

'We can help you with that, Marian. We could help you become more confident.'

'I don't need help. I don't want to take tablets that turn me into a zombie and that I might get hooked on.'

'Is that your fear?'

'No, it's not a fear, I'm not scared. I know what I have to do, but I'm really tired now and I need to sleep.'

'That's probably the best thing you can do for now. I'll leave you to rest and I'll be back tomorrow to see how you feel.'

The psychologist gathered her papers and left the ward.

She can come back tomorrow, but she won't find me here.

The following morning, Marian slipped out of the ward, carrying a plastic bag containing clothes and other essentials. She found a toilet on the ground floor where she dressed, catching sight of her weary face in the mirror. She was shocked at how pale she looked, how *dead behind the eyes.* She pinched some colour into her cheeks, gathered her belongings and walked out into the hospital grounds, disorientated and tired. Tired of overthinking, she needed to escape.

When Marian got home, she felt even more like a stranger. She couldn't connect with anyone, nor did she want to. The conversations she had with herself, in her head, were endless. She talked herself into and out of doing things that might have made her feel better. Everything seemed like too much trouble. She no longer voiced her thoughts but sat there looking at life through gauze.

Each day began and ended with struggle. Debates in her headspace began as soon as she awoke. She fought the lethargy, made her sack of useless bones get up and do what it must. It was becoming increasingly difficult to leave her nest where she could rest her aching head.

She had a child she needed to chivvy through each day. She went through the motions of being a mother without feeling anything. No love, no connection. She knew she should have been enthralled by everything about Dolores, but she just wanted her duties to be done so she could crawl back into her head, back to bed.

She shuffled around the kitchen like a zombie, brain fog making everything numb. When she had fed Dolores, she slipped on her coat over tea-stained pyjamas and pushed her to nursery, relieved she faced away from her, so she didn't have to make inane faces or spout gibberish. When she returned, she crashed on the settee and battled with the voices until they convinced her she should eat.

Sometimes, when the voices receded enough to allow her to move, she could manage a short walk, but this was becoming more difficult as she didn't want to interact with others, didn't want to be bothered with small talk, baby talk, any talk.

Nothing appealed. Nothing seemed worthy of her energy. She was short-tempered with everyone, especially those she moved around the house with.

Each day, when her husband returned from

work, she would hand over the child and slope off to bed where she nursed the chaos in her head. She used to feel guilt, so much guilt, but now she knew he could do a better job, as he was so keen to remind her every day: 'You might as well crawl back in your pit for all the good you're doing here.'

What have I become?

When they first met, she'd felt like a new Christmas tree fairy, all sparkly and white, that everyone would look up at and sigh. Now, her hair was matted, her head on a slant and the magic dust had disappeared long ago.

She couldn't blame James for feeling frustrated, angry even. When she'd fantasised about being a mother, she'd been sure she could do a better job than her own mam. When her child had stirred inside her, the love she felt was overwhelming. She couldn't wait to show her child all the love she was storing up, couldn't wait to show her baby how much it was wanted, how precious it was. Now, she didn't even have the energy or patience to talk to her, couldn't seem to shake away the lethargy. She knew history was repeating itself around her, but she was too tired to stop it.

She needed to put her plan into action, the one she'd decided on when she was 'temporarily out of action', like in the song *Killer Queen*, except *she* felt like a killer mum slowly smothering the life out of everyone around her. She could snuff their lights out merely by being there.

She needed to go, it was best for everyone, but it was not going to be easy, because she no longer had an income. She would have to withdraw funds from the joint account. She planned to do it over a few days until she had enough to manage for a few weeks. She just had to hope James didn't check.

Then, she would need to find somewhere to stay. This would be tricky as her friends were all local, so it wouldn't be a good idea to stay with them. As for her family, they were the root of all her problems, and she needed to make a clean break. That meant moving away as far as she possibly could, but where to?

She went to the sideboard, pulled out the road atlas and flicked through the pages until she came to one showing the coast.

That's it! Southport!

She had vague memories of being taken there by one of the neighbours, walking along the sea-front and eating doughnuts. She wondered if she could recapture that magic. She doubted it, but she was still going to go, and she didn't know if she felt scared or excited.

She had many doubts about leaving her child, but she reasoned that she was leaving her with a capable father who worked and provided, while she just sat day after day, wallowing in her own sweat and self-pity. She couldn't ruin their lives as well as her own. They deserved more than that.

Dolores needed to be looked after, cared for and loved. Marian could do none of these.

Things will be better without me souring the milk.

Although Marian was heading off into the unknown, she felt calm and more in control than she'd been for a long time. Soon this episode in her life would be over. It was surprisingly easy to pack up her bags and arrange for her mother-in-law to look after Dolores for the afternoon while she supposedly went to an appointment.

After two endless bus rides, she pushed the buggy down the driveway in Worsley, passing neatly arranged pot plants and manicured hedges. Her mother-in-law opened the door but turned and walked into the living room without a greeting. Dolores started to chatter as she tried to get out of the buggy. Marian popped the fastener, and she clambered down and ran into the house. Marian followed and stood in the doorway, leaning against the jamb.

Connie's face lit up at the sight of her granddaughter. She held out her arms and lifted her onto her knee. She started to sing nursery rhymes, clapping hands and laughing, doing the things Marian should be doing... *if I could be bothered.*

Dolores giggled and looked happier than she had done all morning. This both compounded Marian's misery and reassured her she was doing the right thing. She could see the beauty of her child, but she couldn't feel it. Every moment she spent with her made her hate herself more. She despised the way she'd turned out, hated the mindset she was trapped in.

Why can't I love this little being who brings so much joy to others?

'Why are you crying, Marian?'

'I don't know, I'm just down, that's all.'

'I don't know how you find time to be down with this one. She's a bundle of energy, she is. I didn't have time to be down when James was little. I was too busy caring for him.'

Connie seemed to be looking right through Marian, and she couldn't stand being in the path of that judgemental gaze any longer, so she sloped off without speaking.

'What time will you pick her up?' Connie called.

'When I'm ready,' Marian shouted back.

The train ride was tedious but soothing, giving Marian a welcome break from the stagnancy of a home she could only glide through and a role which didn't fit her.

What kind of mother leaves her own child? My mother. And me.

Her head sank back into the seat and she closed her eyes, conscious of her racing heartbeat. She tried breathing deeply.

I feel like I've been caught stealing, except I've not taken anything, just left it behind.

She imagined what they'd say when they found out. They'd say they always knew she was no good. She imagined James being so angry, so disbelieving, and Connie saying, 'I told you so'.

But what did they expect of someone like me?

When she arrived in Southport, she was tired, but the need to find accommodation spurred her on and she found *Tourist Information* nestled between a coffee shop and *Mothercare*.

'Can I help you?' asked the assistant.
I doubt it.
Marian told her she was looking for a place to stay for a few days, that it needed to be cheap and near the town centre. The woman busied herself looking through files and consulting with her colleague. Marian imagined the

bedlam going on at home. Connie's irritation when she didn't come back, James' irritation when he found the note. She wondered if he'd be shocked or relieved.

'The only room I can find is about a mile out of town. It's cheap and cheerful, but I believe it's clean, and the lady who runs it is very nice.'

'I'll take it.'

The assistant handed Marian a piece of paper with the address and a hastily drawn map of how to find it. She thanked her and pulled her case out onto the street. She decided to walk the mile, rather than spend money on a taxi. The bags were heavy and awkward, but she reckoned she deserved to suffer for what she'd done.

CHAPTER 13

FRESH START

The guesthouse was small and basic, but clean. Marian spent two weeks there in all, resting, thinking, licking her wounds and trying to forget. The last thing she saw every day, before sleep, was the face of her child.

She didn't deserve to call herself a mother; she'd not really been one for a long time. Not since those first few months when the bond had been strong and safe, before the cloud came. She would hold Dolores, then, and nuzzle her face into her creased little neck which smelled of talcum powder and sweetness. The weight of her tiny body in her arms or over her shoulder felt like nothing she'd ever held before. She would reach down and stroke her baby's waxy little feet, whisper into her ear, tell her 'Mummy loves you.' Dolores would try to focus her blinking eyes on Marian's face, her head wobbling, Marian holding it, keeping her safe.

I need to stop thinking about the past. It's doing me no good at all.

It had been six weeks since she arrived in Southport and, thanks to the owner of the guesthouse, a lovely lady called Marjorie, she now had a little job at the local pub. Her funds were running low and she was glad of the work, but she needed to find something more permanent. For the time being, she was renting a tiny box room in the home of one of Marjorie's friends. It was cheaper than the guesthouse, but she felt she was being watched all the time.

Apart from that, she was happy with the way things had turned out. She'd formed a bond of sorts with Marjorie, although their friendship was based on lies. Marjorie thought Marian was heartbroken by a failed love affair, which wasn't that far from the truth. And it would explain her fluctuating moods, any tears and her desire to be alone.

Marian was beginning to feel better about life, maybe because she was not responsible for anyone's wellbeing, not responsible for hurting anyone. The job at the pub had given her a purpose and she enjoyed serving people from different walks of life. They knew nothing about her, and she could pretend she was a carefree thirty-something enjoying life in a different town. Serving beer and passing the day with small talk suited her. There was no need to disclose anything at all: not where she'd come from, nor who she really was. Any questions about her past were met with a coy smile and flippant comments: 'That's for me to know.' Her confidence soared because she was doing something she could do well. She had done the best and the worst thing she could ever have done, but she was focussing on the positive.

After a couple of years working behind the bar, supplemented by shop work, a chance meeting and a flippant comment led her along a different path.

She was on the bus back to her bedsit for another evening cooped up with only her books for company, when she spotted a lady at the front of the bus, paying her fare. She was carrying a briefcase and a hessian bag loaded with books. She flopped down next to Marian, trapping Marian's skirt under her leg. Marian tugged it out and shuffled closer to the window, unable to see the outside world through the fog of condensation.

'Sorry about that. It's a bit murky out there, isn't it?'

'Yeah, I can't see a thing.'

The woman settled into her seat and took out a book, opening it and squinting to find her place.

'*The Colour Purple*,' said Marian. 'I read that a while ago.'

'What did you think of it?'

'I couldn't believe the injustice. It was sad how those people were trapped in a life they had no control over. It wasn't even that long ago, either,' said Marian.

'Did you study it at A-Level?'

'I didn't do A-Levels.'

'Really? You seem like an intelligent girl,' she said, smiling almost pityingly.

'Hardly a girl,' replied Marian.

'Well, compared to me.'

'I wish I *was* a girl. I wish I could do the girl thing all over again,' Marian said, then wished she hadn't.

'Don't we all?'

A silence followed and Marian pretended to look out of the misty window.

'I was a bit of a sad case when I was a girl. I had a rough start in life, you could say,' said the woman.

Marian looked at her expensive briefcase, her glossy hair, perfect make-up and designer boots.

'You don't look like much of a sad case now.'

Marian wondered why she was speaking so openly to someone she'd only just met. Maybe she felt a connection?

'Something someone once said to me changed my life,' said the woman.

'Pray tell.'

'They said, "Never let your past determine your future" and I didn't understand it.'

'I can see why. I mean, however much we try to hide from the past, it still makes us what we are,' Marian replied.

'That's exactly what I used to think until that comment finally made sense.'

'So, what did you do?' Marian asked, surprised she was confident enough to question the life of a stranger.

'I decided I wasn't going to be that lost little girl anymore. The very next day, I booked some counselling sessions and an assertiveness course. I've never looked back. It was the kick up the arse I needed. Sorry for swearing.'

The conversation continued in the same vein until the bus reached Marian's stop.

She stood reluctantly, not wanting to leave this fascinating lady and her story of hope. 'It was great to meet you. You've certainly given me food for thought.'

'Great to meet you, too. Now go get 'em, girl!'

When she got home, Marian searched her cupboards for a book she'd been given a long time ago, a kind of self-help manual which she'd dismissed as rubbish. The woman's story had struck a chord. She felt the beginnings of a fire in the pit of her stomach, one she wanted to feed, to exploit. By the time she'd finished reading the first couple of chapters, it was midnight and she was revelling in thoughts of making her life count.

When she finished her morning shift at the shop, she took the bus up to the university campus and searched for information on courses. It turned out she had enough O-Levels, but she would have to take a couple of A-Levels at night school. She made a hasty decision: she would take English and Sociology as soon as she possibly could. After all, her evenings often stretched out before her if she wasn't working, so this would be a sensible way of spending them. Who knew where it might lead?

Surprisingly, she found both courses interesting and quite easy to get through. She came out with a Grade A for English and B for Sociology, which opened the door to several options at university.

She settled on Law.

She'd heard Law was not the easiest subject to study, but she was grateful when she was finally accepted onto the course. Life was beginning to feel a lot better. She found she could talk to people more easily, instead of shying away from conversations. She joined a debating society and spoke passionately on subjects which ignited a spark in her. Her previous life was becoming more and more of a distant memory, the image of her child fading.

While some of her younger peers enjoyed the full university life of drinking and partying, Marian preferred to dip in and out as and when it suited. Most days, she would go back home to study, living close enough to campus to do so. On the odd occasion she did join in the fun, she always made sure to keep a tight control on what she said, afraid of giving away the person she really was.

She had concocted a story about her past: she had been put in a care home at a young age and had never wanted to find her parents. Most people didn't probe and, if they did, she would change the subject.

University life suited her well. When she looked back at that person who had run away, she hardly recognised her. She had done such a good job of hiding herself, it worried her; but she knew it had been necessary to her healing. Whenever she doubted herself, she would think of the woman on the bus: 'Don't let your past shape your future'.

Marian eventually came out of university with a 2:1 and a confidence she had once thought she could never wear. She had many mantras she repeated whenever negative thoughts tried to take root. They helped her through, reassured her that she deserved a new life, that she belonged here. The person she used to be was disappearing with every new avenue she explored.

After months of filling out application forms, she started her career at a small back-street firm, learning the rudiments of her chosen field of Family Law. It was a tough world, and it took an abundance of tenacity and willpower to survive the first two years.

Eventually, she moved to a bigger firm, and so began a new chapter in her life.

CHAPTER 14

DIVERSION

Harry Watson strode into the office and plonked himself in the chair opposite Marian.

'You're a mystery to me, so you are, Miss Marian,' he said, trying to hide his nerves with a smile.

'Really? Good,' she replied, not looking up from the file she was buried in.

'A true mystery. I know this sounds corny, but I've been pondering why someone as attractive as you doesn't have a husband, a partner even.'

'You work in Law and you think it's a mystery? It's only like working in a school then deciding not to have kids.'

'Smart, as well. I really don't know how you've slipped through the net.'

'I've never swum near the net.'

'See? You're witty, you're charming, and beautiful to boot. How about making a young man very happy? Come for drinks after work?'

Drinks after work led to dinner, theatre visits, pub lunches and, before long, they were in a relationship. They both had busy workloads, but Harry fascinated her enough for her to want a commitment.

They'd been seeing each other for about a year before he asked her to move in with him, 'You can't spend the rest of your life in bedsit land.'

Marian needed to think but after a few months she agreed and moved her belongings into his place.

They settled into an easy kind of life together, making the most of weekends when the constraints of the office lifted a little and they could relax on long walks or over lazy Sunday lunches in country pubs.

The inevitable discussions about marriage and children came and went. Marian explained her reluctance to start a family had always been because she couldn't give a family the attention it deserved, having such a busy job. And she certainly didn't want to think about having a child now, well into her forties. So why would they need to get married if they weren't having children?

Harry persisted though and, eventually, she snapped and told him it had to stop. It was never mentioned again, but he stopped being so caring and considerate. He never spoke of his resentment, but it was clearly eating away at him. Every time they passed a pram or a toddler, she caught him peering inside at the tiny bundle or the rosy-cheeked tot.

He stayed at the office later and later, citing workload, but she knew it was because she was denying him access to the world of family.

They discussed adoption after Harry conceded that Marian was probably too old to consider pregnancy. Harry wanted to give it a try.

'You can't just give it a try,' she would say. 'We're talking about little beings whose lives we would be fully responsible for. They don't come on approval; you can't send them back if you're not totally satisfied.'

Then she would break down, go up to bed, shut down and shut him out.

They carried on, trying to convince themselves they had a decent life. They wasted the next decade skirting around each other.

CHAPTER 15

BUMP IN THE ROAD

Marian had taken a short break from a particularly challenging meeting. She needed a breather to gather her thoughts. She stood on the glass platform outside the meeting room overlooking the main reception.

This platform was thick and safe, but she did not trust it. When she peered over the edge, the ground below swam up to greet her. She steadied herself and edged her way along the corridor, grasping the handrail for support. She caught sight of her distorted image in the curve of its shiny brass, dancing back and forth, anorexic and obese in turn, looking like *The Scream* on Ecstasy. This was bloody frustrating: *how can a woman in her fifties still be having panic attacks?*

A sharp dig in the shoulder demanded her attention, and she turned to see Dominic Matthews, heir to this empire, privilege oozing from his every pore. Her eyes held his for a second too long and she mentally kicked herself. Despite how much she despised him, he had just saved her from sinking into the panic.

'Hey gorgeous, can't take the pace?' he asked.

Conceited git.

'I'm just a woman, Dom,' she said, flashing her best enigmatic *is it a smile or a smirk?* look. She turned away sharply, her stiletto grinding into glass. She could almost taste the resentment following her like a bad omen, ready to floor her. Dominic Matthews was not used to anything but fawning adoration from the women who surrounded him, and he hated to be ignored.

As Marian stepped back into the conference room she realised with relief that most people had gone, and the meeting was all but over. She collected her note pad and smiled at the doodles she'd scribbled earlier during particularly tedious and rambling speeches. She collected her Perspex name-holder: *Marian Benson, Senior Partner*. The cold glance Amy Dwyer cast her way didn't go unnoticed, but she pretended not to see.

Back in her office, she again savoured the opulence of the place and had to make a big effort not to get distracted by comparisons with her past. She used the technique she had honed over the years to clear her mind of intrusions: deep breaths in, longer breaths out. A rap at the door snapped her out of her quiet time. She beckoned entry, then wished she hadn't. Amy Dwyer stood before her, blonde locks straightened to perfection and framing the glowing beauty of her face. If she smiled, she'd be lethal. As it was, she was merely stunning.

'Hi, Amy. What can I do for you?' Marian asked, her professionalism masking a more negative inner response.

'Me and Dom are having drinks after work tonight and wondered if you'd like to join us?'

Me and Dom. Silly bitch thinks she's really caught the slippery toad but I, for one, know better.

'What's the celebration?' She knew Amy's agenda was to gloat, to show him off. Mr. Desirable, the most sought-after shag in the firm.

'Nothing much. Just seems like ages since we got together, that's all.' Amy pushed her hair back and looked down at Marian through a flickering fan of false lashes.

'I've got so many documents to browse, it's not even funny but, if I get through a decent amount, I might see you there. *Cross Keys*?'

'Yeah,' Amy said. 'About seven.'

She pushed out her ample chest, sucked in her tiny midriff and lazily ambled out, her pert backside swaying as she went. She stopped for a moment, flicked her head back sharply to face Marian and smiled sweetly. Her eyes said it all: *Keep away from him. You can never compete with me.*

Poor cow. She really believes she's everything he wants. She doesn't suspect that, soon enough, he'll cast her aside like he's done all the others, bored with the banal exchanges and self-adoration.

But Marian wasn't lying about the amount of work. She picked up the first folder, a new case of an older woman trying to sue the NHS for negligence. Dominic had dropped it by earlier with a brief verbal outline of the history.

The woman in question was dying of bowel cancer, metastases just about everywhere. It seemed she'd had symptoms for years, but the GP put it down to Irritable Bowel Syndrome and didn't investigate until it was too late. Marian couldn't help but think about the futility of taking this case on. There was little chance of it being settled before this poor woman died, if it could ever be settled at all. The best she could hope for was that her family would get justice.

As Marian pulled back the manila cover, a name swam up and knocked the stuffing out of her. A band of pressure threatened to crush her chest. She stood and paced the room, not knowing what to do, until she was forced by dizziness and panic to sit down. Beads of sweat formed on her forehead and it felt as if an elephant was sitting on her chest.

She looked at the name again and slowly rolled it around her tongue, but it didn't change into someone else's. She frantically skimmed the page for clues. The date of birth confirmed her fears: the woman was her sister, Sylvia.

Marian was blindsided by images she hadn't asked for and didn't want. The past she'd buried so well, for so long, was rising from its murky depths to drown her in its deathly swamp.

Palpitations made her giddy and she walked over to get water from the dispenser, trying in vain to gather her thoughts. Gone was her confident stride, replaced by a slow shuffle and the hunched shoulders of her youth. Inside, she was flapping around like an escaped balloon. She needed to rein it in, regain her composure. She took a sip of cool water, but it made her retch, so she eased herself back into her seat and sat very still for who knew how long?

Dominic's entry made her start. He seemed to flinch at the sight of her.

'Hey Marian, what's wrong, babe? You look like you've just caught a glimpse of old man Matthews himself, come to haunt us.'

Before she could protest, Dominic moved behind her and started to massage her shoulders in a spontaneous show of support and affection. She wanted to scream: *leave me the fuck alone!* But, instead, she crumpled, and the tears flowed.

'Hey, you really are upset, aren't you?' he asked with genuine concern, and it struck her that this former conquest, someone she'd thought meant nothing to her and vice-versa, cared more for her than she wanted to acknowledge. She slumped further down into the chair. If only she could go back to where she'd been a couple of hours ago when her life was still on track.

Dominic's back rub lasted about two minutes before Marian politely told him to sod off.

Who needs a social viper when your world's about to be ripped apart?

She didn't know how much time had passed, but the office was eerily quiet. She hadn't seen or heard a soul since Dominic went, which probably meant she was the only one left. She needed to move, if only to stretch her legs and restore at least her exterior to some sort of normality.

She stepped into the adjacent washroom, looked in the mirror and thanked God she didn't have to see any of the others, looking like she did. Black streaks laced their way down her sunken cheeks. How Amy Dwyer would gloat if she could see her now.

But am I any better? If I fused her fake body with my fake life, would I even exist at all?

As she reapplied make-up, she wondered how she could stop this discovery from destroying everything she had built. How could she avoid a future meeting with the past? She was used to finding answers, sorting out dilemmas, but this one was beating her.

When she calmed down enough to function, she finished applying her mask and felt slightly better. Any papers needing attention would have to wait until the next day: she couldn't face anything that required any amount of thought or effort. She looked at the woman in the mirror and a frightened child looked back. She needed to take back control. She needed a drink. Mature response or not, she had to escape from this negative mindset before it dragged her under. A glass of wine would lift her mood enough to make a start.

She gathered her things, the image on the plastic ID card mocking her.

'Take a last look,' it seemed to say. 'You're about to disappear.'

CHAPTER 16

LAYBY

She was losing herself, and she needed a drink. She strode out to the main office and passed row upon row of empty desks. It must have been after nine, as even the die-hard workaholics had gone. The lift took her down to reception. Tom looked up and nodded in recognition.

'Night, Tom,' she said as evenly as she could. 'See you tomorrow.'

'Good night, Marian,' he responded as he opened the main glass door for her.

Marian stepped out into the grey of late evening and started on the familiar route to salvation, the walk to *Room 58*, the wine bar a few streets down.

The rush hour had passed so there wasn't the usual throng of people going for the bus or train. She was so distracted she almost tripped over a homeless person, nearly joined him on his tatty blanket. Perhaps it was the fear of losing her identity that made her reach into her purse for change. She crouched down to drop it gently into his cup.

'Thanks, love,' he said.

Marian looked at the bearded man who had almost disappeared inside the furry hood of his grubby parka and, for once, she wondered what his story was. She was even tempted to crawl under the blanket with him and share tales. Instead, she held his hand and patted his shoulder. Then she walked towards the bright neon sign which beckoned her forward to oblivion.

The bar buzzed with chat and laughter and she was relieved to reach the counter without being recognised or harassed.

On any other day, she would have stood confidently, shouting her order above the clamour of evening drinkers, but tonight she slipped quietly to the edge of the revellers and waited for the bartender to notice her. She stood there for ages imagining she was transparent and people could see right through her core to her grubby secrets. Finally, she caught his eye and ordered a large drink. When it arrived, the honey liquid dropped easily down her throat and she wished she'd ordered two. She savoured the taste, took a second gulp, closely followed by a third. She waited for the drink to take effect, but it didn't, so she raised her hand to call for another.

'Looks like you needed that.'

One of the suited and booted brigades was slouched on the stool next to her. Typical of the men who came in here, he looked like he worked hard and drank harder.

'You could say that,' she said, turning her back on him, not wanting to talk.

She could feel eyes boring a hole into her back. Most of the men in here had egos to match their cars: big and invincible.

She could have downed that second glass in one, but she resisted. As much as she wanted to drink to forget, she chose instead to sip and savour.

As the effect of the wine weaved its magic, she felt an incongruous smirk rise at each corner of her mouth at the thought of what was about to unfold. She made her way to the back of the room and found a seat in the corner. She sat down and held her wine like it was treasure, not wanting to put it down for fear it might disappear.

She ran her finger down the side of the glass and moved her face closer, then further away, closer, then further away, but *The Scream* wasn't there this time, just a fuzzy image. A man was watching her with curiosity, and she realised she must look deranged, so she put the wine down gently. He took the seat next to her.

'Sorry to disturb your little love affair with your crisp white, but I thought you might like some human contact?'

'Whatever gave you that impression?'

'Sorry, I don't mean to intrude, but I saw you come in and you looked quite devastated. Then when your first drink didn't touch the sides, I thought you might have had some bad news, thought you might want to talk. I'm sorry, I don't mean to pry. I'm Jack, by the way.'

Marian looked him in the eye, trying to fathom whether he was worthy of her time, whether she should tell him to sod off, or allow him into her confidence. But he may have been right about wanting to talk and who better to talk to than a stranger?

'Bad news is a bit of an understatement, I'm afraid, but my crisp white friend is helping a bit. She's more fruity than crisp actually, with honey undertones.'

'Really? What's her name?'

'Chardonnay.'

'Good choice. Want another?'

'Why the hell not?'

While he was at the bar, she finished the rest of her drink. She'd normally stop at two large glasses, especially on a week night.

Tonight's more like a weak night.

She had no intention of stopping just yet. The glow was beginning to rise. She could feel its fuzzy blanket warming her.

'You're smiling, that's progress,' he said as he returned with the drink and placed it next to her empty glass.

She resisted reaching for it straightaway, didn't want him to think she was some sort of lush who made a regular habit of this, not that it was any of his business and not that she cared.

'Thanks for that. I love a good Chardonnay. I see you've gone for red.'

'I prefer a red, especially a Merlot. I like the fruity, oaky tones. I like the warmth of it as it slips down your throat. Oh, that sounded a bit rude, didn't it? What have we here then, one old lush and a rusty old letch?'

'Less of the old, if you don't mind,' she said and, to her surprise, she found herself giggling at his comment.

Three glasses became four, then five and when she got up, she felt so unsteady she needed to sit down again. Using the tables to regain balance, she made her way slowly across the bar and pushed open the first door. The stench hit her first, then the sight of pinstripe trousers, and she stopped. She heard a stifled laugh and realised she was in the Gents. She stumbled out and fell inelegantly through the next door. A row of beauties craned their necks to see what the fuss was about, then continued with their preening, the sight of a middle-aged woman tottering in being nothing of note.

She used the toilet and washed her hands, managing to splatter herself spectacularly. She wafted her blouse under the hand-dryer, rubbing at the wet patch on her skirt so that she didn't go out looking like she'd peed herself. The thought made her giggle, but when she caught sight of herself in the mirror, she was almost rendered sober. Hair dishevelled, mascara smudged and clothing askew, she wouldn't have looked out of place under that blanket, after all.

There was one girl remaining and, seeing the look of shock on Marian's face, she offered a hairbrush and a smile which said, 'we've all been there'. Marian brushed her locks back to something which resembled acceptable.

If only I could do that with my life.

With a damp tissue, she removed the black smudges, then applied a fresh coat of lipstick. Her beautiful silk blouse was marred by water stains, so she tucked it into her skirt and reached underneath to pull it down. Despite her best efforts, the blouse, stuffed into an already tight skirt, ruined the smooth line. She yanked it out again. Now it was both crumpled and sullied.

Her mood had changed from buoyant to morose and she slumped back to her seat, edging too close to her new companion. He shuffled away discreetly, muttering something about space invaders, and giggling into his drink. Suddenly, he was not sophisticated, but stupid, and she wondered what she was doing here.

'Maybe I should go,' she said, patting the side of her seat in search of her handbag.

'Maybe you should stay,' he said. 'Just for one more. It's been fun. Let's have one for the road.'

'One for the road, then I really need to go,' she conceded.

He went to the bar and she was left staring into her empty glass as if she could will it to be full again. Tanned, spindly legs approached, and she looked up to see Amy Dwyer, hand on hip, looking down at her.

'We missed you at the *Cross Keys*.'

Her screeching voice made Marian shrink into the seat. 'Fuck off,' she said.

Amy shuffled off, but not before Marian saw the shock register on her perfect face. Even Botox couldn't stop that reaction. Marian stuck up her middle finger as Amy shimmied off, to join Dominic and his cronies, no doubt. Marian's friend returned, but her finger wasn't retracted quickly enough.

'Steady! What's that for? I've only bought you

a drink.'

'It wasn't aimed at you. It was aimed at her.'

'At whom?'

'At Amy fucking Dwyer.'

'Name rings a bell,' he replied.

'She probably has.'

'What?'

'Rung your bell. And the rest.'

They collapsed into a fit of giggles, which somehow resulted in an embrace. As she shook with laughter in the arms of this stranger, she caught sight of Dominic striding past, Amy Dwyer hanging off his arm like a spider monkey. He looked at them in disbelief and disgust.

CHAPTER 17

BACK ON THE ROAD

She awoke to the sound of a teacup rattling in its saucer and she opened one eye, fearful of where she might be. Thankfully, or not, she was at home. She just didn't remember getting there. Harry was looming over her.

'Thought you might need this. Are you not going in work today?' he asked.

'Why, what time is it?'

'About five hours later than when you rolled in.'

She could feel the resentment oozing from every pore in his body.

'It was a tough day. I went for a drink. It's not a crime,' she said, wondering what had happened to her sense of reason. How would *she* feel, boot on the other foot and all that?

'It must have been bloody tough, judging by how many drinks you had. You were so wasted, you couldn't even find your key, never mind put it in the door.'

'And who are you, the bloody fun police?' she asked

Why am I so nasty?

'You know, Marian, you want to take a long, hard look at yourself. You are by no means perfect, yet you think you can treat me like your little whipping boy. Yes, I'm annoyed, but so would you be if it was me who rolled in at that time.'

He was right, she knew he was, but the words she should have said stuck in her throat. He stalked off back to his office, and she sat up, grateful to be alone.

'Thanks for the tea,' she said into the void.

She sank back into the pillow and stifled a giggle. How could she go from remorse to mirth so quickly? *I must still be drunk.*

The previous night's events suddenly presented as flashbacks. Staggering down the stone steps, leaving the bar, being held up by Merlot Man. Some woman's face, right up in hers in the taxi queue. *What happened there, did we have a row?* Trying to get in the taxi and the driver coming around to pull her out again. Looking down at her leg and watching blood trickle from a scratch. Merlot Man hoisting her up, not gently, and plonking her on a wall.

She had no clue what happened next, no memory, but suddenly it didn't feel funny and bile rose in her throat. She swung her legs out of bed and just about made it to the loo, into which she spewed the entire contents of her stomach. Instead of feeling better, she felt disgust and shame. *What is it that makes someone of my age and standing allow themselves to be reduced to this?*

Then she remembered Sylvia's file, the reason she got into this state, the reason the walls were closing in on her. Self-pity was not going to get her out of this mess, though; it never had before. Closing the door on the bathroom, she went downstairs. She had an apology to make.

She pushed the office door open and edged in. Harry didn't look up from the screen.

'I'm sorry. You're right; if it was you, I wouldn't be happy at all. I'm not very happy with myself, so, yeah, I'm sorry.'

The anger melted from his face, leaving only sorrow, which she found much more difficult to deal with.

'I don't own you, Marian. All I ask is a bit of respect and consideration. For one, it isn't like you to stay out so late during the week. I was worried. And, for another, the way you speak to me stinks.'

'I know, I wasn't thinking, still a bit drunk, but that's no excuse. You were being the bigger person, bringing me a drink and what I should have said is "thanks". You had every right to be annoyed with me; I would have been fuming.'

'You probably would have chucked me out,' he said, smiling.

Marian walked over and put her hand on his shoulder. He held it, squeezing slightly.

'I got a case at work. I can't discuss it but let's just say it's pulled the rug from under me. I know I'm always going on at you about not letting work affect us, but this is a big one. Sorry.'

'I know how hard it is for you to say that word, so I accept. Next time, message me or something.'

He slipped his hand out of hers and carried on typing.

'I'll leave you to it then, she said, slipping out and gently closing the door.

She went back upstairs, and the stench hit her as she opened the bathroom door. The toilet was splattered with vomit. A wave of shame came over her and she scrubbed that bowl as if her life depended on it, scouring away the night's misdemeanours, her shame and stupidity. Not until it sparkled, did she stop.

Turning her attention to getting herself clean, she grabbed her toothbrush and smeared it with paste. She didn't like the grey person who looked back at her from the mirror. She wondered if, like *The Portrait of Dorian Gray*, her face would crack and crumble as the wrongs of her former life caught up with her.

CHAPTER 18

WHERE PATHS MEET

Marian escaped in drink for a while, but that didn't help. Then she buried herself in work to minimise the time spent at home. Life with Harry had become unbearable. She couldn't look him in the eye. *I'm with him under false pretences and soon he'll know what a fake I am.*

Marian had decided she could no longer run. She needed to face this head-on: her sister was dying. *Funny how death overrides everything else.* There was a chance Marian might have inherited the disease too, but that was another problem for another day. She had to take this one step at a time.

This was the day she was going to face her demons and meet up with the past she'd buried under layers of lies. This was the day when reality would drag her kicking and screaming from her bubble of pretence.

She checked the number on the door and

walked up the path, not knowing if she wanted to knock or run. She had arrived at the home of Sylvia and her husband, Paul. Ironically, they had settled in the same area she had escaped to.

Her sister Sylvia who had tended to her needs as a child, dressed her, fed her, cared for her, and who she had so thoughtlessly dumped along with the others.

Marian's nerves were in shreds and she needed to take back some control of the feelings which ran rampant and threatened to undo her. She tried to focus on her breathing, but she couldn't push away the fear. There was so much at stake. If her sister were to judge her for what she'd done, then she didn't know how this would affect her, how she would cope with the negative impact.

She'd not even plucked up the courage to tell Harry the whole truth of what went before, nor explain where she was going this day.

What good would it do anyway? He doesn't do drama.

But even though their relationship had deteriorated to the point where they hardly had a relationship at all, she still wanted his approval.

A shadow appeared at the glass and the door opened. Marian offered her hand to the man she assumed was Paul, hoping he didn't ignore it. To her relief, he took it gently in his and beckoned her in.

'You have to be Marian, you have the same eyes,' he said.

His warmth went some way to easing her anxiety, but still she fussed with her coat and scarf, avoiding eye contact, delaying the need for small talk, the inevitable questions. Paul offered to take her things and, as she handed them to him, she caught sight of a figure sagging in an armchair in the living room.

Sylvia was almost swamped by the cushions which surrounded her, but Marian could see the family likeness, *their* family likeness. Sylvia didn't get up, but she did manage a smile. She looked thin, frail and wan. Marian wanted to turn and run away from the shame that hit her as she registered just how sick her sister was. Sylvia started to cry, and Marian went to her and hugged her gently.

'Alright, our kid?' Marian managed, amazed at the ease with which she slipped back to her Mancunian roots.

But any fool could see Sylvia wasn't alright: her cheeks were sunken, and she was thin, so thin. Marian perched on the arm of Sylvia's chair and took her tiny hand, not letting her frail fingers escape.

'I'm so glad you came, so glad I got to see you again. I've missed you! We all have. We had no idea you were planning to leave, no idea at all.'

'I'm sorry,' said Marian, but it hardly seemed enough for a lifetime of desertion.

'We didn't understand why you went without saying anything. We knew you were down, but we didn't expect you to leave, honestly we didn't.'

'It wasn't me who walked out that day, it was someone else. That's the only way I can explain it.'

'Well, I'm glad you came back, whoever you are.'

Their laughter broke the tension, and the years of absence melted away. Sylvia talked about the family she had made, nodded to the pictures of her children and grandchildren, their beaming faces smiling for the camera, her and Paul behind, proud and parental.

Marian told her about her escape and recovery, and how she could never find a way back.

Sylvia reassured her it didn't matter; the important thing was she was back now, and she was alright.

'When James found out you'd gone, he was fuming.'

'I bet he was.'

'He didn't know where you could have gone, how you could have left Dolores. I must admit, I found that hard as well, especially having kids of my own.'

Marian took a deep breath, 'Like I said, Sylvia, I was someone else then. I didn't understand what was happening to me, how could I expect anyone else to?'

'I know. I struggled when I had my first.'

'It looks like you've made a better job of it than I did. I honestly thought everyone would be better off without me. I realise now that I was ill, but at the time I thought I was mad, and maybe I was.'

'I've told you it doesn't matter. It's a wonder any of us have turned out normal after what we went through.'

For Marian, those words were like a soothing salve on an open sore. She had always thought it was no use blaming your upbringing for all your shortcomings, but now she realised that you can't escape it. Like a bee sting, you need to tease it out so it can stop hurting you.

'Now don't get upset when I say this, but I've not got long, Marian. I'm dying, our kid, and there's nothing anyone can do.'

Sylvia collapsed further into the chair and there wasn't anything as important as that moment.

'I'm so sorry for running away, for not being here. I don't expect you to understand, don't expect anyone to, but it's what I had to do.'

Sylvia lifted her head and looked directly at Marian, who couldn't fathom whether it was pain in her eyes or sorrow, but she looked completely broken.

'It's the kids, the grandkids too,' she whispered, 'I can't cope with not being there for them.'

Marian's heart broke for her and withered with the guilt at what she had done.

Paul came back into the room carrying two cups and a look of concern. 'Come on love, try not to get too upset.'

Marian took one of the cups from him, mouthing 'I'm sorry' as she did so. Paul slid onto the other arm of the chair and there was an awkward silence, but nobody could find the right words to fill it.

What do you say to a sister who is losing her fight for life?

'Sylvia, I can't begin to imagine how you feel.'

'I hope you never do. Which reminds me, you need to get the test, Marian, you all do. I thought I had IBS; thought I'd be alright if I managed my diet, but nothing changed. Then I found out I had this bloody bowel cancer. It's her, you know, me mam. She's passed it on. The only thing she's ever given me!'

Marian let out an involuntary laugh. 'I'm so sorry, Sylvia, it's not funny. But that's exactly what I thought: the only thing she ever gave you is a sodding disease.'

Sylvia's eyes crinkled and she squeezed

Marian's hand. It was as if all those years had dissolved, and they'd never lost touch.

'I'm so glad I came today, Sylvia. I mean that with all my heart.'

Sylvia squeezed her hand again, and promptly fell asleep.

While she slept, Paul kept himself busy making tea and filling Marian in on the many years of their lives that she had missed. They looked at family photographs and Marian felt more than grateful he found her worthy to share those moments.

She had been in denial all these years and, for all these years, lives had carried on, family history had been made and people had made a mark on this earth for themselves and their children.

But what have I done? Hidden myself away and become a non-being, living a non-life.'

Looking through those pictures brought home to Marian how naïve she had been to think running away was the best thing she could have done. She could see with great clarity now that it was probably the worst thing. She realised how warped her mind must have been to think she could escape her past. *She* could have been the one in these pictures with her kids and grandkids. It could have been *her* making history and making a mark. Instead, she had scuttled away, lived a charade.

She watched her sister sleeping in the chair. She seemed small and lost. It took Marian back to when they *had* been small and lost, to when they needed to be rescued. She thought of the irony of life: how someone like Sylvia, who had battled against all the odds to make a stable family life, was now having it taken away.

Where's the justice? It should be me.

Marian cried for what could have been, for how their adult lives could have been different had they found each other sooner, had she not been so consumed with the idea of disappearing. But she reminded herself that life is full of what ifs. She couldn't imagine life being good for her daughter if she'd stayed, couldn't imagine ever getting better if she hadn't taken herself away. How much longer would it have been before the madness completely took her? What would life have been like then?

She looked across at Paul who had resumed his perch on the other arm of Sylvia's chair. He was crying quietly, and Marian put her arm around him so that they formed a human cradle around Sylvia.

'She's been such a good mum, a wonderful grandma,' he said.

'She always was a good mum, even when she was a child herself.'

Marian was tempted to add: 'I wish I could

have been,' but it seemed self-indulgent, and she was there to see Sylvia, not to analyse her own failings.

'Sylvia told me a bit about why you went away, how you were ill,' Paul said.

'At the time, I didn't think I was ill. I thought I was incapable, not cut out for it. I thought I would go under and take everyone else with me if I stayed any longer.'

'Yeah well, times change, and we know a lot more about it now, don't we?'

'Do we?' asked Marian.

CHAPTER 19

A PATH WELL TRODDEN

Back at home, Marian sat in a dazed state. Reuniting with her sister had caused no end of memory flashes, and she felt mentally vulnerable. She was afraid that the episode during her thirties, the stay on a mental health ward, was going to be repeated.

She rested for a few days at home, not sure if she was doing the right thing or not, because she'd been overcome by a stultifying lethargy. Tasks like washing a few pots were strung out over hours, while an internal debate played in her mind. Should she move or stay in the armchair? Yesterday, changing the bed had completely wiped her out and she had crawled into it and slept for hours.

Then there was the relentless vice that gripped her head and squeezed with no mercy until she felt her skull would burst at any moment. When thoughts and voices from the past subsided, they were replaced by that song on a loop, that incessant repetition of those innocuous, but strangely frightening words: 'this could be the last time, this could be the last time, maybe the last time, I don't know'.

She decided to go to the doctor sooner rather than later, because this time she knew the warning signs. The doctor looked up at her over his glasses and asked what he could do for her: déjà vu.

'It's a long story, I don't know where to start, but I feel awful, like there's a vice gripping my skull and a constant song going around and around in my head.'

Marian looked at him, waiting for him to ask those inane questions, but he didn't, he just waited. She shifted in her chair and bowed her head. She wanted to go home but she knew she needed to sit this out.

'I think I had a breakdown in my thirties, and I'm scared I'm going there again. I can't seem to do anything without a massive effort, and I feel like my head will explode. I've tried painkillers, hot baths, watching crap TV, sorry for swearing, but nothing works. I feel like I can't escape from my own head!'

'How long have you felt like this?'

'For a while, but especially since I met my sister recently. It triggered memories of the past, of who I was before. It made me realise why I ran away in the first place, but I had no choice but to meet her. She's terminally ill, you see, and she had information for me.'

'Right…'

'She has bowel cancer, the only thing our dear mother ever gave her. Sweet Christ, she looks awful, all thin and grey and wasted, like those beautiful lilies that flop over the vase when they're spent, all the life sucked out of them.'

Marian stopped talking, aware that she was losing her composure, losing focus. She didn't want the doctor to think she was a bumbling, irrational mess.

'You say she has hereditary bowel cancer?'

'She's been told that, yes.'

'How old is your sister?'

'She's sixty-six, but she won't see sixty-seven, or even next month.'

'I'm so sorry to hear that. Look, the priority here is to get you tested, keep you monitored and to address your other health issues. I can start by taking a stool sample today. The receptionist will sort you out with the necessary kit. Regarding your present state of mind, we have a couple of options long-term, but I think for now you would benefit from some mild tranquilisers to get you through this trauma.'

Marian nodded and fell into herself. She didn't want any of this, but she knew what had happened last time she rebelled against the pills, so she took the prescription and the test kit and went home, curled up like a hedgehog, and wept. So many tears. She didn't know how long she lay there, but when Harry arrived home from work, he looked shocked.

'Bloody hell, Marian, are you still crying? You look terrible. Don't you think you should stop this now? You need to think about going to work, getting back to normal.'

'Normal? Tell me what normal is and I'll get back to it.'

'Oh, very funny. There's no helping you, is there? You're always the victim, aren't you? Never want anyone to comment or help. I might as well not be here.'

Marian looked at him in disbelief, not understanding how he could be so cold and out of touch. He went upstairs, flashing her a scowl which served to worsen the tightness around her head. She reached for the tablets, hardly able to control her shaking, but managed to pop one out of its bubble and swallow it. She could hear banging and mumbling upstairs but couldn't muster a response to it.

When she awoke, her neck was sore, and her head felt thick. Her throat was so parched, she felt she could drink a reservoir. She tried to stand, but her legs wobbled, and it took three attempts. She stumbled to the kitchen with the gait of an old woman and, on automatic pilot, put the kettle on. She listened at the bottom of the stairs for noises above, but there was only silence and she was relieved she didn't have to deal with any more confrontations. She went into the bathroom and saw the test kit taunting her.

Oh yes, I know you're there. I'd forgotten about you for a minute, but I know you're there. I'll deal with you later.

Her body was doing things it hadn't done for a while and it frightened her. There was heaviness in her chest, weakness in her arms. She reached for the medication and read the instructions this time: *one to be taken four times a day*. She could not quite work it out through the fog, but she thought it might be too soon for another one just yet. *Not to be taken with alcohol*. She couldn't even be bothered with getting dressed, never mind putting her face on to go out, and, fortunately, she'd never been one to drink in the house, especially alone.

She wondered where Harry was, what he was doing, but decided she wasn't going to waste time fretting about it. She continued to make the tea. As she poured scalding water onto the bag, she frightened herself with thoughts of pouring the boiling water over her body. She quickly replaced the kettle.

Then she took every one of the kitchen knives off the metal strip on the wall and hid them in the drawer. Quivering, she stood for a moment hunched over the worktop; the cold granite reminding her she was able to feel *something*.

Sometime later, she felt Harry tossing around his half of the bed, huffing and puffing, pulling at the quilt. She got up and wordlessly relocated to the spare room. She had no energy to deal with this. She couldn't think with a head like concrete. She wanted to hide and sleep.

He shouted through the wall, 'That's right, just walk away!'

Not this time.

CHAPTER 20

CAR CRASH

In the hospital waiting room, a week later, she chose a seat in the corner and sat with her head down. With plenty of empty seats around her, she was less likely to get some dull person rattling on about the shortcomings of the NHS.

She avoided eye contact with the others, not wanting to engage in any way. She couldn't be bothered with talking – it used up too much energy – so she sat and looked down into her lap.

Finally, her name was called, but she was so distracted that it took a few seconds to register. When she clicked it had been her name, she jerked and cursed, like someone with Tourette's, and her phone dropped to the floor. The cover pinged off and flew under the chair of the lady opposite, the battery landing under her own seat. She felt tears at the corners of her eyes at the lack of control, the sense that all eyes were upon her. She got up slowly, side-stepping the disassembled phone. Like the phone's battery, her brain had taken up temporary residence somewhere else. She got down on hands and knees to gather each piece, and the lady opposite passed her the cover with a look of pity. It took all of Marian's willpower not to snatch it from her and mutter expletives.

Does she not know I'm a fucking lawyer and I'm perfectly fucking competent?

When she tried to put the phone back together, her hands shook so much, the best she could do was bungle it into her bag still in bits. The young nurse beckoned her, and skipped ahead. Marian shuffled slowly behind.

The consultant, all grey hair, glasses and pompous bloody manner, looked up from his file as they entered. Marian wanted to run, but she knew that would be stupid.

'Come in, take a seat. How have you been feeling?'

'I've felt better.' She hated this non-person she'd become, always down and depressed. 'I'm normally as sharp as a tack, you know.'

'You've had a lot on your mind, I'm sure. Now, we do have the results of your test back and it does show some blood in your stools. So, given the family history, we need to undertake further investigations, get a clearer picture.'

'What does that mean? Does that mean I've got the same as my sister?'

'I'm sure you'll understand that it's impossible to say at this stage. Blood can be present for all sorts of reasons which we need to rule out. The next step is to do a CT colonography, which will give us a clearer idea of what we're dealing with. We'll book you in for that and you should get your appointment in the next couple of weeks.'

Marian stood and said her thanks, glad to leave so she could scurry home to be alone, to nurse her thoughts.

She had thought she could re-invent herself as a success, carry on through life being admired, people looking up to her, coming to her for advice, respecting her. She had succeeded for a while. People had bought into her act, believed she was confident, secure and knowledgeable, while all the while she was hiding the truth. They had all been taken in by lies, by the veneer, the façade. She hated this being she had become, this floating ghost leaving poison in its trail. This thing that could not call itself a mother.

The last few months had seen her real self slowly revealed, coming out from behind its smokescreen to take residence in her befuddled mind.

After what had seemed like an endless wait, she

was at the hospital again, in the same chair, awaiting the news that would guide her next chapter.

She was hoping perversely for the worse possible result, so that she could slip away, and it wouldn't be anyone's fault. She was alone. Harry had given up on her, leaving her to deal with it, as he couldn't do right for doing wrong, apparently.

Her solitude was heightened now by the presence of couples, holding hands, chatting, offering reassurances. Marian was trying to read one of the hospital magazines, but she couldn't focus, so she slipped it back onto the pile. She watched the TV, where a cheerful presenter flashed his beaming smile from the miniature screen, but this only served to highlight her misery. *What is wrong with you?*

'Marian Benson,' called the nurse, and Marian rose to follow her like a little lap dog into the sterile office where her future would be revealed.

'Sit down, Mrs Benson,' the consultant said.

The nurse sat beside him, and Marian guessed the news was not good.

'We have the results of your tests and investigations, and I'm afraid they do suggest an invasive tumour.'

The nurse relocated to the seat next to Marian's. Marian frowned, and the nurse edged away slightly. Marian turned her frown on the consultant. He looked at her impassively, waiting for her reaction, but Marian felt numb, didn't know how to react, so continued to frown.

'This must be very difficult for you,' he said.

She exaggerated her frown, as if he was personally responsible for the results. The silence went on so long, she imagined a metaphorical tumbleweed passing between them. She knew her stare was hostile, but she could not snap out of it. She didn't know what to say.

She thought of the film *Sliding Doors* and wished she had taken the other door, the one that lead to a life more ordinary. The consultant leaned back in his chair, and Marian instinctively did the same. They were having a lean-off and a stare-off. She didn't know who was winning and she didn't care.

'This must be hard for you to take in, Mrs Benson,' he said.

The tumbleweed floated away, and she sat up.

'What happens next?' she asked, finally finding the words. 'When you say invasive, what does that mean? Does it mean that it's spread, that it's spreading right at this very minute?'

'When a tumour is invasive, it has started to infiltrate the surrounding tissue. We would have to do further investigations to get a clearer picture. Then we can suggest a treatment plan.'

'A treatment plan?' She was reminded of the last time she'd been offered one of those. 'What if I refuse a treatment plan?' she spat out.

The doctor looked suitably affronted. 'Treatments do vary between individuals. Let's see what the scan reveals and take it from there.'

'Shit,' was all she could muster as a response.

She hung her head and tried to process what had been said.

The nurse took her hand. 'We'll put it all in a letter, and we'll send you details of your next appointment, so please don't worry if you can't remember what's been said today. Is there anyone with you?'

'No, but I'm fine,' said Marian.

She stood up to leave.

'I'm so sorry, Mrs Benson,' the consultant said.

'It's not your fault.'

She left the hospital and walked towards the car park, but began to feel dizzy, so she sat down on a low wall and tried to breathe through it. She stretched out her legs and noticed her tights were laddered, there were splodges of dried-up tea on her shoes and her skirt was creased. She swallowed any pride she may have had, and phoned Harry to see if he could pick her up; she didn't trust herself enough to drive home.

'Is it bad news?' he asked.

'Yes,' she said, and he agreed to jump in a cab.

Once he'd arrived and they were both in her car, she told him about the tumour. His response was not to hug her or to reassure her that everything would be alright.

He asked one question, 'What about our trip?'

'It's your call,' she replied. 'It wasn't the first thing that came into my mind, our sojourn to the Caribbean, so I haven't thought about what will happen with the trip. I have bowel cancer.'

'God, I know, I can't believe it.'

He turned on the engine and, without another look, drove home.

When they arrived, they didn't quite know what to do. Marian had an urge to tell everyone her news, like it was a piece of priceless gossip. She messaged a colleague – *It's cancer* – then took herself into the spare room and sat in the dark for a while.

It was strange not having a partner to reach out to at a time like this. She drifted off wondering if she could have been wiser in her choice of men.

When she awoke, Harry was perched on the

end of the bed with a cup of tea. 'I thought you'd like a brew.'

'Thanks, I'm parched.'

'So, what happens next? Will you be going in for surgery soon?'

'I suppose so.'

'Have they given you a recovery time?'

'No, but it's a major op. I'm guessing everyone is different, but from what I can glean, I could be off work for six months or more.'

'We'll struggle if it's more.'

'What do you mean?'

'I mean, you get paid for six months, but after that we'll struggle.'

'What will be, will be. I might not even be here in six months' time. Have you thought of that one? I haven't thought about the money aspect. I'm still grappling with the disease.'

'I know, so am I, but we have to be practical.'

'How about planning my funeral then? That would be practical, wouldn't it?'

Harry left the room and Marian wondered if he knew how much his cold practicality hurt. She found it odd that someone could be so lacking in compassion and empathy.

Then she realised, with a jolt, it had been cold practicality that made her leave Dolores. Lack of compassion and empathy? She ticked those boxes, too. Her child must have felt hurt a million times more powerful than this when she grew up and realised her own mother had deserted her.

Marian needed her daughter to know how much she had lived to regret that day.

CHAPTER 21

DRIVING THROUGH FOG

The date for surgery dropped through the letterbox one dull day in October. Marian picked up the brown envelope. As she did so, she was distracted by something moving in the garden. A single magpie: portent of bad luck and thief of happiness. The letter informed her that a bed had been booked for three weeks' time.

In those weeks, she dealt with a few phone calls about important cases at work, but most of her time was spent trying to relax and escape her maudlin thoughts.

Harry skirted around her, not knowing what to do. Although they'd grown apart over the years, she had hoped something as serious as this could bring them together. But he wasn't forthcoming with affection or kind words. She knew she'd not been very nice to him either, but she thought he might have seen past her nastiness to the fear beneath. It hurt, but she was too proud to tell him that all she needed was to be his someone special, especially at a time like this.

She did a lot of thinking during her time at home and she'd come to the sad conclusion that she never had been his someone special, that he was always a bit of a loner and things were always destined to be this way. The cancer diagnosis served to make her acutely aware of the shortcomings in her life and to emphasise how lonely she really was.

The wait was finally over, and Harry was dropping her off at the hospital. He had decided not to have time off work as her surgery was not until the next day. Marian knew his boss: she would undoubtedly have let him take as much time as he wanted, given the circumstances. He swung the car up to the main entrance, and kept the engine running, his hand on the gear stick. Marian reached for her handbag and reminded him not to drive off before she'd got her other bag out of the boot.

If he can't be arsed with emotional partings, then neither can I.

'Who are the chocolates for? And the pink fizz?' she asked, spotting them in the boot.

'What chocolates?'

'The ones in your boot with the pink fizz.'

'Oh, they're for Charlotte at work. It's a big birthday.'

'Bloody charming.' Marian walked to the hospital entrance muttering about big bloody birthdays and big bloody operation days.

He hadn't offered to carry her bag or help her to find the ward. He didn't even grace her with a backward glance, just drove away. She followed the signs to the ward and showed her letter to the staff on the front desk.

'Do you have someone with you, love?'

'No, not in body, nor mind, it seems.'

'Sorry?'

'I'm not down for surgery until tomorrow, so he's gone to work.'

The nurses looked at each other, then back at Marian.

'We'll take you into the waiting room. It's going to be a little while before your bed's ready. There's a snack bar down the corridor if you get peckish, and just shout if you need anything else.'

Marian settled into a chair in the corner and mindlessly picked up a magazine, which she flicked through, not really taking anything in, just looking at the pictures as a small child would do. She checked her phone for the elusive 'I'm so sorry, how thoughtless of me' message. But it remained elusive.

For a couple of hours, she sat on her perch watching people come and go. Most people had somebody with them, a spouse, a mother or a friend. They all wore the same expression of concern. Marian felt, once again, like a tatty Christmas tree fairy.

What is so bad about me that I'm here alone without a soul to comfort me? Who really cares about me? If I died, who would miss me?

'Mrs Benson?'

Marian almost jumped out of her skin, so engrossed was she in her misery. She knocked the magazine off her knee, which knocked a teacup off the side, spilling its contents all over her and the floor.

She pulled out a tissue to clean up the mess, crouching, trying to balance on her haunches, but failing miserably. She toppled over and her foot twisted beneath her. She fell onto her elbow, which gave way.

'Shit.'

Everyone in the waiting room was looking on in disbelief.

I'm a fucking solicitor, you know!

She sat there, marooned, holding her elbow and crying like a baby. The nurse took her arm and tried to pull her up like she would a toddler who'd thrown a tantrum. But the only way Marian could raise herself was to kneel on all fours, her backside sticking out inelegantly. With the help of the nurse, she managed to regain her composure, at least physically. She grabbed the bigger bag and threw her handbag over her shoulder. Tepid tea dripped on to her skirt and trickled down her leg.

'Let's get you to the ward, shall we?'

Marian was led away, shuffling along like a confused elderly person.

All I need now is a pair of tartan slippers with pompoms.

She laughed and the nurse smiled at her. She shuffled along, giggling and crying at the same time, feeling like she'd completely lost her mind, but not really caring.

I just want to get that scratchy, starchy gown on, get in that bed, pull the sheets up and wallow in my own miserable tears.

She would have said she'd never felt so isolated, but that wasn't true. During her marriage, and her relationship with Harry, she had always felt like a solitary tourist. She had never understood how that could be, how you could live in the same house with someone but feel lonelier and more cut off than ever.

This disease seemed to have given her the ability to see things clearly.

If I've only got a short time left, why spend it with someone I don't love and who doesn't even care about me, let alone love me?

She needed to break away to find peace while she still could. She needed to challenge her past, to find answers. When it came down to it, blood ties were everything, and there was more than one child she needed to make peace with.

When you come back, you'll be free, Frank had said, but she never had been.

After a fretful night, she was woken by the moans of the lady in the opposite bed, who was clearly in pain. The nurse went to her assistance, sitting her up and handing her some tablets. She guided the cup to her mouth so she could swallow the pills. Marian watched wordlessly from her pit and more self-pitying thoughts of dependency, drugs and illness engulfed her. When the nurse had finished, she came over to Marian's bed and wheeled the blood pressure machine round. Marian offered her arm but no words. After the rubber sleeve inflated then released the air, the machine bleeped.

'Your heart rate is on the low side,' the nurse said.

'Yeah, I'm practically dead,' said Marian.

The whole procedure was repeated with the same results.

'Are you an athlete?' the nurse asked.

'No, just an Olympic champion at failure,'

replied Marian.

The nurse, clearly well-trained in dealing with all types of responses, patted Marian's arm, tidied away and told her breakfast would come round soon. She quickly apologised when she remembered Marian was *nil by mouth*.

The rest of the morning went by in a blur. Marian got to the point where she didn't really feel anything and didn't care.

Is this what the pre-med has done to me? Or is it because I'm resigned to my own failure of mind and body? Either way, I can't even be bothered to feel sorry for myself.

When she came round, she was back in her bed, the curtain drawn. There was a blissful moment before she remembered.

A head appeared in the gap in the curtains. The young nurse stepped through and asked how Marian was feeling.

'I'm not.'

The nurse explained she needed to check underneath the covers to make sure everything was ok. She carefully lifted the counterpane, then the sheet, had a quick look and smiled reassuringly.

'Is everything alright?' asked Marian.

'Everything looks fine. Do you need any painkillers?'

'I don't feel any pain,' said Marian as she sank

into the oblivion of sleep.

Her slumber was deep, and her dreams vivid and disturbing. She dreamed of being chased by a faceless shape, of trying to lock the door but the bolt kept bouncing back out.

She woke up sweating, her heart racing. She tried to sit up, but the pain felt like she was being cut in two. There was a faceless shape at the foot of her bed. It came into focus: not a faceless shape, but a soulless one. Harry.

She slumped back and closed her eyes, not knowing what she wanted to see less, the nightmares or him.

'How are you feeling?' he asked.

'I'm not,' she said.

He looked puzzled and she wanted to tell him not to bother trying to figure her out after all these years, because it was futile.

'The traffic wasn't too bad getting here. I was surprised.'

'Fuck off,' Marian said, closing her eyes so that she might drift back to nightmares.

CHAPTER 22

PATHWAY TO HEALING

It was a long wait at the train station. Marian fussed with the contents of her handbag, checking she had the essentials, then checking again. That morning, she'd agonised over what to wear, changing twice, before settling on a plain pair of trousers and a white shirt.

When the train finally pulled into the station, she had a mild panic about where her ticket was. Taking deep breaths, she found a seat near the window and hoped that nobody would sit next to her.

Her nerves took her by surprise as, despite the challenges, the transition from respected lawyer to ill person had been surprisingly smooth. It was as if Marian's brain had been reset so that it filtered out all the needless detritus and allowed only the important stuff through. No longer fretting about missing the morning alarm, deadlines or whether she had clothes ironed, she now breathed in life.

Those long months of recovery had given her time to reflect on her life and to rethink what had gone before. Bit by bit, she had allowed past scenarios to unfold so that she could re-examine their meaning in the context of what she now knew. She had blocked their content for so long that their meaning had become blurred, distorted and unwelcome.

She thought about the time she had dropped her phone. It had fallen apart, like she'd been falling apart, its powerhouse separated from its other components so that it no longer functioned. But when she reassembled it, all systems were restored. And that's how it felt now for her; like she had rebooted her central memory store and reset its default systems. Her memory now allowed the downloading of images so that she might look at them again and see them with fresh eyes.

She had mulled over the reasons behind her decisions and actions, and she was trying to understand her younger self, to be a little kinder to her.

She had built a close bond with the sister who'd raised her as if she were her own, this bond cemented by their present and past connections. Sylvia's perspective on their younger lives had helped with Marian's recovery, helped her to see another side to her childhood. Where Marian had shut the memories out, Sylvia had kept them alive. Neither way was the right way or the wrong way, just their way.

They had laughed and cried their way through their childhood recollections. They took each one out of its box and held it up to the light. Each painful chapter was brought before them and they were the judge and jury of it all.

For Marian, it was as if someone had slowly released each screw from the vice around her head, allowing goodness to seep in. They joked about dropping their surnames and changing them by deed poll to Freud. They shared that ability to use humour to salve even the most painful open sores.

Those abusive episodes would never be normalised, never be forgotten, but the sisters were now getting nearer to understanding why they happened.

During this process, with her sister's support, Marian had been able to open up about the rapes by their brother, her shame and the child she bore as a result. Sylvia had no idea that Marian's trip to Ireland all those years ago bore such a sinister secret. Marian had expected her to be shocked; instead she cried. Soft tears for her little sister, for the injustice, the hurt and the scandal; for the little child at the centre of it and for Marian's torment.

This soul-baring resurrected painful memories of her first pregnancy and the desolation she felt as she handed her child over to their cousin. It also released the massive burden of guilt she had carried all this time. Now she could look forward.

However, Marian's future was not something she could easily imagine: her life was more uncertain than ever. Having to face her mortality made her realise how much precious time she had frittered away on things that didn't matter. The thought of going into the next world, or into dark oblivion, without reconciling with her abandoned daughters had become unbearable.

I need to see my girls.

My girls. The words rolled around her tongue and danced in her head, but she was not brave enough to say them out loud.

How can I dare to call them mine when, for most of their lives, I have been absent?

The pain of being abandoned by one's own mother was a hurt she would not wish on anyone, and yet that's what she had visited on her own children. She couldn't absolve herself of those sins. *Forgive them Father, for they know not what they do.* But Marian did know. Her childhood years had been one long episode of pain and she had inflicted the same fate on her guileless daughters. She could only hope her girls had the strength and capacity for survival, and that they had come through without too much ill effect.

Marian wished she'd had someone to shake her and tell her how stupid she was to think Dolores would be better off without her. She wished she'd given someone the chance to tell her that. She had carried the burden of her actions and inactions throughout her life, and it was only now, near death, that she felt strong enough to redress the balance.

She tried, in vain, to find the child she had left behind in Ireland. With every address, there was a dead end, but she would never stop looking.

Marian was consumed with excitement and fear, but mostly she was grateful. If she had to choose one positive outcome from being terminally ill, it would be that it had given her the courage to get on this train and face her daughter. After all, what did she have to lose? Sylvia had been the vital link between Marian and Dolores, acting as messenger and counsellor, but most of all as the voice of persuasion. She had done a wonderful PR job: she should have been in politics. It cannot have been an easy task but, because of Sylvia, a meeting was agreed.

The train rocked, as if to comfort and calm, but Marian's stomach churned, and she had to sit on her hands to stop them shaking. The voice on the Tannoy announced the next destination would be Manchester, the one place she'd always avoided at all costs. A tear came from nowhere. She eased her hands out from under her legs, so she could rummage in her bag for a tissue. The woman opposite was staring, and Marian realised she must look a mess.

'Are you alright, love?'

You wouldn't call me love if you knew what I was. 'I'm fine thanks.'

'It's just you've gone pale, and you look a bit shaky.'

'Do I? I've got an interview and I'm a bit nervous.' *Well, it is an interview of sorts.*

'No job's worth getting yourself worked up for. I always think if you do your best and they don't like you, sod 'em.'

Good old Manchester grit, how I have missed it. 'You're right, but I really want to get this one.'

'My advice, for what it's worth, is just be yourself.'

And who might that be?

When Marian got off the train and started to

tread the once familiar streets, she thought of her own mother, of how she had travelled the same paths in her youth and her adulthood. Visions of her mother and father came unbidden: of them fighting, her mother's face a mass of bruises. Marian shook her head to clear her mind. She stopped to take a breather, thinking what an injustice it had been for her to have erased her mother from her memory. It was too late now. *Sorry, Mam.*

They had chosen a quiet place to meet, Manchester Art Gallery on Moseley Street. Neither of them wanted onlookers and Dolores had assured her it wouldn't be busy on a Monday afternoon. Marian paused on the steps and took the photograph from her pocket. She stroked the pretty face and studied those beautiful eyes, trying to read what they said. From what she recalled, from that lifetime ago, Dolores looked like her dad, the same strong features. Marian took one last look, tucked the photo away, and climbed the stairs to the museum entrance.

Straight ahead, there was an imposing staircase which split and went off to the left and to the right. It reminded Marian of the *Sliding Doors* scenario again.

Just once, let it go the best way.

She tried to compose herself, told herself to be positive, and had a mild panic when she couldn't remember all the things she was intending to say. She looked at her watch: another twenty minutes before the agreed time. *Good, I've got time to calm down.*

She looked for the café sign and saw it to the right, so she went through and joined the queue at the counter. Suddenly cursed by the shakes, she needed to steady herself on the bar that held the trays.

But where are the trays?

She looked around fitfully, but someone had joined the line behind her, so she couldn't come out of her place to get a bloody tray.

Stop! You're getting worked up again. The lady will help you.

'Yes love, what can I get you?'

A Valium? Double G & T? Absolution from my sins?

'A tray, please,' she blurted.

'Anything else?' the server asked, amused.

'A cappuccino, please.'

'Would you like to try the Rocky Road for an extra pound?'

Marian spluttered, and smiled to herself. 'No thanks, I don't think I could stomach it today.'

She was glad she could still see the funny side of things; humour had helped to make her feel a little more human, less trapped. She paid for the drink and found the most remote table for four she could see, tucked away in the corner. A table for two would be too intimate, too constrictive.

She set her drink down, the cup rattling in its saucer and spilling brown liquid over the sides, making a messy puddle on the table. It looked dirty and ugly, and she tried not to relate it to her present mood, but her thoughts were spiralling down a rabbit hole of gloom. So, she looked away.

Then she saw her, already seated at another table. An involuntary gasp escaped her, but the irony that Dolores had chosen a table for two didn't. Marian hurried over; all shakiness gone. She stood in front of her daughter, mouth agape, eyes fixed, lips aquiver, feet rooted firmly to the spot. Dolores stood slowly – Marian drank in her beautiful face, her graceful body – and said, 'Mum.'

Just that one word and Marian sank into a chair at the table before her legs gave way. Dolores scraped her own chair right up next to her and held both of her hands. Marian could do nothing but weep.

She wept ferociously but quietly, internalising the sound, her body shaking. Dolores squeezed her hands and her beautiful eyes wrinkled with concern. That's when Marian took deep breaths so that she could stop crying and spluttering.

'My girl.'

Now it was Dolores' turn to sob and shake. Marian held her very tight and for a long time. People stared, pretending not to, but she didn't care; there was nothing more precious than this moment. They clung together and shuddered. They sobbed and struggled for breath. Finally, exhausted, they were still. They parted slightly and looked at each other. They looked into eyes that were the same, and they saw each other's pain, and they knew they should have done this a long time ago.

'I've missed you so much,' Marian said.

And at last, she realised this was true. All those years she had tried to forget, to put thoughts of Dolores out of her mind, her efforts had been futile. Every decision she had made, everything she had done, had been attempts to bury all traces of her daughter, so that she could believe she didn't exist at all. Now she understood that, if you bury something alive, it will try with all its might to claw its way back to the surface.

'I kept seeing you in my head, in your little red shoes with your chubby little legs, walking towards me.'

Dolores studied her mother through tears. 'I only had pictures of you. No one talked about you. They said it was best I didn't know. For all this time I have imagined you as a monster who did a terrible thing, but really, you're just normal, just my mum.'

'For all this time, I've believed myself to be a monster who did a terrible thing. It *was* a terrible thing to leave you, Dolores, but I thought you were better off without me. I was very poorly, mentally ill. I couldn't see any way out except to leave you, so you could have a peaceful life without me. I'm so sorry. That doesn't seem to be enough, does it?'

'It will take time for me to process everything, to understand, but I will try. I'm just glad we've found each other now. You were always the missing piece of my life, even though I've had a good life. There was always something missing.'

'Yes, I know that feeling.'

Words weren't enough and so they simply gazed at each other.

After a while, they fell into easy conversation, just like two friends. Dolores told of how, when she was little, she had spent a lot of time with her grandma when her dad was working. They would go out on nature walks, and she could name every bird she saw by the time she was five. She spoke with fondness about the woman Marian had thought of as her enemy.

They would share milk shakes and fries, visit museums or sit for hours colouring in and playing snap. Grandma would tell her stories, take her to nursery, then school, wipe her nose and pull her socks up. At home time, Grandma would greet her with a smile and a treat, and a 'don't tell your dad'. Her dad had met a lady called Patricia when Dolores was six. She knew Patricia wasn't her real mum, but she chose to call her Mum because it made life easier for everyone. For that, Marian was grateful.

Marian told Dolores about her life in Southport, how she had reinvented herself. She told her about the job in the bar, how the encouragement of people she met gave her the confidence to go to university. She told her about the constant battle with herself, with the past and how she had to keep pushing it back in its box. She told about how she became a lawyer, how she'd kept herself busy, become respected and sought after, all the while feeling like an imposter. She told her all about the reunion with Sylvia, and her subsequent diagnosis. Finally, she told her that the prognosis wasn't good.

Dolores' face dropped and Marian wondered if she should have been so honest, so quickly.

But Dolores said, 'Then we'll have to make the most of the time we have left, Mum.'

PART 3

SHAUNA

Everything she had been led to believe was an almighty lie. Nothing was how it seemed, and someone was going to pay.

CHAPTER 1

GREYNESS

It was the early 1970s in Ireland and Patrick O'Shea was going nowhere in particular. There was nowhere in particular to go. His village was a nowhere kind of place.

He trudged along the grey street away from the grey factory where he had spent the last two years putting grey components into grey boxes.

My life is fecking grey, he thought as he turned the corner.

His breath was taken by the wind coming off the sea and he pulled his jacket across his chest as he made his way to the bench. He came here when he was fed up, frustrated. Which was most of the time. He especially liked coming here on a Friday after work when he could shake himself free of the oil and the grime, the deafening sounds and the drudgery of factory work. It was autumn and the sea was grey and wild; the only grey bit about this place that lifted him. He felt an affinity with the sea, with the elements.

Colleen closed the door to the café and locked it. She put the keys safely into the inside pocket of her handbag and zipped it up quickly before checking the door handle for good measure. Walking quickly towards the pier and gripping the handles of her handbag in the crook of her arm, she spotted Patrick. She'd thought he might be here today. He'd seemed solemn the last time she saw him; now he sat stock-still, staring out to sea with the world on his shoulders.

Would you look at him? So young, so serious.

'Hey Paddy, what's with the face?' she asked as she plonked herself next to him.

'Oh jeez, Colleen! Do you have to do that?'

'What?'

'Scare me half to death with your screeching, that's what.'

'Well, begging your pardon, mister, if I won't send you an airmail next time, warning you of my coming,' she said, shoving him and standing up to leave.

'Sorry,' he said. 'I'm a bit of a misery today on account of my grey life.'

'Really? Grey, is it? Sure, your hair will be turning grey before long if you keep fretting everything.'

Taking her hand, he pulled her back to the bench. 'Do you want to meet up later?' he asked. 'Come to mine, listen to some music?'

'Sure, if your old man doesn't mind,' she said.

'You know he likes you, and Ma will be working the bar as usual, so what do you say?'

'I'll be round about half seven,' she said. 'I'll be off home now; else they'll wonder where I am. See you later.'

It had been six months since Colleen first met Patrick. They had collided one evening on the corner where Nelson Street meets the sea front. It had been a warm spring evening, but Patrick's head was down, his parka hood up. He'd apologised, said he hadn't seen her, to which she replied, 'No wonder, buried as you are in your hood.' They had laughed and gone their separate ways, but she'd watched him go to the bench and sit there like an old person with the weight of a lifetime on his shoulders.

They had said hello a few times after that, finally arranging to meet one Friday after work for a walk. She told her parents she was going to tea at a friend's so as not to prompt their questions. But, after a couple of months, she came clean and told them she had met a nice boy. Of course, they knew his family, inevitable in a place like this.

'Be careful,' her mum had said. 'They're a troubled lot.'

Colleen hadn't asked what that meant, didn't want to know; she was having a bit of fun, that was all. They were young and there wasn't much to do around here. It was good to hang around with girlfriends but having a boy in the mix added a bit of excitement for Colleen.

It had been fun at first, but she found him a bit solemn at times and now she was beginning to wonder if it was worth carrying on. As much as she liked the boy, their meetings were becoming more about her trying to convince him that life was good, rather than enjoying her time with him.

When she got home, tea was all laid out on the table as usual, the serviettes folded into fancy shapes, her mother's nod to middle-class aspirations.

Mammy stood at the stove. 'Hey Colleen, how was work?' she asked as she stirred the big iron pot.

Stew again.

'Sure, it was good. The usual Friday crowd: few oldies in the morning, then the kids in after school for their milkshake. Same old, same old.'

'It's a job though, Colleen, we can't be too

choosy.'

'I know, Mammy, and it's grand for now, until I become a doctor or something.'

A splutter came from the living room and Colleen popped her head in, knowing her dad would be in there with his paper. Sure enough, he was in his favourite chair in the corner with the paper almost swamping him.

'Hey Daddy, what's happening in the world?' she asked, flicking the paper.

'Too fecking much!' he said, shaking the paper closed.

'Tea's nearly ready, Da. Let's go through, eh?'

He struggled to get up from the sunken cushions. 'Yeah, your mammy's grub always cheers me up, girl. Take no notice of your grumpy old pa.'

'Not so old, Da, you're on the right side of forty.'

'Feeling eighty.'

They sat at the table, taking the serviettes and arranging them with a flourish on their laps, winking as they did so.

'Tell me then, Colleen, how's it going with this Patrick boy? Being good to you, is he?'

'It's not like that, Da. We're having fun, is all.'

'Aye, well make sure it's careful fun, if you know what I mean.'

'Da!'

'You may well blush, Colleen, but I mean it; be careful. And I don't just mean the obvious.'

'What's that supposed to mean?'

'It means that family are troubled.'

'Most of the families in Ireland are troubled, Da.'

'Just be careful, Colleen, is all.'

Despite her father's warning, Colleen carried on seeing Patrick for the next couple of years. They talked about a future together, despite their youth. It wasn't always a smooth path, but Colleen became expert at dealing with Patrick's bouts of depression, eventually helping him to find a better job and a healthier mindset. Occasionally, though, he would go off on a downer and she wouldn't see him for days. Eventually, he would come out of it and appear on her doorstep as if nothing had happened, and Colleen would accept this behaviour; it was a flaw in his character she had learned to deal with, believing he would always come back to her. And he did.

CHAPTER 2

LIGHT

They married two years after meeting. Colleen's family agreed to the wedding, fearful of her falling pregnant out of wedlock and causing a scandal.

They tried for a couple of years for a child, but to no avail. After several tests and exploratory surgery, Colleen was told it was unlikely she would ever have children. Patrick's response was to go on a bender with his cousin Frank who was visiting from England, leaving Colleen at home, alone and unsupported.

Cousin Frank lived in Manchester and used to visit as a boy with his father, Cyril. Patrick's dad was Cyril's brother. Whenever Cyril came over, they would go on huge sessions. Patrick's mum used to moan at them when they eventually rolled home drunk, but sometimes the pair of them were aggressive, so she learned to stay upstairs.

Patrick heard about Uncle Cyril's sudden death, but the two families weren't particularly close, so it hadn't affected him much. He remembered his mum referred to Cyril along the lines of 'no love lost there', then he had been all but forgotten.

Until Frank turned up out of the blue.

He made contact just at the right time and arrived on the Friday they had the news about Colleen. There was a strange atmosphere in his uncle's house when Frank arrived. Nobody seemed to know what to say until Patrick suggested he come over to meet Colleen. Sensing his stony reception, Frank was glad of the invitation.

'What's wrong with your mum? She was always pleased to see me as a kid,' Frank asked on the way over to Patrick's.

'I don't know, but you know what women are like. I think it's because your dad and my dad used to go out on those huge benders and it always caused trouble at home.'

'Yeah, I can see I might remind her of that time.'

'Anyway, we don't need to think about that now. We're grown men with troubles of our own, so we are,' said Patrick.

'You can say that again,' said Frank.

The reception wasn't exactly frosty at Patrick's, but Frank definitely picked up on something not being quite right. Colleen didn't get up to greet them when they walked in, and she didn't look in the best of moods.

'Colleen, this is Frank, my cousin from England,' said Patrick quietly, in contrast to his enthusiasm on the way over.

'Hey Frank, nice to meet you,' said Colleen.

Patrick suggested he take Frank out for a pint and Colleen didn't object.

Once the cousins were in the pub, they got on like a house on fire, sinking pints and laughing about family events, memories from past visits.

'What was wrong with your missus earlier?' asked Frank. 'She looked like she'd lost a pound and found tuppence.'

Patrick laughed, spluttering his drink all over him, 'Never heard that one. Funny, you are.'

'I don't feel very funny, if I'm honest,' said Frank, staring into his pint.

'Me neither, Frank, I can tell you. Truth is we were told today Colleen can't have kids. Sure, I'm not that bothered to be honest, but you know women: their feckin' lives revolve around family.'

'Yep, they sure do. Look what happened to

me mam. She had four kids, but then the old man dies, she leaves us, then drops down dead herself a few years later.'

Patrick patted him on the back, 'I heard about that. I'm sorry for your loss, Frank.'

'It was ten years ago for my dad, two for my mam. We manage.'

'Jeez, but it must be tough! What happened to you all?'

'Nothing much. Our Sylvia took over where me mam left off, and does a better job, truth be told.'

'You're lucky to have her, so you are.'

Frank had his head down now and was looking solemn.

'It must have hit you hard, Frank. Are you alright now?'

'Course I am, but we have a new family problem and I have no clue what to do about it.'

'Sure, you can tell me, Frank, what is it?'

Before they left the pub that night, they'd hatched a plan that would solve everyone's problems and get Frank off a nasty sharp hook.

CHAPTER 3

OUTCAST

Shauna had been sent out to play. She wanted to scuttle up to her room where she felt safe, but her mum and dad had insisted she go outside.

Shauna wasn't always happy at home, but outside, she felt unsafe. She had always felt different somehow from everyone else, found it difficult to make friends. She sat on the front doorstep, wondering how long it would be before she could go inside.

Mary and Siobhan Flynn were walking towards her. She hung her head, hoping they'd ignore her, but as they got nearer, the usual taunts started.

'Weirdo,' said Mary, sniggering.

'Bastard weirdo,' said Siobhan.

Shauna scowled at them, but this only made them laugh.

'We hear your da isn't your da, weirdo.'

'Get lost,' said Shauna.

'Why don't you, little bastard child. You don't belong here.'

'Leave me alone!' cried Shauna, as the front door opened.

Mary and Siobhan hurried away, laughing.

'What were those little sluts saying to you?' asked Shauna's mum.

'The usual. That I'm a bastard, that Da isn't my real da.'

'What else?' asked her mum, wringing her hands.

'Nothing,' said Shauna.

'Take no notice of them, they're jealous, is all. You'd better come in now,' said Colleen, dragging Shauna up and pushing her through the door. 'Go and get your breakfast. You're late for school.'

Colleen went back to the lounge, where her father stood red-faced. It was clear they were in the middle of one of their humdingers.

'Get out my fecking way, Colleen, or help me God I'll throttle you!'

Shauna reeled at her father's anger. She looked out of the kitchen window, longing to go and run in the fields, to get out of this box of pain.

Finally, the argument stopped. She heard the door slam and watched as her father stomped up the path, pulling on his jacket. There was only one place he was heading.

Shauna was shocked to find her mother pouring vodka so early in the morning. When she saw Shauna, she hurriedly put the bottle back in the cupboard. Her eyes were red, and she was shaking.

'I suppose you'll be wanting some breakfast,' she said, without warmth.

'It's alright, Ma, I'll make my own,' said Shauna, opening the cupboard.

'There's no cereal, not until payday,' said her mother.

Shauna went to the bread bin. There was a crust and nothing else. She took it and put it under the grill, then turned on the gas and lit it with a match. She knew not to question her mother, not even to ask if she was alright. The response was always the same: 'None of your business'. Despite her earlier attempt at concealing the drink, her mother was now taking a long swig from the tumbler of vodka. Shauna busied herself with finding a knife, a plate and margarine.

'Do you want some toast, Ma?'

Her mother looked right through her.

Shauna knew that life for her mother was tough. Her father had lost his job, and it was left to her mum to put food on the table. Now that was taking its toll.

Shauna understood, but it didn't stop her longing for the mother she had lost. She used to be so loving, so happy, but the arguments had become worse, and even violent, recently.

She had watched her mother change from a happy housewife to a miserable drudge as her drinking became heavier. Her father had never been very loving, but now he was positively hateful. And in the heat of their many arguments, he said hateful things, things he didn't think Shauna could hear.

'Why should I care about a kid that isn't even mine?'

CHAPTER 4

MADHOUSE

Shauna was woken by her mother's screams. Grabbing her dressing gown, she ran downstairs and reached the hallway as the front door slammed shut. She could hear her mother's pathetic sobs. She went through to the lounge and the sight that met her was shocking.

Her mother was cowering on the floor in the corner of the room, holding her nose which was bleeding all over the carpet. Her eyes were swollen, her top was ripped, and she was whimpering like a stray dog. Shauna stepped over beer cans and the contents of ashtrays, the detritus of one of her parents' heavier sessions.

'What's happened?' asked Shauna, knowing the answer.

Her mother didn't move or speak. Her eyes looked weird, the pupils small and fixed, staring ahead at nothing.

'Come on, Ma, we need to clean you up. You

can't stay here all night.'

Shauna was used to the rows, the slaps and shoves, but she had never seen her mother in this state. Hooking her arm under Ma's elbow, she was shocked at how light she had become. She helped her over to the chair, where she plonked down.

Ma looked Shauna in the eye. 'It's all your fault!' she slurred. 'If it wasn't for you, things would be better.'

Although Shauna was used to being ignored, and feeling unwanted, this direct stab was hard to take.

'What do you mean? Why is it my fault? It's not my fault I was born, not my fault you had me.'

Her mother made a sound like a dog yelping and cried hard into her hands. Shauna went to fetch a cloth, but Ma grabbed her arm.

'Get out of my sight, you little bitch!' she said. 'He's not coming back, and it's all your fault!'

Shauna wasn't hanging around to hear any more. She climbed the stairs slowly, wracking her brains for reasons why her mother should blame her for what had happened.

CHAPTER 5

MISERY

It was Shauna's fifteenth birthday. No banners and balloons here. Her classmates had celebrated theirs by gathering in the park, drinking and having a laugh, if what she had heard was true. She had never been invited.

For much of her time at high school, Shauna had struggled to get through each day, counting the minutes until home time. Home wasn't much better. Her father never did return, and her mother continued to drink.

Shauna closed her bedroom door and headed downstairs. The living room was a tip, as usual, but today she ignored it.

She didn't expect anything from Ma, knew better than to get her hopes up, but she couldn't deny the stab of hurt at the lack of a card. A simple, cheap card would have done, to reassure her that she was somewhere in Ma's thoughts, that she'd at least remembered her birthday.

Closing the front door, swallowing down the familiar rising panic, she headed to the bus stop. Today she was going to treat herself to a fry up in the café she had been working in after school. She'd had to lie to her mother about how much she was earning, so that she could keep a little for herself. She should have been working today, but they had agreed to let her have the day off and work Sunday morning instead.

It wasn't yet ten o'clock when the bus pulled up in the town centre and Shauna got off, patting her pockets to make sure her purse and keys were in there. Keeping her head down, she made her way to the café. She hadn't walked more than a few steps when someone pushed her so hard, she fell backwards onto the pavement.

Teresa Murphy and her mate Alison James were standing over her, clutching their stomachs with laughter.

'Where are you off to, greaseball? To buy some shampoo, are you? Scruffy mare,' said Teresa and she spat on the ground.

Shauna knew better than to say anything: it was two against one and it would only make things worse. She took a deep breath, tried to calm the anger and hurt.

'What's up, Shauna? Have your mates all ran away?'

The two girls doubled over with laughter. Shauna slowly tried to get up, but Alison James pushed her down. It took all her willpower not to cry. Then a stranger came over and told the girls to leave Shauna alone. They walked away, making rude gestures and sneering.

The man helped Shauna up. 'Are you ok, love?' he asked.

Shauna muttered that she was fine, she wanted to be away from there. He accepted her answer and left her alone. Her backside was sore, and she limped to the café, glad of her boss's familiar face behind the counter. Reg had guided her through the job, correcting her gently, never losing patience. This was the only place she felt human.

'Hey Reg, I thought I'd celebrate my birthday with a fry up,' she said, easing herself into a seat tucked in the corner.

'Are you on your own?'

'Sure am. Thanks for reminding me,' she said, trying to hide her embarrassment.

'That won't do. Where's your ma? Is she busy?'

'She's not well, but it doesn't matter, I like my own company.'

'Breakfast is on me then. It's the least I can do.'

Shauna had got good at lying about her mother. It was bad enough being bullied at school; she didn't want to be pitied at work. She had learnt to say very little about her situation, but Reg was not stupid. He had witnessed the taunts and dirty looks from the local girls. He had stopped a couple of them coming in, but they still laughed at her through the window.

Shauna had developed a hard shell against it all, but inside she was festering. She was sure that one day her anger was going to rise and explode.

CHAPTER 6

VULNERABLE

Shauna got the key to the door on her twenty-first birthday, but not in a good way.

She had been woken by a commotion downstairs. Shouting, screaming, smashing glass: nothing unusual for the early hours of Sunday.

Ma's latest man, Jim, had moved in a few months ago and Saturday night was when their drinking reached a peak. Inevitably they would argue. Tonight, the row was particularly loud and heated, but Shauna had stopped intervening after receiving a nasty cut to her hand, trying to stop Jim from knifing her mother. He had calmed down eventually, but it was as if a switch had turned off for Shauna. From then on, she decided she was going to put her own safety first.

She nodded off and woke up to silence a few hours later. She checked her clock: ten-thirty.

Happy Birthday, Shauna.

If she got up now, she'd have plenty of time to have breakfast and get ready to meet Jack at twelve, as arranged.

She didn't know why she bothered; he was never on time anyway. Maybe today he would make an effort; it was her twenty-first, after all. *Who knows, he may even get me a present.*

She threw the covers back and gathered the empty beer bottles, kicking aside the clothes and dirty plates; she'd sort them out later.

She stepped carefully downstairs and kicked open the lounge door.

She dropped the bottles.

There lay her mother, eyes staring, covered in blood. Shauna knelt beside her, checked for a pulse and calmly called an ambulance.

Although it was clear her mother was dead, Shauna felt nothing. She sat motionless until the crew arrived and took Ma away after confirming that she had indeed passed away.

Shauna sat in the armchair until the police arrived. She answered their questions, giving Jim's name willingly.

They searched the house and confirmed he wasn't there. Then one of them left, leaving Shauna with a female officer who said she would help with arrangements. Between them, they contacted Colleen's parents and Patrick's mum. All of them were heartbroken, even though they hadn't visited for years.

When Jack arrived, an hour late, Shauna told him to get lost. He shrugged his shoulders and walked away without question. He didn't appear to have a present. Not that it mattered to Shauna; she had more than enough to think about today.

Today, her Ma had died, and she felt about as numb as a rock. She always knew that she would end up on her own, so it was no big shock. She felt strange, like she was on a boat in the middle of the sea with no anchor, no oars.

It was then that she started to question who she really was.

CHAPTER 7

PSYCHOTIC

Since her mother's death, Shauna had become increasingly confused and reclusive. Unsure of her roots, even of her sexuality, she had drifted through relationships, each one more destructive than the last, until she had given up altogether.

She knew it didn't help, keeping herself cooped up away from the world, not one little bit, but she couldn't face other people. Slowly, she withdrew further and further into herself.

Why should I be punished for their mistakes? What have I ever done?

She made a few attempts to socialise with colleagues, but she always felt out of place. Life went on, and Shauna grew increasingly bitter.

She eventually decided to do some digging. What she discovered changed her, destroying what little self-regard she had managed to cling to. Her life was based on a giant lie.

Through some covert questioning of various family members, she managed to glean that the people who had raised her as their own were not her parents at all. In fact, her birth mother had given her away, and everything after that was falsehoods and deception. Colleen had faked pregnancy, faked the birth certificate, faked every bit of Shauna's life.

This knowledge festered and grew like a malignant stone in the pit of Shauna's stomach until, after many years, she could stand it no more and decided to take matters into her own hands. She was in her forties now, with a string of failed relationships behind her.

If it wasn't for the actions of a silly girl, Shauna wouldn't have had the life she did.

How could a mother leave her child? How could a child be abandoned like an unwanted puppy?

So help me god, I'll make that woman pay.

Clicking on the dating profile, she cringed into her seat as her target's face appeared. She typed into the dialogue box:

Let's stop all this pussyfooting around and meet. It's about time.

A pause. Then came the response:

You would have to live so far away.

She typed back:

Blackpool isn't exactly the other side of the world. Go on, you know we can't put it off forever and I'm dying to meet you.

I suppose you're right, Andrew. No harm in meeting, if only for a chat. I'm not quite up to anything else just yet.

What about we meet here, on Blackpool front? We could have fish and chips and a bracing walk up the beach. It's not too far for you to come. What do you think?

Sounds good to me. I'll look at train times. We'll make it an afternoon, then I can get back at a decent time.

Afternoons are not good for me. I could be free from about 6pm, then you could get the last train after supper and a walk. What do you say?

I love fish and chips on the front.

So do I! That's settled then. What about next Saturday?

A pause.

Yes, alright, why not?

Perfect, thought Shauna.

Deleting her profile, she shut down the site, then googled flights to the UK.

PART 4

DOLORES

Scrambling out of the concrete hole, she blinked at the brightness, clutching her chest, taking deep gulps of fresh air. She knew she must get away, but how could she run when someone lay dying?

CHAPTER 1

SETTING SAIL

Dolores felt the familiar prickle of irritation as she stepped inside the coffee shop. Her date had suggested the venue for their first meet, and she had agreed, not wanting to appear difficult. He said it had a 'relaxed atmosphere' and 'easy vibe'. Not for Dolores: she couldn't see beyond the stacks of paper cups and plastic lids piled beside them. She shuffled towards the vast glass counter, the cakes taunting her in all their creamy, sugary splendour. Aware of her sour demeanour, she altered her expression: the barista wasn't to blame for the ills of the modern world.

Dolores ordered tea. The server wordlessly tapped the machine and silently indicated for Dolores to pay.

Everything's going contactless.

She waited at the end of the counter near the hissing machines, their noise competing with chatter and clattering crockery. The wait seemed endless, possibly because, as always, Dolores was overthinking.

'Would you like milk with your Earl Grey?'

'No thanks, just how it is.'

Once her drink arrived, she scanned the busy room, looking for the impossible: a seat which was free and tucked away in a corner. A young family huddled around the centre table, heads hooked over technology, not one word exchanged. A couple in their twenties swiped phones and smiled to themselves, but not to each other. Others wore earphones, wireless and discreet or large ones covering their ears; all of them completely shut off from the world.

Easing her way between tables, stepping over shopping bags – images of children making cheap clothes in sweat shops running through her mind – she cursed Carly for setting her up.

A blind date in a deaf and blind world.

But she reminded herself that life was essentially good. She took deep breaths and made for the stairs, hoping there would be more space up there and less reason to inwardly rant about all and sundry. There was a vacant table in the corner, and she squeezed in, surveying her purchase as she sat: one cup of tea, no snacks, no extra sugar or plastic spoons, just the tea.

Good girl, Dolores.

But she couldn't feel completely smug; she was here, after all, endorsing the place simply by being present. She had recently begun to question every aspect of her life, including her friends, and even her choice of footwear. She looked down at her favourite leather boots and vowed to buy plastic next time.

'Plastic, though?'

She'd said it out loud, and her timing was impeccable. In front of her stood the bearded man Carly had described. He was looking down on her, one pierced eyebrow raised, bemused. She stood up and offered her hand, at which he let out a hearty laugh.

'I didn't think people shook hands anymore, except at interviews. I'm Joe.'

He plonked himself down next to her.

'Dolores. Nice to meet you.'

'Likewise.'

There was an awkward silence while Dolores fixed her gaze on the plastic top of his disposable cup. It was amazing how many thoughts a piece of plastic could trigger: *does he know about the damage these things do? Why has he even got a takeaway cup? Maybe he's hedging his bets.*

'So… we meet at last, Dolores. Cool name. Are

you Irish?'

She hated it when people started every sentence with a 'so'.

'I'm not, no. It was my great-grandma's name, apparently.'

'Cool.'

Not cool. Traditional.

Another one of her bugbears: everything was 'cool'.

I really must shake off this grumpiness.

She took a sip of tea to avoid saying the wrong thing. She wished she could keep her views to herself, but she felt passionate about these things.

'Were you not planning on staying?' she asked.

'Sorry?'

'The plastic, I mean the cup, it's takeaway.'

'Force of habit. I always get coffee-to-go.'

You and thousands of others, it seems. 'I'm sorry, I don't mean to be a killjoy. If I told you I'm a recent convert to veganism and saving the planet, would that make it any clearer?'

'Ah, yes. I see now. That's why you were staring at my cup. I thought you were expecting a white rabbit to jump out of it or something.'

Dolores laughed. 'Sorry, I'm a bit obsessed.'

'No worries, I've seen the programmes. I just forget, you know?'

'I know, I slip myself sometimes.'

'That makes me feel a whole lot better. So, do you fancy something to eat after this?'

'Thought you'd never ask. Where do you fancy?'

'Maybe it's best if you choose,' said Joe.

'Cool,' she said, then kicked herself.

'So, what do vegans like to eat?'

'We eat lots of things. Most places cater for us now, but *Zen's* is good.'

'Cool, *Zen's* it is.'

As they walked, Dolores bit back comments on the state of the streets. Stepping over the hated plastic and cardboard mess, she kicked aside cartons and tutted inwardly at crisp bags. When she was out with Carly, they'd both have a good moan about all the wrongs of modern living, but she had to keep a lid on all that for now: just not a plastic one. Joe was a good-looking bloke, and she didn't want to put him off.

'I like your style, Dolores. The vintage look. I suppose that's what attracted me in the first place. Do you have any body art?'

'None at all. I like vintage, but I'm not into tattoos and piercings,' she said, then remembered the bar through his right eyebrow.

'So, yeah, I have piercings and some body art. Thought I'd put that out there from the get-go.'

'Oh, it's not that I judge people who have them, I just don't fancy them myself.'

'Cool. Free country and all that.'

They smiled, and he held her hand, which surprised her, given her grumpy tone. They arrived at *Zen's* and asked for both menus. They chose a quiet booth and discussed choices.

'So, I have a friend who's vegan. He seems to live on chickpeas and spinach.'

'Yeah, I'm not denying it can be restrictive, but you get used to it.'

'Just like everything else, I suppose. So, what do you fancy?'

'Chickpea and spinach curry, please,' she grinned, another ice breaker.

They chatted easily, finished their meals and drinks, and mutually decided to 'call it a day'. It had been intense for them both, even taking first date nerves into account. They arranged to meet again the following week and parted with a chaste peck on each cheek.

Dolores hopped on the bus, her head throbbing.

She was certainly attracted to Joe, but they were so different she doubted it could work. It was too difficult to hold back negative comments whenever he said 'so' or 'cool,' and dating a non-vegan was not ideal. To insist on it, however, would narrow her options to almost zero. Trying to mould someone into a different version of themselves had never been her style. She wondered if Joe would change his way of thinking naturally if they stayed together.

Listen to me, we've only been on one date. It's early days.

Resisting the urge to check her phone – cutting down on screen-time was another aim – she watched the blur of the city as it passed across the window. She didn't like the way life was changing at a rate of knots. There were so many things that worried her. Friends and family told her to 'lighten up' or 'get a life', but she had a life and she liked it the way it was. It was everyone else's lives that bothered her. The list of annoyances grew daily. Everywhere she went seemed to trigger a gripe. So many things made her sad. She often wondered if she should have been born in a different era.

The bus stopped at Fletcher Street and Dolores hopped off so she could call at Carly's on the way home, as arranged. She preferred to talk in person, rather than message. She was sure they'd invent an emoji for 'first date doubts' at some point but, for now, she'd express it in the old-fashioned way. She lifted the brass knocker on Carly's door and gave it a couple of raps. The door swung back and there stood Mrs Barton in all her Caribbean glory, beaming her wonderful smile.

'The lovely Dolores. Always nice to see you, diamond. Come in, come in. We're having tea. Would you like some?'

'Thanks Mrs B, but I've just eaten in town. I'm stuffed.'

'Always room for a bit more, sweet girl. Come in, Carly's through here.'

Dolores loved the Barton household. She loved the infectious energy, the laughter, the endless mealtimes, the random art and the upcycled knick-knacks dotted about the place. She loved the passionate exchanges on topics close to their hearts: mostly kindness, good manners and the environment. Mrs B had been a big influence on Dolores. She had a lot to thank her for.

Carly sprang from her place at the table. 'Dee! At last! How did it go? What did you think of him, honestly?'

'Woah, woah, woah,' said Mrs B. 'Let the poor child get in. Here, give me your coat, precious.'

'Thanks, Mrs B. Yeah, it was good. He's good-looking, like you said, and I'd say it went kind of alright, for a first date.'

'Excellent. I know it was a blind date, but what is a girl to do these days?' said Carly.

Mrs Barton discreetly left the room to busy herself with chores, leaving the girls to catch up on their news.

'Come on then, spill,' said Carly when her mum had gone.

'There's not much to tell, really. It was a bit awkward, to be honest. I know it's my fault but, at first, everything he said irritated me.'

'Oh no! He didn't say 'cool' a lot, did he?'

'All the time, and everything he said started with 'so'

'But he's good-looking, so you let him off, right?'

'Right, but it was hard. It's a wonder my tongue wasn't bitten to shreds. Why am I such a grump, Carly?'

'Let's not start that again. Don't be hard on yourself. What do we always say?'

'There's plenty of people who will do that for you,' said Dolores.

'Right. You're not a grump, you just care.' Carly tucked a stray piece of hair behind Dolores' ear.

They hugged and carried on chatting about

the day, exchanging a couple of new recipes and arranging to meet for a night out next weekend. Dolores made her way home, not sure about how she felt. The date had been good, and her friend supportive as ever, so why did she feel like the world was closing in on her?

CHAPTER 2

JELLY FISH

Their next date fell on Grand National Day, not the best day for an ardent defender of animal rights, and Dolores felt uncomfortable in the pub they'd agreed on. Hoping to move on as soon as Joe arrived, she hung around in the shadows, people-watching.

The place was buzzing with both habitual and once-a-year punters, their faces reddened by alcohol and excitement. She spotted Joe as he lumbered in wearing a shabby old combat jacket and jeans which sagged below his groin. A chain hung from his backside and looped round to his front pocket. She let out an involuntary sigh as he beamed back. Despite the groans from within, she had to admit he had one hell of an infectious grin. It seeped through her prissy exterior and found a much warmer place.

'Hey, Dolores. Good to see you.'

'You too,' she said. 'I wondered if we could find somewhere else. It's a bit packed in here. The races are on.'

'Which is exactly why I suggested it. So, have you had a flutter?'

'No, it's not really my bag,' she said and, noticing his face drop, decided not to go on about it.

'Cool. Shall we have a drink here first before we move on?' said Joe, obviously trying to sound upbeat.

Dolores pondered a moment. She settled on going with the flow just this once; she could always expand on her reasons for being anti-racing another time.

'I really don't mind. We can stay in here if you want. I'm quite peckish now,' she said.

Indicating a small vacant table in the corner, she led the way and they sat down. Joe pulled out a newspaper folded at the racing pages.

'So, see what you fancy,' he said, handing it to Dolores.

She took it reluctantly; being here was one thing, but actively betting was another.

'I'll leave that to you,' she said.

Joe went to get drinks. When he returned, Dolores smiled tightly and thanked him.

'Have you had a look?' he asked. 'So, I know

you don't want to bet but, just to humour me, which one would you go for?'

'I suppose it would have to be *Tiger Roll*,' she said.

'Cool, why that one?'

'No other reason than it's the favourite. Oh, and I like tiger bread. I know nothing at all about racing. What's your money on?'

'*Vintage Clouds*, then I've got *General Principle* as a cheeky outsider. You've got to pick a cheeky outsider, by the way.'

'What's one of those when it's at home?' Dolores was warming to his warmth.

'Something with high odds. Mine's 33-1. Have another look, see what you like the look of. You don't have to put any money on it. It's just a bit of fun.'

Dolores took a sip of her drink: *it's not much fun for the horses*. But she reminded herself she was saving that for another day. This was all new to her and she wasn't sure when to voice her thoughts and when to keep them to herself.

She ran her finger down the list. 'Ok, if I had to choose one, it would be *One for Arthur*, my grandad's name,' she said, decisively, then pushed the paper back to Joe.

'Cool. So, do you mind if I pop next door and put mine on?' he asked, getting up to go anyway.

Trying not to focus on the filth ingrained in the cuff of his coat, she shrugged her shoulders. He took a slurp of his beer, smiled and went on his mission.

Dolores looked around the pub, curious to see what kind of people came to a place like this. Preferring quieter places, more intimate spaces, to the chaos and clamour of commercial chains, she had never been here before. There was a good mix of types, that much was evident. A group of students debated passionately in one corner, while an older couple sat wordlessly in another. And there was everything in between: a noisy group of thirty-something trendies, all looking the same with their beards and tattooed 'sleeves'; a couple of forty-something women standing near the bar self-consciously; a young family squashed around the corner bench, kiddies playing expertly on tablets, parents with eyes fixed on iPhones, swiping adeptly. Dolores couldn't help but watch them, feeling sad for something lost.

'Done!' said Joe, slapping his hand on the table and making her jump.

'You scared me,' she laughed. 'I was miles away.'

'Yeah, I noticed. So, they're off in half an hour.

Do you want to order food now?'

'Sounds good to me.'

They scanned through the various choices and offers. Dolores looked for something suitable and realised there was only one option.

'I'll go for the sweet potato and chickpea curry,' she said, without enthusiasm.

'Sure, of course, I was forgetting for a minute,' said Joe. 'Right, I'll go and order. Do you want another drink?' Dolores rooted in her bag. 'Put your money away. I'll get this: first date rules.'

'It's technically the second,' she said.

'Never mind about that,' said Joe as he walked off.

Dolores thought it was quite sweet of him to pay. He didn't appear to be what she would call traditional, so it surprised her. She felt a bit bad for allowing it though, as she was beginning to think she couldn't see him again. He just wasn't her type. But then, who was?

Jonnie was, or so she'd thought, until she went out with work one night and caught him snogging the face off some girl in a corner of the club. He had told her he was staying in with his X-Box. She could laugh about it now, but it had hurt so much at the time.

Sometimes it seemed life was out to get her, but she knew this wasn't so; she had to get out of that mindset. Maybe she would take Carla up on the idea of going to The Buddhist Centre to learn mindfulness as a distraction therapy. Bless Carla, always looking out for her, always knowing what she needed.

'Cool, all done. Sorry I was so long,' said Joe. 'Bloke in front of me was a bit worse for wear.'

'It's fine. I was quite happy, people-watching,' she said.

'I do it all the time,' said Joe. 'There are worse ways to while away the hours. So, I never got to know much about you last time. I didn't even ask about what you do for a living, or is that a no-no on the first date?'

'I don't know, I'm not very well-informed about the finer points of dating,' she said, fiddling with the edge of her shirt.

'I'm not exactly Casanova myself,' he said, his grin seeping through the ice once more. 'Cool, we don't have to be bothered with all that for now. The race should start in five minutes. I just hope that meat-head gets out of the way before it does.'

Dolores flinched inwardly at his crude choice of words, telling herself again this relationship would never work.

'And they're off!' Joe shouted, snapping her out of her misery.

He was on his feet, the most animated she

had seen him so far. 'Come on, my son! Aw, shit! *Vintage Clouds*, down at the first.'

'Oops,' mumbled Dolores.

'Ah well, there's always the other one.'

Dolores stood up to get a better view of the screen, trying to look between the raised arms and bobbing heads. But she decided to sit back down rather than watch horses being brought down or falling.

Joe was excited. 'Mine's doing well. Come on, boy, come on... oh.'

'Was that yours, *General Principle*?'

'It sure was, the little tinker. I thought he'd go further than the nineteenth.'

He slumped into his seat, then rose again to see how the other horses fared. He caught sight of *Tiger Roll* holding his own with the leading few. He grabbed Dolores' hand and lifted it in the air, cheering as he did so, joining in the fun again. The whole pub was going mad. Some were shaking their heads at their losses, but most were cheering the remaining horses on.

'There he goes! Come on, *Tiger*, come on, son! I don't believe it! He's taking the lead. Come on, *Tiger*!' Joe shouted, his voice only just holding out.

Dolores watched as her horse took first place. She was relieved that it was all over.

'That's forty quid, right there. Not bad for a novice,' said Joe, sliding his wallet out of his back pocket to find the slips.

'But I didn't bet,' she said, confused.

'No, but I did. Trusted your instinct', said Joe, tapping the side of his nose.

Their meals arrived, and they sat down and cleared a space for the plates. In all the excitement, they'd forgotten about the food, but were glad of it now. The mixed grill was put in front of Dolores and she flinched, shoving it quickly over to Joe.

'Sorry about that,' he said.

'Don't worry, I really don't judge others for what they eat. How can I? That used to be my favourite,' she said. 'I don't want you to feel guilty for eating.'

'Ah, good,' said Joe. 'I won't, then.'

They tucked in, hungry after a couple of drinks and all the cheering. They didn't speak for the next few minutes, enjoying their food and smiling at each other in between mouthfuls. Finally, their plates were clear, apart from a couple of bits they couldn't manage.

'I have to say, I really enjoyed that,' said Dolores.

'Hey, no problem,' said Joe. 'It's been one of

the best days I've had in a while.'

'Tell you what,' said Dolores. 'Shall we go for cocktails with our winnings, somewhere snazzy?'

'Cool, sounds perfect. But not sure *Harvey Nic's* will let me in looking like this. Sorry, I would have smartened up a bit if I'd thought.'

'There's that great place in the Northern Quarter. What's it called? *Turtle Bay*? *Blue Turtle*? Something like that. I've only been in once, but I loved the atmosphere, and the cocktails were good, if I remember rightly.'

'Right,' said Joe. 'Let's get your winnings and seek out the turtle, then.'

They were shown to a seat in the corner and given menus. There was so much choice and Dolores perused silently for a while, welcoming the calm in contrast to the bustle of the pub. But, without warning, beads of sweat formed on her top lip and she suddenly felt claustrophobic and shaky. Frantically patting the side of her seat in search of her handbag, she tried to take deep breaths, but blackness was forming in her peripheral vision and palpitations were knocking in her chest. Her legs wobbled as she tried to stand and she dropped back in her seat, her bag crashing to the floor, spilling its contents.

'Are you alright?' asked Joe.

A waiter came over. He sat at Dolores' side and offered a paper bag.

'It's alright. Take deep breaths, that's right, in and out.' He turned to Joe, 'I think she's having a panic attack. I'm sorry to interfere, but you seemed to be struggling. My sister has them, so I kind of know what to do.'

'I'm glad you do, mate,' said Joe. 'I thought she was going to faint on me.'

Eventually, with the waiter coaxing her, Dolores came out of her panic, but she was overwhelmed with disappointment and the need to get out.

'Sorry about that,' she said to Joe, as the waiter slipped back to the bar. She felt shaky and weak, but above all, embarrassed and frustrated.

'I'm just glad you're ok, well, kind of: you still look a bit pale. Shall we go?'

'I think that's best,' she said. 'But, if you don't mind, I need some fresh air and to be on my own.'

'Cool,' said Joe. 'But at least let me walk you to the bus stop.'

'No, really, I'm ok,' she said, rising. 'I'll text you when I get home.'

'I can't let you go on your own. What if you

pass out on the street?' said Joe.

His concern touched her, but she was adamant. 'I really need to be alone. It's fine, it's happened before. I'll be ok now.'

Joe looked deflated, but she couldn't hang around any longer. She walked out, nodding a 'thank you' to the bar man.

Stumbling like a zombie to the bus stop, her head felt like it would split in two and all she could think about was getting home to sleep. Mercifully, her bus rolled up within minutes and she buried herself in the back seat, closing her eyes, the sound of the sea crashing against her skull.

CHAPTER 3

MAROONED

By the time Dolores arrived home she was confused and weak. Leaning on the front door, she fumbled with her key, unable to steady the tremors. Finally, the door yielded, and she was back to safety. Tossing her phone aside, she stumbled up to her bedroom and locked the door, a habit she couldn't drop.

After the ambient warmth outside, her bedroom felt cold and eerie. A blue shaft of light cast surreal shadows. Everything felt wrong. She closed the gap in the curtains, making a mental note to get blackout liners for when summer kicked in.

Exhausted, she wrapped herself in the duvet, not bothering to undress. She sobbed and shivered until eventually she succumbed to sleep.

Dark shapes appear from darker crevices, their

creepy tendrils reaching for the woman, dragging her down. She tries to scream, but nothing comes out. The woman is dragged away. Summoning every ounce of strength, she scissor-kicks her way towards the distant light, the darkness trying with all its wicked might to pull her back.

Dolores woke to another panic attack, prompted by yet another nightmare about the sea.

Flashbacks from the date with Joe jolted her back to reality, and she squirmed as she remembered the attack which came from nowhere and drained her dry. She remembered her fumbled departure. She had failed again.

The buzz of her mobile jerked her fully awake and, stomping downstairs, she retrieved the phone from the hall carpet. Ten messages, three missed calls and, the biggest surprise of all, the time: 11.30 am.

It must be Sunday, but she was certain she'd slept for only a short time.

She placed the phone on the hall table and went to the kitchen where she ran the tap for a long time before filling a pint pot with cold water, eager to dilute the brine hanging maliciously around the inside of her mouth. She gulped, taking in the pure liquid, relishing its tasteless flow and allowing it to wash through her.

Feeling slightly better, she plodded upstairs to the tiny bathroom. Its pink acrylic suite was normally a source of irritation, but now the room felt like a haven. She shoved the grubby rubber bath plug in and fought against the stiff tap until warm water spurted and spat its way out. She poured in bath oil and watched as the globules swirled around in the heat of the rising pool, throwing out a soothing aroma which calmed her. She stepped into the warmth, a beautiful contrast to the darkness of her dream. Easing back against the plastic, she allowed her body to melt.

She was woken by the doorbell. She clambered out of the tepid water, grabbed her robe, and wrapped it around herself as she made her way downstairs. She could see through the glass it was Carly. Dolores suddenly felt bad for not checking her messages, so she opened the door and smiled.

'Thank God for that. You're still alive, then?' said Carly, obviously concerned.

'Yes, I'm sorry. Come in.'

Carly stepped into the hallway and noticed the phone.

'You haven't lost your phone, then? Is the battery dead? Bloody hell, Dee, you look like Alice Cooper on a bad day. Are you ok?'

'Kind of. I had another episode right in the middle of the date. So embarrassing.'

Carly stepped forward and took her hand. 'I'm sorry, Dee, I know how it bothers you. I thought it was odd you didn't give me an update. Then, when you didn't answer my texts, I was a bit worried, but I thought you must be having a good time.'

'I was! We had a great time, honestly. Then I went all peculiar like I do and, well, I'm ashamed to say I just left him there, in that turtle place in town.'

'In that turtle place?'

'You know, the one that does Caribbean food, and two-for-one cocktails.'

'You mean *Turtle Bay*. Honestly, Dee, I worry about you.'

'So do I, *I* worry about me.'

'Come on then, tell me all about it.' Carly headed into the kitchen to fill the kettle.

Dolores followed her and sat at the table, waiting for the conversation to start, not knowing how to begin.

'I'm a bit worried about you, Dee. You don't seem yourself.'

'What can I say? I'm absolutely gutted it's happened again. It came from nowhere, no warning at all. I can hardly remember getting home. Oh, and the nightmares are back.'

'How bad? Did you have one last night?' asked Carly, a tremor of concern in her voice.

'Yes. It was so vivid, I felt so bloody helpless. I could taste the salt and the...' She hunched in the chair, her head hanging down. Tears threatened to erupt, but she needed to keep calm.

'Shh now, Dee. Have you been taking your meds?' asked Carly, taking her friend's hands in hers.

'I thought I was ok. I thought I could stop taking them, make a fresh start.'

'You can't just stop, babe. You need to phase them out until you're strong enough.'

'I thought meeting someone would give me the strength to get my life back, to get away from the past and the meds and the whole bloody mess!'

Dolores slumped further and started crying. Carly held her until the sobs subsided.

'Come on, chick, let's get you dressed. I'll treat you to lunch if you want. It might make you feel a bit better.'

'I don't think I could stomach anything. I feel sick and strange.'

'No wonder, stopping your meds like that. Where are they, by the way?'

'Halfway down the Mersey. I flushed them down the loo.'

Carly snorted her amusement, 'Oh Dee, the bloody fish'll be high as kites.'

This made them both laugh, and relief washed across Carly's face. 'Have you heard from Joe? Has he called you?'

'Haven't got a clue. Not checked the demon phone.'

'What are we going to do with you? Go and get your phone and see what he's said. You'll feel better for answering him, even if it's to say you don't want to meet again.'

'But I do want to see him again. He makes me laugh.'

'Well, hallelujah! If he makes you laugh, he's well worth carrying on with.'

'Carry on up the Northern Quarter,' said Dolores, surprised at her own humour breaking through the doom.

'Exactly, and wherever else you may venture. Now, go and get that phone and bring it right back here.'

Dolores fetched the phone and threw it on the table between herself and Carly.

'I can't look. What if he's called me a bad name? What if he's just put WTF?'

They giggled and Carly slid the phone

towards her. She picked it up and went to WhatsApp: four messages from Joe, six from Carly. She read Joe's out loud:

So, I'm sorry about what happened in the café. I hope you get home alright. Please message me when you do, so I know you're ok.

Hi Dolores, I hope you got home safely. So, I'm sorry I wasn't much help to you when you had your attack. The bar man who did help you told me a bit about it. Please don't be embarrassed, it's cool. We had a great day, and I would like to see you again.

Are you ok? Message me as soon as you get time.

Ok. So, I guess you're either poorly or you don't want to see me again. No hard feelings. Honestly. I hope you feel better soon. All the best, Joe.

Dolores shrugged and slid the phone back to the centre of the table. She bit on her bottom lip.

'He sounds genuine, like he cares,' said Carly.

'That's exactly why I should let him go. Who wants to be landed with someone with *issues* like me?'

'Oh, come on, don't start that again. You are the most beautiful person I know. Inside and out. So what if you have the odd panic attack? Who cares?'

'It's not only that, though, is it? It's everything else. The whole sordid kit and caboodle. The nightmares, the –'

'Stop! I'm not having you putting yourself down. Mantra, please.'

Dolores shrugged again. 'Mantra, shmantra.'

'Come on, Dee. Mantra.'

'Ok, but only to shut you up. I am strong, I am worthy, and I can conquer the fear. There, Shitface.'

'That's more like it. Now get that phone and I'll tell you what to write.'

'Yes, miss.' Dolores reached for the phone, tapped in her pin and went to Joe's messages. 'Go on, then.'

'Hi Joe. I'm sorry I left you in the lurch, but I needed to get home. Actually, I've been asleep all this time and have only just got your messages. Yes, let's make another date.' Carly sat back in the chair, pleased with her effort. 'Send it!'

Dolores sent the message and threw the phone down. 'Happy now?'

'Well done you. Come here.' Carly stood and held her arms out. They embraced, which prompted tears from them both. 'Aw, don't get all emosh on me, Dee, I can't bear.'

'I love you, Carly, and I don't know what I'd do without you.'

The phone buzzed and they jumped, breaking the embrace. Dolores picked it up and read the message aloud:

Cool –

They laughed,

So –

They laughed again,

where would be least likely to trigger your panic?

This set them off giggling and they blurted in unison, 'Not *Turtle Bay!*'

CHAPTER 4

SHIPWRECKED

The face looms above her, flint eyes piercing, mouth sneering. An unbearable pressure weighs on her chest; fear strikes her to the ground like a limpet. Like quicksand, the ground gives way, and she's falling into an abyss of black sea.

Dolores woke, arms thrashing, legs kicking, damp clothing clinging and her head in that vice again. She stilled as the images dissipated. She took deep breaths, blowing out each horror. The pendant light came into focus and she realised where she was: stuck to her own bed like a log lodged in mud.

The first light of morning filtered in with the sounds of spring. Birds tweeted their calls to anyone who'd listen; a greeting, a thank you for another day. It soothed her enough that she was able to move, although she could still taste the sea, feel the fear in the pit of her stomach.

She swung her legs slowly to the side of the bed and felt for the floor, her bare toes stabbing the cool air until they connected with carpet.

As she forced herself slowly up, she held her head, trying to stop it exploding, but the pain gripped, making her nauseous. She managed to stumble to the bathroom where she glugged clean, clear water and two Paracetamols. The face in the mirror, that non-person she couldn't relate to, looked back at her and warned her to get a bloody grip.

It was only five thirty; too late to go back to sleep – as if she could – too early to be up and about. It took her a minute to remember what day it was.

'Monday, of course,' she muttered.

A song filtered through the turbulence: *Monday, Monday, so good to me.*

Terrified, she felt her mind unravelling beyond her control: *But Monday morning came without warning of what it would be, and it certainly isn't what I hoped it would be. Tell me why I don't like Mondays, Mister Tambourine Man, play a song for me, take me on a trip upon your magic swirling ship, I'm not sleepy and there is no place I'm going to.*

'Snap out of it!' She stopped just short of slapping herself in the face.

Shuffling back to the bedroom, faint and

confused, she flopped onto the bed where she lay staring at the ceiling, frozen, washed up, paralysed, trying to calm herself.

'It's just a normal Monday,' she chided. 'A normal bloody Dolores Monday.'

She threw her arms wide and laughed at the ridiculous farce her life had become, at the irony of a girl, who worries so much about the planet, sinking into the oblivion of the sea she is trying to save.

The doorbell rang its sharp trill. She staggered downstairs, trying to focus, and opened the door. She was taken aback by a bright light shining directly into her eyes. Holding up her arm, she was shoved forcefully back into her hallway. Desperately trying to stay upright, she grasped at coats, but they slipped through her fingers and, as she fell, her head caught on the corner of the shoe rack.

She was still holding her head when she came to, a searing pain running across her skull. Tentatively, she peeled her eyelids open. Blackness. She thought she was blind, then she realised that she was blindfolded. She lay stock-still, the sweat of fear trickling down her spine and bile rising from her stomach. Unable to move or speak, she remained rigid, waiting for something to happen, for whoever had done this to her to show themselves and let her know what they were going to do next.

The only sound was of her own heart as it banged against her ribs. When she finally realised her hands weren't bound, she slid the blindfold up, blinking at the brightness of a lamp shining directly at her. Clutching her body to protect her modesty, she realised she was fully clothed, still in her pyjamas.

She reached for the lamp and swivelled it round, so she still had light but wasn't blinded. She was in her bedroom, on her own bed. The chair had been dragged from the corner and positioned next to her, but it was empty, a mocking emptiness which gave no clue as to how it had got there. She took a deep breath, then got off the bed, checked the wardrobes, every cavity, but there was nothing. When she was sure she was alone, she fumbled with the key, locked the bedroom door, then tried to phone Carly.

An image of a face inside a black hood flashed through her mind. She dropped the phone, panic rising, and slumped to the floor, meeting the carpet abruptly. She could see her phone, just out of reach. With shaking hands, she reached out, but her ears buzzed, and darkness closed in.

When she awoke, she was lying face down, her mouth twisted into the carpet, drooling saliva, pain ripping through her skull. Terror gripped, rendering her immobile. But she willed herself to move. She rolled over slowly, then knelt, carefully lifting her head, fighting against its heaviness. Using the chair for support, she eased herself onto it and surveyed the room, bright spangles of light dancing across her line of vision. The lamp threw a bright arc into the corner next to the bed, illuminating the only picture she had kept. Her mum looked down, saint-like with a halo of brightness, but her smile looked worldly, troubled.

Dolores felt sadness rise, mixing with her fear, making her helpless, detached. As if floating above herself, she could hear her own pitiful sobs somewhere in the distance. She sank onto the bed and lay limp, resigned to her fate, whatever it was. There was something draped on the quilt beside her and, instinctively, she reached for it. *What the...?* Her mother's silk scarf, the one she'd been wearing the night she never returned. Where the hell had that come from? Its scent and softness evoked a mixture of melancholy and fear. From somewhere, Dolores found the strength to sit up, to at least give herself a fighting chance. She caught sight of her phone on the floor, and whimpered.

Using the least amount of energy possible, she slid off the bed and, not wanting to stand in case she passed out again, she crawled across the floor like a wounded animal. She reached up for the key in the door and checked it was still locked. Fighting tremors, she picked up the phone, but it shook out of her hand and bounced on the carpet.

'Breathe, Dolores, *breathe.*'

Crawling like an SAS commando, she reached for her phone and this time managed to grasp it.

'Shit, what's my shitting PIN?' The number wouldn't come through her mind-fog and she cried out in frustration.

Her mum's gaze penetrated her confusion, and the month of July sprang unbidden, jolting her memory. Of course! Her mother's birthday. Punching the numbers into the phone, she mumbled 'Carly, Carly.' What was her number? The colourful icons danced before her. She chose the green speech bubble with the white phone. Carly's face was there, along with messages, the last one at 12.34 am:

Now sleep!

Dolores tapped the little green phone to the right of Carly's name and was relieved to hear the ringing.

'Hello.' Carly's sleepy voice trickled through

her senses like nectar.

'Carly, thank God. You've got to come, someone's been in. I don't know what's happening. My head hurts. They might still be here; you've got to come!'

'Dee? Are you at home?'

'Yes, I'm at home. Please come Carly, but be careful, they might still be here.'

'Wait right there. I'm on my way.'

Relief flooded through her, quelling the anguish, but not killing it. She relaxed, her arms flopping to the floor, her phone falling to the carpet. Drained, she waited, sobbing into her chest, her throbbing head muffling thought. Terrified they might have heard her and might kick the door down any minute, she pushed her back into it. But she could never be a match for the monster on the other side. The image of that twisted face came unbidden, and she squeezed her eyes shut.

Desperate pounding on the front door made her jump. Her phone was moving along the carpet and she grabbed it.

'Dee, it's me! Let me in, chick. Mum's with me, everything's fine.'

Dolores tried to stand, but her legs would barely hold her. She managed to unlock the door and open it a little. She could see the way was clear. She stumbled onto the landing, her faltering steps finding the stairs. Gripping the banister, she tottered down, catching sight of two figures in the doorway outside, Mrs B's hair forming a beautiful halo. She opened the front door and fell into them, shaking her head and sobbing.

Carly and her mum guided her into the lounge, where they sat her down and tried to calm her. Her hair was a matted mess, her pyjamas damp with sweat, and her face looked much older than it had just a few days ago.

'You've got to help me,' she sobbed, 'they came for me. They came here.'

'Who did, sweetheart?' Mrs B's lilting voice cut through the heavy air.

'*They* did. He did. She did. I don't know. Someone was here!'

'Where did you see them, babe?' asked Carly.

'A face inside a hood. They blindfolded me. When I pulled it off, the lamp was shining in my face and the chair was next to my bed.'

'Was there anyone in the chair, Dee?'

'No, they must have gone.'

She saw Carly catch her mum's eye. 'Show us where you saw them, chick.'

'It's all mixed up, the face, the blindness, the light, the chair!' Dolores held her head in her hands and pressed on a tender spot: 'I fell! Yes, I fell in the hallway.'

She showed them the back of her head, desperate to make them believe her.

Carly went into the hall and knelt to inspect the lino. There was no sign of blood, no sign of a struggle; the coats were hanging neatly, the shoes in tidy pairs on the rack. She stood up and fiddled with the lock on the front door. No sign of a forced entry. She walked back to the lounge, discreetly shrugging her shoulders at her mum.

She sat next to Dolores and held her hand gently. 'Remember when we talked about your meds yesterday, babe?'

'No, it's not that! Someone was here! The chair, the lamp. And the scarf! They brought Mum's scarf, the one she was wearing when...'

Carly exchanged worried glances with her mum.

Mum took the lead. 'Let's see what's going on upstairs, shall we, sweetheart?'

Dolores was pitifully pleading with them to believe her, but this was all too weird. Carly guided Dolores up the stairs while she continued her frantic account of what had happened. When they reached the bedroom, Dolores stiffened, and they held her a little tighter.

'See? Look at the chair. It doesn't live there; it belongs in the corner. And there's Mum's scarf. They blindfolded me with it! Look at the lamp. It was shining in my face and, and...'

Mum guided Dolores gently to the bed, where she sat, looking defeated. It was heartbreaking.

Carly wondered how to phrase what she was about to say. 'I think you may have had a nightmare, Dee. You know how sometimes they seem so real, like they're really happening? Then you wake up.'

'No! It wasn't like that! It *was* real!'

Mum intervened. 'I'm taking you back home with me, at least for today.'

Her motherly tone brought a semblance of calm to Dolores and Carly, both. Dolores nodded her agreement, fear giving way to a pathetic resignation that was distressing to witness.

Carly tried for briskness. 'Come on, miss. Let's get a bag packed. I'll take the day off, sort your meds out and we'll take it from there.'

Again, Dolores nodded as she rose from the bed and shuffled to the bathroom. She closed the door on them. They were about to return to the bedroom when Dolores shrieked. Carly rushed in, closely followed by her mum. Dolores was staring into the mirror, horror-struck.

Carly scanned the room. 'What is it, chick?'

'Nothing. Just me,' Dolores said.

CHAPTER 5

FLOATING

Dolores spent a few days cocooned in the warmth of the Barton household, allowing them to look after her. It was clear they didn't believe an intruder had been in her home: she could tell, the way they nodded while looking at her with pity. She didn't want them to feel sorry for her, she wanted them to take her seriously, but she was beginning to doubt herself now she felt safe. The meds were working, bestowing a sense of calm and allowing her to think straight, or as straight as she could, given the circumstances.

It would soon be time to return home. Like getting back on a bike after a bad fall, she knew it needed to be done, but she couldn't face it on her own. Although she now doubted her own version of events, she knew something bad *had* happened. How could all that have been a dream, a hallucination? She had a sore head as evidence, although Carly could be right:

she could have fallen onto something in her confusion. Carly would come with her and stay the weekend, then go back to work on Monday, leaving Dolores to get used to being alone again. They had been so patient with her, so good to her, and they were only a phone call away. But she was terrified of going back, of being in the presence of something evil, whether it was a figment of her over-active imagination or not.

Joe had messaged a few times during the week of her stay with the Bartons. With Dolores' permission, Carly had messaged back brief replies, not wanting him to lose interest, but not wanting to disclose what was going on, either. Dolores sent the last message, telling him she had been busy with repairs on the house. He seemed to buy it, but you could never be sure with messages. Being a technophobe, it didn't sit right with her that all their communication was by phone, so, stupidly or otherwise, Dolores agreed to meet him the following Tuesday. That would give her time, between now and then, to get accustomed to her home again and get her sense of self back.

When Carly got back from work on Friday evening, they all sat down to a meal of jerk chicken, rice and peas, washed down with Mrs B's special rum punch. Dolores scanned the faces of the two people who had anchored her to sanity over the past year and she felt a warm glow, a confidence which told her she was ready to move on.

Clever Mrs B. Better than any meds.

Although Carly was putting on a cheerful front, Dolores knew this whole situation had caused her grief and worry. This didn't sit right with her, either. The last thing she wanted was to be a burden on this family.

When I feel better, when this nightmare has passed, I will repay your kindness.

As if in response, Carly drained her glass and let out a loud belch.

'Oh, pardon me, I'm sure,' she said, giggling.

'How have I brought you up, child?' said Mrs B, grinning broadly.

'It's the rum punch, Mum. Packs a punch in your stomach, it does,' said Carly, patting her midriff.

'The elixir of life,' said Mrs B, draining her own glass and picking the last of the chicken from a greasy wing.

All this happiness. What a lovely, lovely family, and lucky me for sharing in it.

Dolores sat quietly for a minute, wishing she could stay here, but knowing she had to find her own sense of belonging.

'Come on, Little Miss Dreamer,' said Carly,

nudging her arm gently.

'Yeah, time to go,' said Dolores without conviction.

It was late evening by the time Dolores reached home, the sun setting beautifully, casting a warm red glow which didn't quite reach her. Fumbling in her handbag for the front door key, she was secretly scanning the ground for clues.

'Come on, I'm taking root here,' said Carly.

'I'm just getting my key. Ah, found it.' She held it up, her hand shaking slightly.

Carly took the key from her and unlocked the door, swinging it open and entering confidently. Dolores shuffled in behind, looking for shapes in corners.

'I'll get the kettle on. Think we need a strong coffee after that punch, do you?' said Carly, brightly.

But, as if sensing Dolores' fear, she dropped her bag to the floor and hugged her, whispering reassurances: 'You'll feel better after tonight when you've spent some time here, seen everything's ok.'

'But everything's not ok, Carly, it's not ok at all.'

'What do you mean, chick? What's bothering

you? Tell Aunty Carly.'

'Something's not right. I can't put my finger on it.'

Like with those magazine puzzles that show two seemingly identical pictures, Dolores was trying to 'circle' the changes in her home. Something was amiss, but she couldn't work out what. She rubbed her eyes and sat down. But a sharp stab made her jump back up. She picked up the offending object from the cushion and turned it over in her hand.

'What's that?' asked Carly.

'It's a badge. It says *World's Best Mum*. Someone has been here, Carly. Someone left this on my settee, in my house!'

Dolores could feel her anxiety rising, the soothing effect of the rum completely gone now.

'I know what's happened here,' offered Carly. 'You bought this settee second-hand, right? That badge has been stuck down the cushions for ages, left by the last owners. Then, in all the kerfuffle, it's worked itself out, that's all. Da-da! Inspector Carly strikes again.'

She took a bow, then waltzed into the kitchen to fill the kettle noisily whilst humming the *Pink Panther* tune.

Dolores picked up the badge and placed it on the mantelpiece behind a glass candlestick.

Carly was probably right. She wandered into the kitchen, holding her arms out wide. Carly walked into them and they hugged.

'What would I do without you? I'd be a paranoid mess.'

'No, you wouldn't, Dee. You're stronger than you think. You just need time, that's all.'

'Ah, the magic *time*.'

'Since when did I start talking in clichés?' asked Carly. 'And exactly when did I turn into my mother?'

They laughed; the tension broken once again by Carly's light spirit. Dolores drifted back into the lounge while Carly finished the tea. She slumped into the chair and scanned the walls.

'Stop it right now,' said Carly, juggling two teas and a plate of biscuits.

'Stop what?'

'Don't act daft with me, miss. I saw you looking around for something else to worry about. Stop it!'

'I wasn't. I'm glad to be home, that's all.'

'So why do you look like you're having your teeth pulled? You can't kid the kid who kidded the kid, Dee.'

'I know. Clever, you are,' said Dolores, taking a custard cream, grateful for Carly and her common sense.

The rest of the evening was spent watching chick flicks and chatting about things that didn't really matter. Dolores needed to rest her mind, give herself chance to adapt to the meds again, get comfortable being back at home. They didn't have a glass of wine. She wasn't supposed to drink, and she'd already had the rum punch, fooling herself it was mostly milk.

When they could no longer stifle their yawns, they went upstairs. Carly would 'camp out' in a sleeping bag at the foot of the bed. Dolores knew it was best if she slept alone, but it was reassuring to have Carly in the same room. This way, she could sleep reasonably well, and she knew this would help her state of mind. Once the weekend was over, she was hoping to be back to where she'd been a few days ago, looking forward to the future.

They muttered their good nights, and Dolores switched the lamp off, throwing the room into darkness. Once her eyes adjusted, Dolores could make out faint shapes as the streetlamp cast a pale light through her thin curtains. Smiling, she shook her head at her own silliness and fell into a deep and, for once, dreamless sleep.

Bird song woke her and she opened her eyes. For the first time in forever she felt rested and refreshed. Breathing in the calm, she lay still for a while, enjoying the peace. Since that episode in town, while she was out with Joe, she had been waking up in a cold sweat, terrified.

Maybe that incident caused paranoia. And maybe the paranoia built up and convinced me my nightmare was real.

It seemed like a logical explanation, and she wanted so much to believe it. Slipping out of bed, she gently nudged Carly's sleeping bag with her toe.

'Hey sleepy head, do you want a brew?' she asked, and waited for a response. Nothing. Crouching down, she peeled the quilted bag from the side of Carly's face. It was a shame to wake her, she looked so angelic, so Dolores decided to leave her there for a while longer.

She slipped her feet into flip-flops, and went to the bathroom, still feeling strange. The face looking back at her from the mirror certainly looked a lot healthier than the one on Monday. It seemed so long since she had worked herself up into that frenzy, and all because of a stupid nightmare, a silly notion that someone was out to get her. Wondering how she could have allowed herself to become so paranoid, she cleaned her teeth vigorously. Turning the shower to full pelt, she waited for the welcoming steam, then stepped in and stood soaking up the warmth. After drying herself, she put on the soft towelling robe Carly had bought her for Christmas, bless her.

Feeling at least a hundred percent better, she stepped lightly down the stairs, humming as she went. There was a letter on the mat, her name scrawled in red spidery handwriting across the envelope, but no address. She took it through to the lounge and propped it on the mantelpiece. She would read it later with Carly. She wouldn't speculate now and ruin her mood.

As she looked up, she noticed the empty hook on the wall. Her insides turned cold.

CHAPTER 6

CASTAWAY

Dolores is rocking gently. The boat must have slipped anchor and drifted. She can hear her name floating on the sea breeze: a faint voice trying to reach her. 'I'm not alone,' she thinks. The rocking becomes stronger, more persistent. She tries to open her eyes, gritty from the salty spray. A familiar face looms and she blinks, the grit scratching at her eyes.

'Dee, are you ok? What are you doing on the floor?'

'The boat, it's… '

'It's ok, you must have gone back to sleep for a minute.'

Dolores felt heavy, like a sack of potatoes. She sat up trying desperately to remember what had caused her to feel this fear, this dread.

Eventually, she lifted her head and scanned the wall. She focussed on the empty hook.

'That's it. The hook, it's empty!'

'It's always been empty, hasn't it? I've never noticed anything up there.'

'So, why is there a hook? There was something up there, I know there was!'

'Have you taken your meds today?' Carly asked as she helped her up onto the settee.

'Yes... no... I don't know.' Exasperated, Dolores began to sob pathetically.

Carly went into the kitchen and came back with the medication and a glass of water. She sat next to Dolores and read the instructions. She popped one capsule from its bubble. 'You need to take this now, and you must have them regularly throughout the day.'

Dolores nodded her consent and took the capsule. Taking a sip of water, she started to swallow but spluttered and nearly choked, wafting her arm frantically.

'Did it go down the wrong hole?' asked Carly, taking the glass from her.

'Look!' Dolores waved at the letter on the mantelpiece. Carly rose from the settee, seeming reluctant. She picked up the letter and handed it to Dolores.

She took it, her hand shaking.

'Can *you* open it?' she asked, handing it back.

'Are you sure? What if it's Joe declaring his

undying love?'

Dolores looked at her balefully.

Carly sat next to her again, and slipped her finger under the flap, breaking the seal. She removed a single card and turned it over. There was a seashell motif in one corner, embellished with gold glitter which caught the light.

Carly read the message:

We need to meet.

It was written in the same red, scrawled writing as the envelope.

'Aw, that's sweet. I told you it was Joe.'

'Let me see,' said Dolores, taking the card. That shell glinted at her, ominously. 'This isn't Joe.'

She'd seen this card before. Or something very like it. She tried desperately to summon the memory, but it was no use. 'It isn't Joe.'

Over the phone, Joe confirmed the note hadn't come from him. 'You must have a secret admirer. How are the repairs going?'

'I've nearly finished. I'll see you Tuesday, after I've sorted a few more things out.'

'No worries. I understand. So, how about going bowling on Tuesday?'

Dolores had him on speaker with Carly listening in. Carly gave manic thumbs ups, so Dolores agreed. She needed some fun to balance out the fear, so she agreed to go.

But if Joe didn't sent the card, who did?

The friends speculated until Dolores was exhausted and threw the card in the recycling bin. She tried to think of something else. Carly prompted her to take her second lot of meds with lunch. They ate in silence, all out of things to say. When they finished eating, Carly cleared the pots and suggested they get dressed and go for a walk in the park. It seemed like a reasonable idea, so Dolores slouched upstairs.

The walk took her mind off things, as she distracted herself with people-watching. A young mum, her eyes fixed on her phone, scrolled avidly while her little boy tugged at her leg to show her the worm he had found. Mum was oblivious. Dolores murmured her disapproval and Carly agreed how sad it was we were losing the joy from the little things in life. Their usual rants about the dangers of social media and the total disrespect of people who discarded their litter in such a beautiful oasis were aired and put to bed once more. Dolores was beginning to feel a little more relaxed when a sudden vision of that red scrawl danced before her eyes. And the seashell. It seemed too much of a coincidence for it not to be connected to her nightmares. The hairs on her neck prickled. Shaking it off, she saw the ice-cream van and suggested they get a Ninety-Nine. She tried to sound chirpy.

Rather than retrace their steps along the park path, they strolled down the high street and back through the estate, slurping at their cones as they went, enjoying the sweet stickiness of the chocolate flakes before they melted.

It was a beautiful day, warm for October. Spurred on by exotic pictures in the travel agent's window, the girls talked about taking a holiday soon, if Dolores was feeling up to it.

'That's if you don't end up going away with Joe,' Carly joked.

Dolores shrugged. 'I very much doubt he'll put up with me for much longer, so I wouldn't hold your breath.'

Carly looked at her sternly and elbowed her gently.

When they arrived back at the house, they dragged a couple of deck chairs out from the storage shed and set them up in the back yard.

'Is it too early for gin and tonic? Dolores asked.

'We shouldn't really, Dee, not with the meds and all.'

'Oh, yeah, I forgot about those.'

'It won't be for long, just until you're feeling better.'

Dolores didn't answer. She closed her eyes and lay still, wishing everything would go away.

They sat out for a couple of hours, dozing and filling the gaps with chit-chat. It was early evening, when the sun disappeared in a fuzzy haze, that they felt the chill and packed away. They retreated indoors, their eyes adjusting to the darkness.

'God, it feels depressing in here after such a lovely autumn day,' said Carly, looking through cupboards to see what they could throw together for tea.

Dolores didn't reply. Coming into the house had brought back the fear. A trickle of sweat ran down her spine.

'Dee? What do you fancy to eat? I could knock up some pasta and veg if you want?'

'Do you mind if I go and lie down for an hour? I'm not feeling that good.' Dolores rolled her shoulders to ease her tension.

'No, of course not, it's been a long day. Shall I bring you a cuppa?'

'I don't think I'll stay awake to drink it, to be honest. I'm whacked,' said Dolores, already making her way to the stairs.

It was almost two hours before Dolores went back down, her pyjama top clinging to her back with sweat. Carly fussed over her and ordered her to rest on the settee while she warmed up the tea she had made. Eating slowly and without relish, Dolores stared into space. Each tasteless mouthful made her want to retch, but she knew she had to keep up her strength. Her throat constricted, making her splutter with gasping sobs. She spat out the half-chewed food and handed the plate to Carly who took it from her and placed it on the carpet. Then she hugged Dolores tight, as if she was trying to squeeze the life and happiness back into her.

'It's good to cry, Dee,' she said when the shuddering and spluttering had stopped. 'You'll feel better for it. And when the meds kick in, you'll be dancing on tables again.'

'I know you're right, but just now I feel like a wet dishcloth,' Dolores said, feeling the misery in every cell.

Carly held her tighter still.

They sat huddled until Carly suggested some crap TV before bedtime. Reluctantly, Dolores agreed: it was preferable to going back to bed, back to nightmares. They watched a couple of reality shows, remarking on the self-obsession and vanity of those 'stranded' on *Love Island*. They laughed at the lack of talent on the talent show and, finally, when they could no longer stay awake, they trudged upstairs and undertook their ablutions quietly. Dolores sank into bed, listening to Carly struggling with the zip of the sleeping bag.

'Thanks for today, mate,' she said, pulling the quilt up and snuggling down.

'No problem, chick, you're worth it. Night.'

Dolores reached for the lamp and pressed the switch, fearing the wave of darkness. As her eyes adjusted, she identified each shape until she could dismiss them all as harmless.

Finally, she sank back into her pillow, exhausted. Something was tapping at her memory. Something dark and sinister. Something was reminding her that all was not well.

CHAPTER 7

HOOK, LINE AND SINKER

One Year Earlier.

Dolores watched as her mother applied the finishing touches to her make-up, her hand shaking as she swept the mascara wand over her lashes. Dolores felt a dread she couldn't justify.

'Going anywhere nice?' she asked, pretending not to be concerned.

'Just to Josie's for supper, nothing special,' Marian replied, not looking her in the eye. Her cheekbones had sunken slightly over the past few months and her beautiful eyes had lost their sparkle. As if looking at her for the first time, Dolores noticed how her once-tight pencil skirt hung slackly around her waist.

'Do you want me to walk to the bus-stop with you?'

'No!' Marian said, too sharply. 'I mean, it's

good of you to offer, but who would walk you back, Dolly?'

She zipped up her make-up bag and gathered her purse and key.

'True,' said Dolores, that nagging doubt gnawing at her insides. 'Have fun, then. What time will you be back?'

'Not sure, love, but it won't be late. Have a nice evening with Carly. Is she staying? There's some curry left if you want it.'

'Thanks, yeah, she'll probably stay, if that's ok?'

'Course it is! You know it is,' Mum said, taking her handbag and cramming her purse, lipstick and keys inside. She softly kissed the top of Dolores' head. 'I love you, Dolly. Be good.'

'Always. Love you, too. See you later.'

Dolores watched her leave, knowing she shouldn't be worried – it wasn't her job to worry – but she was worried, anyway.

Taking out her phone, she messaged Carly:

Mum's gone, come any time.

Switching on the TV, she settled back in the chair, suddenly feeling weary. Although Carly was usually a breath of fresh air, she could do without her tonight. Allowing her eyes to close, she drifted off.

There was a sound, a distant knocking, and it took Dolores some time to come to her senses. She opened her eyes and realised the knocking was at her front door. It must be Carly. But when she opened the door, there was no one there. She looked around, walked to the end of the small path, making a mental note to pull the weeds out soon. She looked left and right but saw only a couple of kids at one end of the street and a young couple at the other, linking arms on their way out.

Turning around, hoping she hadn't missed Carly, she noticed a small white card on the doorstep. Puzzled, she picked it up. It was embellished with a single shell in one corner. In red scrawl was written:

You will soon know how it feels

Thinking it must be a tag from someone's Valentine's flowers, she popped it in the paper bin, wondering why it wasn't grubbier as it was now July. She shook off a cold shiver and went back indoors.

Carly's text buzzed in as she entered the living room:

see you in 20 with wine and a smile

Glad she hadn't missed her, but baffled by the knocking, Dolores tried to dismiss the nagging doubt chipping away: *who could it have been?* Shaking her head, as if this could shake away her unease, she went to prepare for Carly's arrival. From the display cabinet in the corner, she took out two large wine glasses and carried them through to the kitchen. It was annoying how Mum never changed the tea-towel, always left it until it almost walked to the basket by itself. She rummaged through the bottom drawer and pulled out a freshly ironed towel. She rubbed the glasses until they sparkled, then placed them on a tray along with a small bowl of peanuts. Finally, she went upstairs to apply make-up. Although they weren't going out, Dolores liked to look decent; otherwise, Carly would fuss and tell her she looked ill.

The knock at the door made Dolores jump, but this time it was Carly, and she came bounding in full of optimism, as usual.

'Are you alright, chick?' She unscrewed the wine and poured them each a large glass.

'Why wouldn't I be?' said Dolores, taking the wine and clinking Carly's glass. 'Cheers!'

Dolores gulped the wine, glad of its velvety

warmth.

'Hey, steady,' said Carly. 'I thought you said you were fine. You look like you needed that drink.'

'It's probably just me, you know what I'm like, but...' said Dolores, rolling her eyes.

'But what? What is it? Yes, I do know what you're like. Little Miss Worry, that's you.'

'Before you arrived, I was asleep and there was a knock at the door. I thought it was you, but when I opened it, there was nobody there.'

'And?' asked Carly. 'It was probably kids playing 'knock a door run'.

'Yeah, you're probably right,' said Dolores, taking another swig of wine.

'Probably? You know I am.'

Surprised at how quickly they had managed to get through a bottle of red, Dolores went to get another and came back into the lounge, her brow knotted.

'What are you fretting about now?' asked Carly. 'Don't worry, we'll go easier with this one.'

She took the bottle and poured modest amounts this time.

They spent the next few hours watching TV, then a rom com which neither of them could stay awake for. Dolores looked at her watch, thinking it must be getting late, she was so tired.

She gasped. 'I can't believe it's half past twelve already.'

'Half twelve? I wonder where the lovely Marian is. She usually gets the last bus, doesn't she?' Carly stretched and yawned and pulled an empty crisp packet from under her thigh.

'She does, but I have a horrible feeling,' said Dolores, fresh anxiety nudging its way through.

She felt a pang as she passed her mother's room, catching sight of the empty double bed, the nightie laid on top. She cleaned her teeth and hugged Carly goodnight, before going into her own room and closing the door gently. It wasn't easy being in this position, living with a terminally ill mum, feeling responsible. When they had finally been reunited, Marian had insisted that Dolores moved into the little house she had bought when she'd left Harry: 'When I go, it will be all yours, love.'

Dolores swallowed.

Knowing she wouldn't fall to sleep easily, despite being dog-tired, she slipped out of bed, opened the bottom drawer of her dressing table and pulled out a large photo album. Lifting it over to the bed, she snuggled back under the quilt and flicked through the photos.

Her parents looked so happy in the snaps of them holding her, feeding her, playing, singing, being a family. A fat tear escaped as she looked at herself as a chubby-cheeked baby, a cute two-year-old.

The creak of the bedroom door, the following morning, roused Dolores from a fitful sleep. Opening one eye, she was glad to see Carly with a cup of tea. 'You are a star; do you know that?'

'I know, but you're worth it,' said Carly, gathering up the album. 'Reminiscing?'

'I know I shouldn't, but it's hard. I can't help wondering what it would have been like if she hadn't left me and Dad when she did.'

'Well, families come in all shapes and sizes,' said Carly, tucking her curls behind her ear.

'God, I'm sorry Carly, I can be so insensitive at times.'

'Don't worry. I do wonder sometimes what it would have been like to have a dad around, to have a proper family.'

'Enough of families. At least we've got our mums,' said Dolores. 'Speaking of Mum, is she up?'

'How can I put this?' said Carly, chewing her lip.

'What?' Dolores sat up.

'Her bed's not been slept in,' said Carly, trying to sound casual.

A heavy dread descended, and Dolores leapt out of bed. 'She'd never do that! She'd never stay out without letting me know!'

'Check your phone. We were a bit pissed last night; she might have messaged.'

Hands shaking, Dolores picked up her phone and tapped in her pin. No messages. She threw it onto the bed and paced the room. 'Something's not right, Carly.'

'You're worrying about something that hasn't happened, chick. You need to count to ten, take deep breaths, and let's think about this rationally. We could start by contacting Josie. She said she was going there. I know you don't think she did, but she could have. She might have fallen asleep on the sofa, could be snoring away as we speak.'

Retrieving her phone, Dolores scrolled down her contacts and found Josie's number. Quickly composing an opener, she tapped on the dial icon and waited as it rang through.

After an eternity, Josie's voice came through: 'Hello?'

'Hi Josie, it's Dolores. Did Mum come to yours last night? Is she still with you?'

'No, love. She said she was busy last night. Are you ok? You sound a bit shaky.'

'She went out last night, Josie, said she was going to your house for drinks, and she's not come back.'

'That's not like your Mum. She always comes home, doesn't she?' said Josie.

'That's why I'm bothered. It's just not like her. There's something wrong.'

'There's always a first time, pet. She may have decided to stay out on the last minute.'

'But why wouldn't she have messaged me? She always messages me!' The panic was rising now, replacing all rational thoughts, replacing them with thoughts Dolores couldn't say out loud.

'Have you got someone with you, love? Do you want me to come over?' said Josie, the concern unnerving Dolores further.

'Carly's here. It's ok. I'm sure you're right. There's bound to be a simple explanation. Mum's really rubbish at keeping her phone charged, so you're probably right. I'll be ringing you back at eleven, when she turns up looking for her egg butty.'

'Let me know when she does, please, Dolores. I'd appreciate it.'

'Sure,' said Dolores, still struggling to suppress dread, 'I will do. Thanks Josie, and sorry for bothering you.'

'No problem, love. You take care now and I'll speak soon. Bye.'

What should she do next? There had been something different about Mum in the last few weeks, she now realised. Cursing Marian for being so bloody private, she tried not to conjure up worse-case scenarios.

'Think, think!' she said, tapping the side of her head. 'Where could she be?'

She flopped back on the bed and jumped up almost immediately at the sound of someone knocking at the door. Grabbing Carly's arm, she pulled her out of the bedroom, and they staggered downstairs. Dolores made out the broad black outline of a policeman in the doorway, and fell into Carly's arms, shivering and weeping, at the foot of the stairs.

CHAPTER 8

DRIFTWOOD

Present Day.

The medication had started to do its work making a difference to her mood, to the point where Dolores felt ready to meet up with Joe again. The nagging dread was still there, despite her attempts to rationalise each strange incident; but Carly was a great friend, as ever, taking each worry and putting her common-sense stamp on it.

This morning, Dolores had woken to a beautiful autumn day, and, closing the door gently behind her, she stepped out into its warmth, vowing to enjoy it. Joe had been more than patient, and she wanted to have some fun, to forget what had happened. Walking to the bus stop with a smile which for once didn't feel false, she stepped up her pace and held her chin in the air, like someone unburdened.

Joe was sitting on a bench outside the bowling alley when she arrived. She thought he looked apprehensive, but when he saw her, he jumped up and beamed that smile.

'So, Dolores, how are you? It seems like ages since I saw you,' he said.

'Not too bad,' she said, not wanting to be too bright, too false.

'Cool,' said Joe. 'So, are you ready to be thrashed by the ten-pin demon?'

'What? Oh, the bowling!' she said. 'Yes, I suppose so, but be warned: I'll put up a good fight.'

'Cool, let's do it.'

The usual dilemma over who would pay was settled by going Dutch, and they laughed at their ridiculously oversized clown shoes as they flopped their way over to the lane.

'Joe, there's something I want to get out of the way before we start,' said Dolores, wondering how much to tell.

'Cool, fire away,' said Joe, taking a seat and holding the heavy bowling ball on his lap.

Sliding next to him, Dolores tried to formulate her words, not wanting to sound dramatic.

'The thing is, Joe, as you've probably gathered, I've had a few issues with anxiety.

You know, panic attacks and stuff.'

Looking earnest, Joe nodded.

'I don't want to go into detail, but it's been a tough year, and I've had some things to deal with, and, well, I want to be honest with you.'

'Sure,' said Joe. 'Look, I'll understand if you want some time on your own.'

'I think that's the last thing I want. Like I said, I don't want to go into detail, but I think it's only fair to let you know that I'm on medication for the anxiety. Not that it really concerns you, but just in case I'm acting a bit weird, you know, or if you're wondering why I don't want a drink.'

'Sure,' he said, lifting the bowling ball into the rack and sitting back down. 'I'll be straight with you, too. I really like you, I think you're great company, but I'm happy to take things slowly, have a bit of fun. I understand about anxiety, believe it or not, so don't worry about it. We can take it one date at a time.'

'That's settled then. Let's get on with the game.'

He wants another date!

She tapped her name into the console: 'Ladies first.' She lifted a bright orange ball from the rack, and sent it spinning down the aisle, almost going with it. She regained her balance just in time to see the ball career down the side gulley.

She shrugged: 'Beat that!'

She thumped Joe playfully, and dropped onto the seat to watch his shot. All feelings of dread dismissed, she watched Joe as he psyched himself up, eyeing the pins. He lunged forward and launched the ball down the centre of the aisle. Just as she thought he was heading for a strike, the ball veered violently to the right and clattered noisily down the gulley, out of sight.

'Classic,' she said, laughing.

'So, that was just a warm-up. No mercy from now on.'

After winning the game by a very small margin, Dolores suggested lunch at the café next door. She linked her arm through his and felt lighter than she had for weeks. There was still that niggle, the feeling of impending doom, but it wasn't overwhelming and didn't domineer her every thought.

Right now, life is good.

As they entered the shop, she took her reusable cup from her bag, noticing Joe's look of confusion. 'So I don't have to keep getting a throwaway one; saving the planet and all that.'

'Cool. I thought that was just a trend,' said Joe, shuffling on the spot.

'One of my things, as you know' said Dolores. 'I have a few more, but we'll talk about that when we sit down.'

'Cool. Sounds ominous. Should I be scared?'

'Maybe a little bit,' she said, smiling.

'You'd better go and get a seat in a quiet corner if I'm going to be told.' Joe took her cup. 'What would you like?'

'I'll have a coconut cappuccino, please,' she said, and went in search of a seat.

There were things that needed to be said if she was to carry on seeing Joe, and she tested ways of saying them, in her head, while she waited for him to sit down. A young couple, maybe in their late teens, sat down at the table next to her, plonked down their drinks and, without exchanging a word, got out their phones and swiped merrily away.

At least they'll be quiet.

She shuffled sideways, putting as much space between her and the twosome as she could.

Joe arrived with a tray laden with goodies.

'Thought we might need some fuel,' he said as he slipped in next to her. 'And, just for you, I've bought one of these cups.' He grinned broadly.

Touched by his gesture, she patted his thigh in thanks. 'Not wanting to put the dampers on your lovely feast, I might as well start by explaining some of the delights of being vegan. Most goodies here contain animal products, so they're a no-no for me. Fortunately, there's one that doesn't, and it's this one here. I hope you don't mind if I take it?'

She picked up the flapjack and took a bite.

'So, it's the vegan thing you want to talk about? I thought you might be pregnant, for a minute,' said Joe, laughing at his own humour.

Dolores spluttered out crumbs and laughed too. 'That would be a modern-day miracle. Yes, it's the vegan thing mainly.'

'Please tell all,' said Joe, sheepishly taking a bite of his sausage roll.

'Horse racing,' she said. 'I can't condone it, because it uses animals for our own gains.'

'Oh, I get it,' said Joe. 'I never thought, sorry.'

'It's ok,' she said. 'I need you to know in case you're planning any more race-day extravaganzas.'

'Do you really not mind me eating meat and stuff when I'm with you?'

'Like I said, it's your choice. Obviously, it would be ideal if you were vegan too, but, no, I don't mind.'

'I'll try not to be so blatant and, who knows, I might even try the chickpeas and spinach next time we're out.'

'That would be sweet,' said Dolores. 'Plastic.'

'Plastic what?' asked Joe.

'Plastic is the next topic. I might as well get it all off my chest in one go. I don't know if you've watched the documentaries about how plastic affects marine life?'

'So, I vaguely remember something on the telly about it getting into the stomachs of fish?'

'Yep, that's the one. It's really awful the way animals suffer because of it, so, in case you think I'm weird for avoiding plastic at all costs, I need you to know that I feel really strongly about it, to the point where it brings me out in a cold sweat to see people drinking from single-use plastic bottles.'

'Not a problem. In fact, that's something I could well get into myself. To be honest, I've not given it much thought. I'm as guilty as the next person of mindless consumerism. I'm not materialistic, as you may have guessed from my attire and lack of car, but I do kind of buy things without thinking, you know? So, I'd be more than happy to support you with that one. It would be good to challenge myself to find alternatives.'

'Great,' said Dolores. This was going better than planned. 'That's veganism and plastic covered, so there's just one more thing, for now. Panic.'

'Panic?' said Joe. 'Do I need to?'

'As in my panic attacks. The thing is, they really embarrass and frustrate me, so I need to know if you're ok with all of this or if you want to do a short, sharp exit. I'd totally understand if you think it's too much like hard work. I'd like you to be honest.'

'I'm fine with it all, as long as you let me help you next time you feel a panic coming on. I really worried about you getting home safely last time. I'm not good at expressing myself, but it freaked me out when I didn't hear from you. I was imagining all sorts.'

'I know. I should have at least texted when I got home, but I felt so bad, I put myself to bed thinking I'd have an hour, then slept all night. I'm sorry.' She smiled, 'I just, well, panicked.'

'So, let's get this right. You don't eat any animal products whatsoever, you won't support activities involving animals, and you have panic attacks for which you take meds. Is that about the sum of it?'

'Yes, basically,' said Dolores. 'And the plastic.'

'Of course, the evil plastic. Cool. If that's all, I think we'll be good for another date.'

'If you don't think I'm too weird, yes, we're good for another date,' she said.

They finished their drinks, chatting about things they'd done since they last met. Relieved to share her thoughts with Joe, Dolores was much more relaxed than she had been on their previous dates. He seemed to take it all in good spirits and she was happy he was willing to support her beliefs, albeit in small ways. It was good to have someone to spend time with, someone who didn't know her history, someone other than Carly. But it would be a while before she could share the other stuff with him.

'So, now we've put the world to rights, shall we make tracks?' asked Joe.

'Yeah, to be honest I'm pretty knackered after all that.'

They stood up. As Dolores edged her way out of the seat, she was knocked off balance by someone passing.

'Sorry,' they muttered from behind their hood.

Turning to look back, a shot of fear bolted through her and she froze: *that face!*

CHAPTER 9

WASHED UP

One year earlier.

'Dolores Walsh?' asked the female officer.

Carly's knees buckled now. 'No,' she stammered. 'But she's here. You'd better come in.'

Carrying their hats in front of them, the two officers, one male, one female, stepped in. Carly indicated the lounge, then came back to Dolores where she sat on the stairs, frozen and reluctant to move, knowing that life would never be the same once she left this perch.

Taking her under the arm, Carly helped her up, nodding solemnly and leading her through the door of the lounge. Sunlight cast a shaft of light down the centre of the room and the birds were chirping merrily. For once, Dolores wanted them silenced. She collapsed on the settee in the bay with her back to the light, holding her breath, dreading what would fill the void. Leaving her hat on the chair, the young woman officer came and sat next to her.

'Are you Dolores Walsh?'

'Yes,'

'Is Marian Benson your mum, Dolores?'

'Yes, she is. Why are you asking?'

'I'm afraid we have some bad news.' She waited a moment. 'There's no easy way of saying this, love, but this morning a body was found on the beach at Blackpool. We believe it to be your mum.'

Dolores let out a primal scream and covered her ears.

I'm not listening to this ridiculous story.

Carly's arm slipped around her back and the officer took her hand.

'Can you make some tea, love?' she asked Carly. 'Plenty of sugar.'

Carly left the room, sobbing.

The male officer, not much older than the girls, awkwardly took out his notebook and pen, but put them down when the female officer shook her head.

'Dolores, I'm WPC Jane Marshall, Family Liaison Officer, and this is PC Grant Evans. We'll be here to support you for however long you need us, ok, sweetheart?'

Dolores shook with fresh grief. *Sweetheart. Mum calls me sweetheart.*

'Where is she? Where's my mum? I need my mum!' She stood up and shouted, 'Where is she?' Then she sank back down.

'I'm so sorry. We can only tell you as much as we know so far. We were alerted early this morning, around 8.00 am, by a dog walker who came across a body on a remote part of Blackpool Beach.'

Dolores shook her head, 'No, no, that can't be possible. She didn't go there! Why would she go there?'

'That's something we need to work out, Dolores. We'll need to ask you a few questions about her last movements. We don't have to do it now, if you're not up to it, but the sooner we can put a picture together, the more chance we have of working out what happened.'

'How do you know it's her?'

'She'd left her bag on the prom, love, near to where she was found. Someone handed it in and, well, there was a note,' said Jane.

'A note?'

'Yes, love, written by Marian. It seems she'd had enough of struggling and wanted to go.'

'That doesn't make sense! She wanted to make the most of the life she had left.'

'We understand it's a lot to take in, but believe me, we're going to do our best to find out more details. It looks as if she drowned, but we're not sure. There's a full investigation under way. We'll be trying to piece together the events of last night, but it doesn't look like there was a struggle. Suicide does seem most likely at this point.'

There was a buzzing in Dolores' head and a splitting pain. Bright lights danced in her peripheral vision, and she felt the room closing in on her.

'It might help to take some deep breaths,' said Jane, handing her a tissue.

A band tightening around her chest, Dolores felt like she couldn't breathe at all. Blinking her eyes to clear the blur, she looked the officer in the eye, 'She would never do that. She wanted to live what little of life she had left, she was terminally ill! Besides, we'd only just got to know each other after a long time apart. She was so grateful, you know, to have me in her life again. She would never let that go.'

'We can only tell you what we know so far, but, from initial findings, it does look as if she wanted to take her own life.'

Dolores had known there was something wrong with Mum, that she'd changed over the last few weeks, but she'd put it down to her diagnosis.

Why didn't I talk to her about it?

Carly returned with a tray of tea and biscuits, her face red and puffy. She put it down on the coffee table and sat next to Dolores. But Dolores jumped up again and started to pace the room. Nothing made sense.

Mum would never leave me, no matter how unhappy she was. She just wouldn't, not when we've only been reunited a couple of years. Not when she knows our time is so short.

'She didn't kill herself,' said Dolores, and she slumped to the floor, banging her head on the coffee table as she went down.

Aware of muffled voices, Dolores tried to open her eyes.

'Don't get up, Dolores, you need to rest now.'

Fighting panic, she opened her eyes, slowly, letting in the light and the world bit by bit.

'Where am I?' she asked, touching her head and feeling a thick dressing.

'I'm Nurse Bennett and you're in hospital, love. You had a nasty fall and banged your head. How are you feeling? Do you have any pain?'

'My head feels like it's going to explode, and my eyes hurt, too.'

'I'm not surprised,' said the nurse. 'You

have quite a bump there. Fortunately, there's nothing broken. Can you tell me what you remember, Dolores? If it's too much, don't worry, you can rest a bit longer and we'll talk later.'

'What I remember?' asked Dolores, closing her eyes again.

The images and words came fast and furious: Carly, the police and –

'No!' Dolores shouted, fear taking hold.

Screwing her eyes tight shut, she pulled the covers up to her neck and lay still. The jumble of images didn't make sense. Had she dreamt it all? She blinked away tears. Wanting to know, but dreading the truth, she looked the nurse in the eye and asked, 'Where's my mum?'

'Can you tell me what you remember?' repeated the nurse.

'I don't know,' said Dolores. 'It's mixed up. There was a note. Mum didn't come home, the police...' Helpless, exhausted, she wanted to sleep so everything would fade away.

'I think you should rest now. I'll let the doctor know you've come round. Try to rest, pet.'

Pulling the covers back up to her chin, Dolores stared at the ceiling. Exhausted, but too confused to sleep, she tried to make sense of what had happened, to put it in some sort of order. But the pain made it difficult to think and the ever-present dread warned her not to. She drifted off to sleep.

She sat up in bed, fear making her heart hammer. There was someone in the chair.

'You have to help me!' said Dolores.

'Dee! You scared me! Thank God you're ok,' said Carly, coming to comfort her.

'Carly, is that you?' she said, taking her hand. 'What's going on, Carly? I keep remembering things, but nothing makes sense. I don't know what's a dream and what isn't. I was drowning, just now, in the sea and someone was calling me.'

'Dolores, I'm here now, it's ok, I'm here.'

Although relieved to see her best friend, Dolores still had that hard knot of dread. 'Is it true that Mum's gone?'

'Yes, it's true.'

'I don't understand. She wouldn't leave me; you know she wouldn't!'

'I'm as shocked as you are,' said Carly, fishing for tissues and handing one to Dolores.

'Something's not right, Carly. We both know it. She wanted more than anything to see me happy. She would never, ever leave me like this. She knows it would break me.' She blew noisily into the tissue. 'She's always telling us to make the most of this wonderful chance at life we've been given, isn't she? Despite all her sadness, she's an optimist, she believes in life. She believes it's a gift. She knew the time we had together would be limited. She wouldn't leave me, Carly, she just wouldn't!'

'I absolutely agree with you, but the police will sort it out. We need to wait until all the evidence is gathered and see what they come up with, chick.'

'None of it will bring her back, though, will it?' Dolores fell back into the pillow. 'None of this shit will bring her back. No one can tell me everything is going to be alright, because it isn't true, and you know it!'

Carly closed in for a hug, but Dolores pushed her away. 'Don't you dare try to tell me that time will heal, or some other such crap. Because it won't.'

Carly had never felt so helpless. She'd always been able to close the abyss which, from time to time, threatened to suck her friend into its depths. But this time she couldn't save her. What could she say? That she'd feel better tomorrow, the next day, next week? She wouldn't insult her. Instead, she went in again for a hug, and this time Dolores fell whimpering into her embrace.

CHAPTER 10

RAFT

Present Day.

That empty hook taunted her. Glinting in the light, it caught her eye as she tried to relax.

Why can't I take my eyes off it?

Something had hung there but, with the meds and everything else, she couldn't think what. She resolved to find something cheerful to put in its place, so that she didn't have to keep looking at the bareness of it.

Her thoughts wandered to her last date with Joe. Bowling had been fun, especially as she'd won. Then having the chat had felt like a load lifted. It had been a relief to tell him about her beliefs and it was reassuring to know they were on the same page, at least as far as their friendship went, both happy to take things slowly. Life had been finally slotting into some semblance of normal, even if it was with the help of meds.

The medication was not sitting well with Dolores, but it was a necessary evil, and she had to admit it was doing its work. That feeling of helplessness, of being overwhelmed, was slowly fading and she was mostly keeping the paranoia at bay, though it occasionally crept up on her, especially when she was particularly tired or emotional. But her sleep pattern had improved, so she was hoping that in time these moments of panic would leave her completely.

And she was hoping to find some work soon, maybe starting with a volunteer role, perhaps relating to the environment. Not only would it help her to feel as if she was making a difference, but it would also get her out of the house and give her purpose. She had too much time to brood and it led her mind down dark paths. Promising herself to start the job search tomorrow, she curled up on the settee.

Her eyes immediately strayed to the hook: *that bloody thing*.

She heaved herself off the settee, walked the few steps to the mantelpiece, and touched the hook's metal curve, rubbing it as if it were Aladdin's lamp.

It wasn't a genie that appeared, but a stark realisation:

Of course! The portrait of me and Mum in that

awful cheap frame.

She had hung it there when she first moved in. It was a memento from an impromptu visit to Blackpool when she was about three. In it, her hair was blowing about, and the wind was clearly taking her breath. Mum was holding on to her in front of the railings on the prom. That picture had always hung in her bedroom, and it was the only thing about Mum that Dad would tolerate in the house. He used to tell her they had all gone for fish and chips after he took the photo, and they'd sipped hot tea, glad of the steamy warmth in the café. It was like a bedtime story, and the picture had epitomised a happy time and place.

Dolores had been meaning to take it down to put it in a better frame but was sure she hadn't. Where had it gone? Had she moved it during one of her crazy days? She thumped the side of her head, trying to prompt an answer. Nothing.

There must a perfectly logical explanation, like there has been for all my other nutty experiences recently.

She paced the room to stop the anxiety gnawing. She needed to escape, get some air. Grabbing her coat, she slammed the door and marched onto the street, as if with purpose but in fact not sure where she would go.

When she got to the end of the road, she

took the left turn, then the dirt path down to the canal, a route she'd normally avoid. Feeling brave, she made her way along the towpath, fixing her gaze on the murky water, forcing herself to carry on.

Unbidden, a memory of something Mum had said not long before she died came to her:

'Don't let jealousy take control, Dolly.'

She'd thought nothing much of it at the time, simply wondered if Mum had been plagued by the green-eyed monster while she was with her dad or maybe when dating. Now, somehow, it seemed relevant.

Am I being paranoid?

Shaking her head, she picked up a discarded plastic bag and began to collect bits of rubbish from the towpath: crisp bags, coffee cup lids, straws, sweet wrappers, bottle tops. She fought hard to quash negative thoughts about the kind of people who dropped litter. It wasn't helpful to keep dipping into depressive rants. Instead, she thought how good it was that people who care still existed. Her bag was soon full of detritus and she pressed it into a nearby bin, not sure if she felt better or not. Most of the times when she litter-picked, she would feel a little lift, but today she felt only frustration.

Beyond this point, the landscape was mainly industrial; dark mills with broken windows from which, Dolores imagined, phantoms of old weavers looked out at this strange new world. Just ahead was the next grassy slope up to the road and she climbed unenthusiastically, not wanting to go back to the noise and buzz of traffic, but not wanting to be reminded of a past more simple, more appealing to her. A truck whizzed past, leaving her breathless in its slipstream.

One day I'll move somewhere green and quiet.

It wasn't a particularly bad area but being close to a city meant it was busy, noisy and grimy. Her wish list was growing daily, and clean air to breathe was near the top, along with finding a job. Maybe she could combine the two. Looking down the high street, she tried to imagine what it would be like to leave this place, these memories, and start again somewhere else.

Times were changing for worse. This she knew, but it didn't mean she had to accept it. *'You can't change the world, Dolly,'* Mum used to say, but Dolores thought she could, if only in small ways. Her teacher had said she was wise beyond her years, which she had taken as a compliment; but sometimes it would be simpler if she didn't think so deeply. She'd seen the blank looks on people's faces when she expressed her views.

I wish I could touch base with Mum and unload

on her, get her perspective, let her help me get things straight.

Feeling exhausted, she trudged back home and put the kettle on. She wondered how she had become so passionate about the ills of the world. When did she lose the joy?

It had started with her own time of change, her teen years when, feeling different from her friends, she had become an avid and insatiable reader, using books to escape the feeling of alienation. She had wanted so much to fit in, but she was bored with her peers' obsessions about self. Even when she had the money, she wasn't that bothered about clothes or make-up. She would often join her father in the front room to watch documentaries, desperate to be part of a world she could feel at ease in. They would learn about threatened species, disappearing habitats, how humans were changing the world.

She started to read up on the environment and became increasingly interested, and saddened, by what she read. It was then she vowed to make a difference, however small. Her love of animals eventually led her to question why and how she could eat them. Despite protests from her step-mum Patricia she went vegetarian, eventually committing to becoming vegan.

As she strolled along a very different high

street from the one of her childhood, she thought about her early life, her dad and how he had shaped her. When he died a few years ago, her assumptions of a future which included him were cruelly shattered. The effect on her well-being was huge. She became obsessive about saving the world, withdrawing to her room for hours at a time, refusing to eat. The panic attacks followed, as did rebellion. Feeling unloved and wanting to escape from herself, she would wander the streets until all hours, worrying Patricia half to death.

Before long, she became involved with a group of similar rebels and they would drink cheap cider in dark places, blotting out the world with every bottle. Cider was replaced by vodka, paid for with money she stole from Patricia's purse, reasoning that if her mum hadn't left her when she was little, and her dad hadn't died, they shouldn't begrudge her a few quid.

'*What are you doing to yourself?*' her stepmum would ask.

Killing myself, so I don't have to look at you anymore, she would think.

'*Escaping,*' she would say.

Patricia would cry, try to hold her, to bring her back, but Dolores was not for being helped. She would retreat to her room, into the dark place.

It would have been a slippery slope downwards if she hadn't met Carly. Feeling particularly rough one afternoon, Dolores had wandered into the local *Greasy Joe's*, as people affectionately called it. Carly had served her coffee with a smile and asked her what she was up to.

'Trying to feel normal?' Dolores said.

Carly had joined her at her table when the queue had all been served. She'd offered a listening ear if ever she needed one.

'Thanks for the offer, but I have lots of friends,' Dolores said.

A couple of weeks later, one of these friends had flashed some drugs during a particularly heavy session and Dolores had been spooked. Next time she was on the high street, she popped into the café and asked Carly if the ear was still available. They had been friends since. Carly had helped her to ditch the drink, get back on track with studies, and see that a better life *was* an option.

CHAPTER 11

THE DEEP DARK

The kettle clicked and Dolores poured steaming water onto the herbal tea bag. As she stabbed at it with the spoon and the water turned green, she asked herself when she had become so bloody boring.

Roughly pushing the cup to the back of the worktop, she shrieked as boiling tea splashed over, scalding her hand. Cursing and shaking, she ran it under the cold tap. She was useless. Wanting to feel that warm glow only a shot of rum could provide, she crouched and grasped the bottle tucked away at the back of the cupboard. She poured herself a generous measure, took a large slug and smiled.

Boring no more.

She grabbed a packet of chocolate rice cakes and her drink, and carried them through to the lounge. A voice in the back of her head told her not to be stupid, but she ignored it, choosing instead an afternoon of selfish indulgence. She would watch absolute garbage on the box and get rat-arsed.

Boring I may be, but I'm not dead yet.

The rest of the drink went down in two glugs. She glowed with it, wanted more.

Better take the meds as well, keep Carly off my back.

She went back to the kitchen, found the packet, and swallowed the pill with a mouthful of neat rum. It stung her gullet as it slid down, but the warm glow was worth it. Pouring another large measure, she added coke, smiling as she did.

Diet Coke. You're such a prick. Next time, live a little, get the full fat.

She carried her drink into the lounge, slouched down in the chair and flicked through the channels. From nowhere, tears sprang, and tightness gripped her chest. Sadness came, stealing the warmth, wiping away her smile. Her chin sank into her chest and she sobbed heartily, slugging the drink between shuddering sighs. The empty hook taunted, the mysterious shell motif card stabbed at her memory, and the panic came in one mighty wave, stealing her breath, threatening to pull her under.

Needing more drink, she staggered to the

kitchen. This time she brought the bottle back with her to save messing about. She poured half a tumbler and drank it neat in three long swigs. Another drink poured, she scrolled through the film channel and selected *Home Alone*, a childhood favourite.

There's no place like home.

A fat tear escaped. The picture on the TV blurred and her head spun. Taking another swig of rum, she closed her eyes, but this made her feel worse. She sat up. Everything swayed, and she wondered when the happy feeling would come.

CHAPTER 12

SEA LEGS

A dark maelstrom swirls as the ship lurches and sways. Rocks press down on her chest and bile rises from the gurgling depths. She spews vile liquid as she tries to stand. Voices play on the edge of her consciousness, cutting through the fog, and salty grit scratches as she tries to open her eyes. Slimy seaweed tangles around her feet and she falls endlessly. Swirling down, twisting and turning, faces flashing past. Her father's, contorted in agony; her mother's, floating away with a helpless haunting look. Dark places, darker thoughts, she twists against invisible straps which hold her in limbo.

What kind of a nightmare is this?

Brightness, shining relentlessly, brought her to her senses. A shrouded creature, scaly and ugly, stood over her. She blinked twice, the grit scratching her eyes, as she struggled to sit up.

The creature did not speak, only stared vacantly. Dolores retched, spewing yet more of the vile liquid until there was nothing more and she lay spent but terrified. A derisory snort came from the hooded thing. She reeled in pain as a heavy boot pressed down on her ribs. Gasping for breath, she tried to move, but it was no use: the boot pinned her to the ground.

'What do you want?' she spluttered.

'Wouldn't you like to know?'

Dolores was taken aback by the female voice. She looked closer and realised the creature's face was a mask.

'I can't breathe. Please, I need to get up.'

'You're not going anywhere.'

The masked face descended, so close Dolores could feel its breath on her cheek. It leaned in closer and whispered, 'I do believe you took something that was mine.'

Dolores desperately tried to reconcile her thoughts. Nothing made sense. She had never stolen, apart from Patricia's money in the dark days.

'I don't know what you mean,' she gasped.

'Oh, you soon will.'

And with one blow Dolores was out cold.

The putrid smell acted on her senses like salts,

and she opened her eyes, her heart beating wildly. It took more than a moment to realise where she was: not in a boat, but here in her own living room, marooned on an island of detritus. The stench was horrendous. Stale alcohol and bodily fluids. Dried vomit caked her nose and mouth, streaked down her front and pooled on the floor.

Then she remembered.

She flapped her arms, trying like mad to beat off the wild beast crouching in her mind's eye, but, however hard she tried to make it disappear, the beast was imprinted.

'You're not going anywhere.'

Dolores tried to move, but that boot held her down still.

Are my eyes playing tricks?

She could feel the boot, but the monster had gone. Gingerly, she lifted her top, and gasped. Her ribs were a mass of red and purple. Tender wasn't the word. Her head throbbed and her legs seemed at odds with her body. She wished she could die here and now, end this torture.

The buzz of the phone made her jump. She tried to move, but the pain was more than she had ever felt. She slumped back, clutching her ribs. The phone continued to buzz. Slowly, she reached for it, rolling onto her front so that her fingers could touch it. She clawed at it until it moved closer. It was covered in her vomit, which simultaneously made her self-pitying and ashamed. The buzzing stopped. As she turned the screen to face her, it lit up with Carly's name and number.

'He –, hello.'

'Dee, thank God! Are you ok?'

'No... I don't know. I don't know what's going on.'

'Dee, it's me, Carly. Are you at home?'

'Home? Yes, I think so, yes.'

'I'm coming over. Don't move!'

Carly reeled as the stench of booze and vomit hit her and made her retch.

'Shit the bed, Dee! What on God's earth has happened here?'

'Carly, listen, you've got to listen! She was here!'

'Who was? What do you mean?'

'Her! She had a mask on. She stamped on me, look!'

Dolores lifted her top. Carly shrank back, clearly shocked by the bruising.

'Jesus Christ, Dee. How did you do that?'

'I just said. It was this masked woman, she was here.'

'Looks to me more like you've bounced off every piece of furniture you own, after drinking every bottle you own.'

Dolores sagged, sobbing and wretched. 'How can I make you believe someone is stalking me?'

'How can I convince *you* that taking your meds properly, and not drinking yourself into oblivion, is the only way you're going to stop these nightmares?'

'It wasn't a nightmare, Carly, it was real. She was shrouded in a hood and she had on this ugly green mask and she stamped on me!'

Carly held up the tumbler. 'And how many of these had you drunk before she stood on you?'

Dolores squinted, trying to remember.

'Let's go and see, shall we?' Carly strode into the kitchen and came back carrying an empty bottle of dark rum.

'Yo-ho-ho, with a barrel of rum. Rule One, Dee: take your meds every day with a glass of water. Rule Two: do not consume alcohol. Christ sakes, no wonder you've had nightmares. Wouldn't surprise me if your nightmares are actually waking hallucinations from drinking so much.'

Dolores thumped the sides of her head. 'Please, Carly. I'm not lying. Someone was here. Someone wants to hurt me.'

'That someone is you, Dee. You're hurting yourself. And, while you're at it, you're hurting just about everyone around you.'

'Please believe me, Carly, *please.*' As she spoke, she spat out stale vomit and saliva.

Carly reeled back, covering her mouth. 'Seriously, you need to get cleaned up. You sort yourself out, and I'll try to salvage the wreck that is your living room.'

Defeated and confused, Dolores limped up to the bathroom. The sight of herself in the mirror made her vomit some more. She listened to Carly sorting out the mess downstairs and resolved never to let this happen again. Soap and warm water removed the outward mess, but her insides churned as she tried to shake off those images.

Downstairs, she found Carly in the kitchen. She shuffled over, wrapped her arms around her friend's waist from behind and rested her head between strong shoulder blades. Carly turned to her. She wore a softer look now.

'I'm really, really worried about you, Dee. I've never seen you hit such a low, even during the worse times. I don't know what I can do to help you.'

'I don't know what to do to help myself. Just as I think I'm getting back on track, something else happens. I can't shake off this stupid sea theme, either. These weird nightmares, they won't go away, and I think they're literally driving me mad.'

'I understand that, but drinking isn't the answer. Rich coming from me, right? Yes, I love a few cocktails, but you've taken it to the next level, and it scares me.'

'I know. It was a one-off, it won't happen again. In fact, you can watch me pour all the drink I possess down the sink. Come on.'

'Well, I wouldn't go *that* far. Someone has toiled hard to make that lot, and you know how we hate waste. I'll keep it at mine; we can ration it.'

Carly smiled warmly and continued with the clean-up. Dolores helped, trying to avoid bending down. When the kitchen was back to something resembling normal, the girls whizzed up a cocktail of juices to replenish lost vitamins.

They sat in opposite chairs, sipping the pulpy drink, Dolores trying not to retch. She put her glass down and hung her head, rubbing the back of her neck and her temples.

'Look, mate, you know you're the best thing that ever happened to me, right?' said Carly.

'I honestly don't know where I'd be without you, Carly.'

'I think I do.'

Dolores hung her head lower.

'Look, I'm not trying to make you feel bad,' said Carly. 'But I can't watch you destroy yourself.'

'I so wanted to break out of the sensible mould for a day.'

'I get that, Dee, but things as they are with you, I think even one drink now is going to send you down that spiral again.'

'I was ok, honestly I was, until that thing turned up and started pressing its boot into me.'

Carly sighed. 'Where is it now? Why would it disappear if it intended to hurt you?'

'I think it's playing with my head. I think it wants me to think I'm going mad. I think it'll come back.'

Dolores could see Carly was struggling to believe what she was saying, but then she remembered something the woman behind the mask had said.

'Oh my God, she said I've taken something belonging to her! That's it, Carly, that's why it, *she*, keeps coming. I've got something she wants.'

'What could you possibly have that someone else wants? No offence mate, but you haven't got a pot to piss in.'

CHAPTER 13

SEA SICK

It was the anniversary of her mother's death. Dolores was fighting the urge to reach for the bottle. Flicking through the album of her life, the time when everything was simple, made her yearn for a family: her family, not a borrowed one.

That's not very kind to Carly and Di.

Closing the book firmly, she looked around the living room. *'You haven't got a pot to piss in,'* Carly had said.

What are you thinking, Mum? If you can see me, what do you think of your daughter wasting her life away?

She opened her laptop. The dead screen seemed to mock her. Grey and full of nothing; or could it be a blank page, ready for a fresh start? She pressed the power button and waited for the machine to buzz into life.

She searched for 'jobs near me' and browsed

the options, none of which appealed. None of them broke the minimum wage barrier. Even the salaried ones, when you broke them down to an hourly rate, were not much different.

She downloaded her CV and wondered how she could explain her lack of employment for the last year. No job, no travelling or volunteering, just a gaping void.

Snap out of it, Dolores.

Typing 'left due to unforeseen personal tragedy' as the reason for leaving her last post, she saved the document and went back to the search.

It was easy to apply online; she simply uploaded her CV and pressed the button. It felt good and lifted her somehow into thinking she belonged again. Realistically, she couldn't see herself having the confidence for bar work, or the strength to resist the wares, but there wasn't much else, and it would get her out of the house.

Carly had been a fantastic friend, more than she deserved at times, but she needed to stand on her own now, face the world. It was a scary thought, but she knew it made sense. It had been a year of sulking around and emptiness.

I've applied for jobs

she messaged Carly, and to Joe:

Do you fancy meeting up this week?

Carly's response was immediate:

Well done you! Time to get back in the world and find yourself again. Love ya xx

Joe's response came in as she was reading Carly's:

Yeah, Thursday good for me. What do you want to do?

She responded to Joe:

Trying to avoid the demon drink, how about a film?

And to Carly:

I hope I like the me I find; hope she can behave. Love ya too, more than you know xx

The rattle of the letterbox made her jump.

A figure passed quickly by the front window, head down, hood up. She froze. Then the sun beamed into the lounge and she sprang up, telling herself not to be so bloody dramatic. An envelope had been pushed through. She gasped at the red scrawl as she pulled the card from the envelope. A beautiful scene of a sunset over water, she turned it over and read the scrawl. Two words:

Sun Down

What's that supposed to mean? Who is doing this to me? Carly can't argue with this.

Shaking, she slipped the card into her back pocket and reached for her coat. If someone was stalking her, she wasn't going to be a sitting duck. She slammed the door and double-checked it was locked. She stumbled down the street, trying to think clearly, and decided there was only one thing to do: go to the police.

Fortunately, there was a local station not a mile from her house and she picked up pace, heading in that direction, adrenaline making her feel strange, like she wasn't quite there. When she got to the station, she swung through the revolving doors a little too quickly and almost fell onto the front desk.

'How can I help you?' the officer asked with a bemused smirk.

Dolores stood up straight, took the card from her pocket and plonked it on the desk.

Raising his eyebrows, the young man on duty turned it over, 'And?'

'Someone is stalking me,' Dolores said.

'Stalking you? With pretty cards?'

'No. Yes. Not just cards, they've been in my house!'

'They? Do you know who *they* are?'

'It's one person – thing, whatever it is – but last time it came, it hurt me. It had these big boots on, and it stamped on me.'

'Was it a person, or a thing? I'm not sure I'm following you.'

'Sorry. I have these nightmares about the sea, so when I came round and saw its face, it was horrible, all green and, well, horrible, and it was hidden in a hood as well.'

'Are you sure this *thing* wasn't just part of your nightmare? I'm not being funny, but have you heard at all about the pressures on the police to attend to serious crimes?'

'*This* is serious! Obviously, it wasn't a thing – I was getting confused for a minute – it was a woman. It, *she* had a woman's voice. Why doesn't anyone believe me?'

'I'm not saying I don't believe you, but we have to have something more to go on than a strange creature who may or may not have been part of a nightmare, who may or may not have been a woman, and a pretty card with two words which are, frankly, not incriminating, are they? You say no one believes you? Who doesn't believe you?'

'My friend. She thinks it may be my meds playing tricks with me, but she's wrong, I know she is. Her mum as well, she thinks I've lost it, but I haven't, I know what I saw.'

'Look, miss, all I can do at this stage is log your visit. My boss will laugh me all the way out of a job if I spend any more time on this. All I can suggest is you take the usual precautions to keep yourself safe and, if this stalking continues, document it. When you have something we can work with, come back to us. I'm sorry I can't help you any further, but we're stretched to the limit here with knife crime, murders and the like. I hope you understand.'

Dolores gaped at him, then turned away, defeated.

'You forgot this.' He held up the card.

She took it, slipped it back in her pocket. 'Thanks.' *For nothing.*

She cried tears of sheer frustration as she

stomped along the high street, her head aching with pain and confusion. When she reached home, she flopped on the couch and closed her eyes while she tried to gain some composure. She must have drifted off, because when she awoke, there was a small package on the coffee table.

That wasn't there before.

Someone had been in her house, could still be here. She called Carly, let it ring twice, then hung up, an agreement they had in case Dolores was in danger and couldn't talk. She had also handed over a spare key.

Leaning forward to take a closer look, she noticed a fishy stench. Tentatively, she picked up the package. She saw the wet patches on the wrapping just as the paper gave way, spilling putrid fish guts into her lap. She leapt up and, as she did, a hand reached from behind and clasped her mouth.

Dolores desperately bit at the fingers, but her attacker swiftly gagged her and roughly dragged her off the settee, flipping her over so that she faced down. She tried to resist, but her hands were swiftly tied behind her with rough rope which cut into her wrists as she struggled. She was kicked in the back as the assailant spilled vile words of hatred onto her.

Then the only sound was her own breath

as it came in ragged bursts. The attacker was silent. Dolores couldn't speak or scream, she could only wait, terrified that at any moment she might be stabbed or shot or pummelled to death.

Dolores awoke to excruciating pain and a loud buzzing which, she soon realised, was in her head. There was no other sound. She tried to prise herself up, but her hand collapsed under the strain, and no wonder, it was black and swollen, her thumb distorted. Her other hand was not much better. Every part of her ached and when she tried to move the pain was unbearable. She couldn't remember how she'd got there, face-down behind the settee. Kneeling up slowly, the stench of vomit made her wretch.

What the...?

This time she knew it wasn't down to drink or madness. Scared the person who hurt her was still there, she turned around slowly. But she was alone. The only evidence that remained of the intruder was a piece of rope arranged in a noose on the carpet. The sight of it made her blood run cold.

Crawling, she searched for her phone, trying to ignore the pain. Finally, she found it underneath the armchair. She couldn't use her right hand, it was too painful. So, with her left, she entered her pin and went to her contacts.

Every name and number had been deleted from the list.

She slumped back against the wall and cried.

When she was spent of tears, she crawled upstairs to the bathroom. A bath had been run.

Did I do that?

She didn't think so. She needed to check the rest of the house.

She pushed her bedroom door open. On her bed lay Mum's scarf, which had been in her dressing table drawer, and the picture, taken down from the wall. The quilt had been turned back, something Dolores never did, and there was another card on her pillow. She picked it up. It was a picture of a mermaid. She turned it over. Written in that now familiar red scrawl was the word: *TSUNAMI.*

As she turned in rising panic, she was confronted by the masked intruder.

'Don't scream, or I'll slice your face off,' said the voice behind the mask. 'It's time for you and me to go on a little adventure.'

CHAPTER 14

LOST AT SEA

Dolores had rung Carly, just two rings then she'd hung up and Carly had immediately contacted her mum to go and check on her. She agreed to get there as quickly as she could, but she was at a friend's house and the next bus was in twenty minutes time. It was faster than Carly could have got there, so they could only hope it was another of Dolores' 'episodes'.

When Diane Barton arrived at the house, the front door was wide open. She quickened her step into the hallway.

'Hey, Dolores, it's Di. Are you there?'

There was no reply. Dreading what she might see, she stuck her head around the lounge door, but there was nobody in there.

She spotted the rope, 'What on earth…?'

She walked into the room, taking in the state of it. The settee was on its back, cushions scattered about. Dining room chairs were toppled on the floor behind it, ornaments smashed, bits of food everywhere. But it was the smell that almost knocked her off her feet. Stale vomit, and another vile stench she couldn't quite place.

'Dolores! It's me, diamond. Are you ok?'

The silence hung ominously while she tried to fathom what had happened. Maybe Dolores had got drunk and had been stumbling around. Diane couldn't entertain the other options.

Taking a deep breath, she pushed the kitchen door and went in. Nothing stood out as being unusual. The morning pots had been washed, apart from one mug. Hating herself for doing it, she opened cupboards, looking for the one with alcohol, looking for clues. She found one sticky bottle of liqueur, nothing else. On the draining board, there were no wine glasses, no tumblers. Closing the cupboards gently, mystified, she went back into the hallway. The coat Dolores always wore like a second skin was hanging there. So, where was she?

Holding on to the banister, Diane climbed the stairs and looked in the bedroom. On the bed was a picture of Marian, with a scarf laid out beside it. Not knowing whether it was the sight of her old friend, or the realisation that Dolores wasn't there, but she was overcome with desperate sadness. She sat on the bed, lifted the picture, held it to her chest and sobbed. There was a small card on the pillow, so small she had to squint to read the message: TSUNAMI. On the other side, a picture of a mermaid sprinkled with glitter, something a little girl would like. The word and the picture didn't sit right with her. Dolores had called for help and now she wasn't here. Diane reached into her handbag and took out her phone.

'Carly, have you heard from Dolores again?'

'No, Mum, why?'

'I'm at her house now, but she's not here. Her lounge stinks, the furniture is all over the place and there's blood and sick in the bathroom sink.'

'Shit the bed, Mum, what's going on?'

'I don't know, child, but the front door was wide open when I got here, and no sign of her.'

'Let me think. Oh God, you don't think she's gone back on the bottle, do you?'

'I did think that at first, but there's a card on the bed. It makes no sense to me. It says TSUNAMI on one side and there's a mermaid on the other.'

'A mermaid? Tsunami? Shit! Is it red writing?'

'Yes, red, and scribbly.'

'I'm not feeling good about this, Mum, not at all. I'm going to get off work and come over. Can you call the police? I think she might be in danger.'

'Yes, I'll do that. I think that's the right thing to do.'

'I'll be over as quick as I can.'

Diane rang off and tapped into her phone again.

'Emergency services, which service do you require?'

'I'm afraid I need to report a missing person.'

'How long has the person been missing?'

'We don't really know. She's not at home and we're worried.'

'When did you last see or hear from her?'

'Earlier today.'

'This line is for life-threatening emergencies. There isn't enough information to treat this as an emergency. I can't send an ambulance if she isn't there, and if she hasn't been missing for at least forty-eight hours it can't be a priority for the police. I'll give you the number of your local station. I suggest you ring them and explain what's happened.'

'Thank you, diamond. So sorry to take your time.'

Diane rang the number and waited.

'Hello, Swinton Police, how can I help?'

'I need to report a missing person.'

'Ok. What relation are you to them, and how long have they been missing?'

'I'm a family friend and they've gone missing sometime today.'

'Sometime today? What makes you think they're missing?'

'She phoned my daughter, let it ring twice, then hung up. We agreed that she'd do that if she was in danger but wasn't able to talk. When I got to her house, the front door was wide open and no sign of her. Furniture all over the place. Blood and vomit in the bathroom sink.'

'Mrs...?'

'Barton.'

'Mrs Barton, we get calls like this every day, and every day we get calls back to say the person was upset, drunk, angry, whatever, but they've turned up. Do you see what I'm saying?'

'Yes, I understand. But if you knew Dolores, you'd know this isn't like her.'

'Dolores? Hang on a minute. Dolores Walsh?'

'Yes, diamond, that's right.'

'She was in this morning. Spoke to her myself. She seemed a little – how can I put it? – confused.'

'Yes, she's not been well at all, been on medication, but she's convinced someone is posting notes and the like.'

'Yes, she said. I told her we couldn't act on the

information she had, and that stands. I'm really sorry.'

'But there's another note, and blood and such in the sink. Something's not right. We're really worried.'

'Look, Mrs Barton, the best I can do is send an officer round when one is available. I'll take your number and let you know when they're on the way. I suggest you leave everything as it is, make sure the door is locked and sit tight. Let us know immediately if she turns up in the meantime. Is that alright?'

'Yes, thank you. I appreciate it.'

Diane gave her number and hung up. She went downstairs and sat at the back of the living room, not wanting to be amongst the mess. She tried to dismiss thoughts of Dolores being in danger. With all her heart, she wanted to believe was that Dolores' meds had got the better of her, nothing more sinister than that.

CHAPTER 15

CAVE

Dolores opened her eyes, just enough. Her legs were bent at an awkward angle, her ankles tied. She had no shoes, and her hands were bound behind her back. She was lying on her right side, her cheek resting on rough ground beneath her. Shivering uncontrollably, she opened her eyes a little more and tried to get an idea of where she might be.

'Oh, awake are we now?'

Dolores stammered, 'Who are you? What do you want with me?'

'Now, that's a fine question to be asking on this lovely day.'

'I don't have a clue who you are. I think you may have the wrong person.' Dolores tried to believe her own words.

'Oh, I definitely have the right person. I'm one hundred percent sure of that.'

'I don't understand.'

'Ah, you will in time, but first I'm going to have a little fun with you.'

'Fun?'

'Well, it might not be fun for you, but, feck, I'll enjoy it.'

There was a scuffle in the corner of the room. It was dark, the only light coming from a small hurricane lamp next to her captor's chair. The cruel-voiced woman got up and shone the lamp into the far corner. More scuffling.

'Looks like you have a visitor.'

The light from the lamp followed a rat running along the side wall. Dolores wriggled frantically, trying to free herself from the ties, but they dug deeper into her. Her whimpers were pathetic, she knew, but it was all she had.

'I brought you where you belong, you sad piece of shite. Where you can die in this shit with vermin.'

Inner alarms exploded.

'You've got the wrong person. I've never done a thing wrong in my life.'

'Now, that's debatable, but I'm not here to talk about you. In fact, I have better places to be.'

Heavy boots crunched over gravel towards Dolores, that fearful mask loomed at her and she screwed her eyes tight shut. A gag was forced roughly around her mouth, then the monster left, taking the lamp and leaving Dolores in the dark. She heard the clunking of a lock.

There was no other sound apart from the rat scratching in the corner. Drawing her knees up as far as she could and using the wall behind her, she managed to sit up. The pain in her right arm was intense as the blood rushed to restore feeling.

The scratching eventually stopped, and Dolores drifted.

Mum, I'm haunted by a vision of you being sucked into a dark, salty void, of you swirling, taken by the deep, drowning, yet not dying. I imagine you half alive, spinning endlessly in a murky maelstrom, creatures clawing at you, sea water cutting into your eyes. Please, Mum, know that your girl loves you very much. All those times I made you feel bad when I asked why you'd left me, and you smiled bravely and told me how you'd loved me but you'd had to go. I never understood how you could leave us. I never got chance to tell you that I understand now, that you were poorly, mentally ill.

I wanted you to be so proud of me, I wanted to change the world, and now look at me.

There was a faint sound of voices, like children playing nearby. Desperately, Dolores tried to scream, but the sound that came out was a faint grunt. The voices faded and the quiet deafened her. Silence and pitch-dark were conspiring to make her lose her mind.

But wasn't I already halfway there?

Her father once told her the people who survive are the ones who stay calm, who make a plan. His voice rang out clearly: *Life will throw some rubbish at you, that's a given. It's how you deal with it that matters. You have to have a good mindset. Instead of thinking how hard-done-by you are, think about what you can do about it. You do that, Dolores, and you won't go far wrong in life.*

There had certainly been challenges, her life had been full of them, and she'd tried her best to overcome them. Her mother's mysterious disappearance, then her death: how could she get over that?

Carly says you don't, you just learn to live with it.

Learning to live with death was not easy, but she had tried. And now she had an even bigger challenge: trying to avoid her own death against what she could only see as impossible odds.

Fumbling about behind her, she felt for a sharp stone, something she could cut the ties with. The thought of what she might find made her nauseous, but she carried on, shuffling around on her bottom and feeling without seeing. This went on for what felt like hours, but the only thing she could find was gravel. Small rounded stones, nothing more. Kicking her legs out in frustration, she heard something fall behind her and she edged her way towards it using what little strength she had left. Stretching out, she felt a rough piece of wood and she winced as a splinter embedded in her finger. Ignoring it, she felt along the length of the plank and almost cried with joy as she felt the sharp jag of a nail. For a long time, she sat on the plank rubbing the rope along the nail until, eventually, she slumped forward, exhausted.

Where are you, my Carly? Are you worrying about me? I hope you believe I'm in danger and you try to find me, because I don't want to die, I really don't. I know we had loads of chats about the evils of this world, but it's our world and we have a place in it, my friend. We belong here, if only to annoy each other. All my rants about social media, plastic, eating meat, rubbish, manners, respect, they all seem futile now. None of it matters when you're about to go into the abyss, not knowing what's on the other side. I hope it's not the hell I imagine Mum to be in. I hope I can see her again, hold her, be held by her. Do you think I will, Carly? If I could, I'd gladly go now. But nobody knows, do they? Not for sure. We have this thing about Heaven being a floaty place where you get to be with all the people you ever loved. They wait for you and they lead you off to Paradise. But that's not the place in my nightmares. Come and find me, Carly, because I don't want to go there. If you save me, I'll be a better person, have kinder thoughts. Please look for me. I'm not that far from home.

CHAPTER 16

SWIMMING AGAINST THE TIDE

Diane Barton sat in the chair thinking if anything had happened to Dolores, she could never live with it. The girl had been through too much grief already for one so young, having her own mother desert her, then losing her to death. No one should have to go through all that at such a young age, it wasn't fair. *Maybe I should have protected you more, but how?* Looking around the room for clues, she felt helpless. All she wanted was for Dolores to burst through the door with a perfectly rational explanation, but that seemed like a fading possibility now.

The sharp shrill of the doorbell jerked her from her thoughts. She stood and shuffled to the front door, able to see the outline of Carly through the frosted glass. They fell into each other's arms as soon as the door was open and sobbed. Finally, they pulled away, wiping away tears but not the trauma.

'No news?' asked Carly, raising her eyebrows hopefully.

'I wish I could say yes, but I've not heard a thing.'

'Oh Mum, where is she? Who's got her?'

'Now Carly, we don't know that anyone's got her at all. You know how confused she's been. Maybe she's gone out to be somewhere quiet.'

'Yes, but she was convinced something was here in the house that time, that it had hurt her.'

'Her mind has been playing tricks on her lately, hasn't it? She doesn't seem to know what's real and what's not. You know she's got worse. I'm worried about her, of course, but I'm still hoping she's going to walk through that door and wonder what the fuss is about.'

Carly paced around the lounge, picking up a chair as she passed it.

'We've got to leave everything as it is, the police say. They'll send someone round as soon as they can.'

'Mum, I can't just stand here and wait for something to happen. I need to find her. What if this *thing* is real? What if she has been taken?'

'By a sea creature?'

Carly smiled. 'Seems unlikely. But what if someone *was* watching her and it wasn't all in her head? The card and the picture – what if she wasn't imagining stuff? Those dreams and the panic attacks and...'

'You said it. Dreams and panic attacks, Carly. The mind can play cruel tricks on you, especially when you're weak and vulnerable. Especially when you've not slept and certainly when you're bereaved.'

'I'm sorry, Mum. This must be so difficult for you.'

After some discussion, they agreed Diane would stay at the house and Carly would walk down to the police station to see if any more information had come to light, if, *God forbid*, anyone had been found injured, or worse.

Maybe the police had a record of what Dolores had said to them.

The desk sergeant looked up from his screen as Carly entered. She strode towards him, trying to give an air of confidence.

'I believe my friend was in earlier. Dolores Walsh.'

'Dolores Walsh? It rings a bell.' He thought for a moment: 'Ah yes, it was me she spoke to. How can I help you?'

'The thing is, she's not back and I can't just sit

there. I wonder if you can remember what she said?'

'Not back?'

'My mum rang earlier to report her missing. You said you'd send someone round.'

The telephone rang and made her jump.

The policeman answered it: 'Hello, Swinton Police Station, how can I help you?'

Carly waited anxiously until the officer had finished the call.

'Sorry about that. You were saying?'

'Dolores Walsh; she's still not back.'

'As I explained to your mum, people go missing every day. It's rare that they stay missing for long, for all sorts of weird and wonderful reasons.'

'I understand that. I also understand my friend, and she wouldn't make us worry like this.'

'As I remember, your friend seemed to be over-anxious, confused.'

'She's not been very well. I wonder if you can remember what she said?'

'I can't share that with you, but what I do remember is a little card with 'Sundown' written in red ink. She said it had been posted through her door.'

'There's another card at her house, same writing, same theme. We tried to explain it away, but for it to happen again, surely there has to be something in it?'

'I understand your distress, but we cannot spend any more time or resources on your friend until we have something more solid. Even if she went missing on her way home from here, it's only been about four hours, and with no real evidence, we can't do anything more than we already are.'

He didn't have to continue; Carly knew the score. She thanked him and walked out, not knowing what to do next, but knowing she couldn't go back to that house.

The air had turned colder, the daylight nodding its last farewell before giving in to darkness. If her friend wasn't missing, if she didn't feel so bereft, she would appreciate the beauty of an autumn sky displaying its reds, golds and lilacs for the briefest time before nightfall.

Leaving the concrete of the town behind, Carly took the steps down to the towpath. Trees blazed their colours proudly against the fading light, and the sight of them provoked tears. She quickly wiped them away and trudged through a beautiful canopy of boughs laden with the riches of a season bearing gifts of colour. For once, Carly looked up into their branches, instead of down at the litter and it occurred to her how much time she had wasted looking at the ugly things in life.

We only looked at life's ugliness because we wanted to put it right, Dee.

The sky was already beginning to turn a murky grey, the last glimmers of light settling on the horizon. Zipping up her coat, Carly quickened her step; she didn't want her mum to be dealing with two missing girls. At the next exit, she left the canal side and made her way back to Dolores' house. When she arrived, she tapped gently on the window.

Her mum looked somehow older without her trademark smile. 'Anything they could tell you?'

'Not a lot, only what they'd told you, but they mentioned another card. They didn't think it was important, but it's obvious that they're connected. "Sundown", this one said. That sounds like a threat to me'

'Yes, and the sea theme again. The sun goes down on the horizon. I don't like it.'

Carly thumped the side of her head. 'I can't think why they're connected, why they're threatening.'

'You mean apart from the obvious?' asked Diane.

'The obvious?'

'The sea. How Marian died. You don't think it could be that, do you?'

Dropping into the chair and pulling at her collar, Carly wiped a bead of sweat from her top lip.

'Are you alright, child? You gone pale.'

'Mum, what if it *is* connected? What if Marian didn't take her own life? When you think about it – and God knows we've done nothing else – why *would* Marian have killed herself when she knew how much her daughter had been through? Especially as she was terminally ill, and they didn't know how much time they had left. As a mother, you must know that doesn't sit right?'

'I've always doubted it, but the police seemed so convinced and there was nothing else to make us think otherwise. I suppose at the time we were all consumed with grief but, with the things that are happening now, yes, it does make me think there may be something else. Why would a woman like Marian choose to leave the daughter she had only recently been reunited with?'

CHAPTER 17

MURKY DEPTHS

The sound of the lock brought Dolores to her senses. She instinctively shuffled away from the plank.

'Hi honey, I'm home.' The voice of her attacker, definitely an Irish accent.

Even the soft light of the lamp made her wince, but she winced more when she saw the figure. The Grim Reaper, complete with hood and scythe. It was time.

'What, you're not pleased to see me?' Then, with a change in tone from almost gentle to downright vile: 'Now that could upset me just a bit, you snivelling little shit.'

With one swift kick delivered to her legs, Dolores slumped back onto her side. She writhed in agony, feeling each crunch of bone, each bruising of flesh, as the boot went in, first to her legs, then her back, her arms and one to the head which made her ears ring before the walls closed in.

'That's right, you silly bitch, play dead. You'll be there soon enough. I want to make you suffer some more, like I've had to suffer all my fecking life.'

'I don't understand. What have I done? How does my life have anything to do with yours?'

'Your mammy, she made a big mistake.'

'What do you mean?'

'It seems she got herself knocked up, dirty little slut. By her own brother.'

Dolores gasped. 'But she, she only had one child, and that was me.'

'One that you know of. I was the dirty little secret. She was put on a boat to Ireland, and I was handed over like a puppy as soon as I was born. Little whore never looked back. My father was her own feckin' brother!'

This was too much. Dolores cowered.

'She liked disappearing, didn't she? See, the fact she'd disappeared once before, left her *only* child,' the Grim Reaper did air quotes around *only*, 'That kind of helped me. Made the idea of suicide a little more believable, don't you agree?'

Realisation hit Dolores like a hammer. 'You killed my mum?'

'I did. And you're next, you little shit.'

'But why? Why would you kill her? Why would you want to kill me?'

'You don't get it, do you? All my life, since that half-wit who called himself my father left, all my life has been miserable. They were a bad bunch, the O'Sheas, always trouble, and my father was no different. Left my mother in poverty and me without a father. And where I live that makes you stand out.'

'I'm sorry,' was all Dolores could muster.

'Sorry, are you? You were brought up in a nice semi, with your nice daddy and his new woman. I was dragged up by an alcoholic. Then I found out you'd been reunited with your mammy; the mammy I should have had!'

'But don't you see that's not our fault! My mum was only a child herself, she had no choice. Surely you can see that?'

'You had what I wanted.'

Dolores was baffled. 'What you wanted? My mother left when I was a baby, then you killed her! What could I possibly have that you want?'

'Well now, all that is true, but *you* were never a misfit, were you? Your mother made me a misfit in a world where misfits don't survive well. You've had a good life. Look at you now, with your blonde hair and your little figure. That's what I want. I want normal.'

'But I can't give you normal.'

'No, but when I bash in that pretty little face of yours, it's going to make me feel so much better.'

Dolores whimpered, and this was enough to make the woman lunge at her. Desperately, Dolores lifted the wood from behind her and brought it down on her captor's head.

She couldn't stop what happened next.

When it was over, she scrambled out of the cellar, into the light.

CHAPTER 18

HOORAH, UP SHE RISES

Judging by the sky, it would soon be dark, and Dolores had no idea where she was. It was some sort of industrial estate: concrete, dirty and deserted. She needed to be as far away as possible from that place, that thing, and from the pain in her head. So, despite her body screaming at her to stop, she staggered on.

For now, she couldn't deal with her maelstrom of thoughts and emotions: she needed to be alone, to rest, to heal. She followed some steps down to a dirt track. It was going dark, but she wasn't scared. Nothing could be worse than the horror of the last few hours.

When her body could no longer carry her, she hid under an old disused railway bridge. There was no sound except for the faint hum of traffic in the distance and birds chirping the end of a day.

Dolores was disturbed, mid-nightmare, by a sniffing sound. She tentatively opened one eye to see a hairy creature pushing its nose into her face. She shook her head and let out a muffled cry.

'Bruno! Come on, boy.'

Not a creature from her nightmare then: a plain, ordinary dog. She heaved herself to a sitting position, as a woman appeared at her feet. The woman looked shocked, a bit scared.

'Are you alright, love? Do you need help?'

'I don't know. Not sure where I am.'

'You're in Salford, lovely. Is that where you live?'

Dolores thought about it. 'No.'

'Right. I'm phoning the police. Let's see if they can come and get you home.'

Dolores screeched and struggled until she was upright. She needed to escape from the gnawing feeling in her gut that something terrible had happened. She staggered away from the woman and the dog and kept going until she could no longer hear the woman's shouts.

The splash alerted the dog walker. She put Bruno on the lead and rushed ahead. Someone was in the water, splashing frantically; no doubt the girl she'd just seen. She ran as fast as she could, tied Bruno up, took off her shoes and coat, and jumped in. She knew the water here was shallow. She was almost able to touch the bottom, but not quite. The girl had gone under. She'd stopped thrashing. Time was critical. The woman dipped under the water and quickly found the body. She placed her elbow under the girl's chin and struggled to the side. By this time, an older couple had arrived. Between them they pulled and pushed the girl out, turning her onto her front and pressing into her back.

The dog walker heaved herself out of the water and caught her breath while the other lady called for an ambulance.

CHAPTER 19

WAITING FOR THE TIDE TO COME IN

By late evening, Carly had grown tired of waiting. She knew something bad had happened, could feel it. She couldn't just sit there and wait for news from the police; she had to be proactive.

'I'm going to ring the hospitals, Mum.'

'Do you think that's wise, Carly? What if...?' Her voice trailed off.

'What if something's happened to her? What if she's alone in a hospital bed, no ID, nobody knowing who the hell she is?'

'Oh Carly, that doesn't bear thinking about. I suppose it couldn't do any harm, though I do think you should leave all the ringing round to the police.'

'But they won't do it, will they? Not enough time has passed. And I can't wait, I just can't.'

Carly googled the number of the nearest hospital and rang, her stomach doing somersaults as she waited to be put through.

'Hello, Hope Hospital, what department please?'

'I'm not sure, but my friend is missing, and I wondered if she'd been brought in.'

'I'll put you through to A & E, love, hold on.'

The usual piped music grated more than ever as Carly waited to be connected.

'A & E.'

'I wondered if you've had a young woman admitted, late twenties?'

'Are you a relation?'

'I'm a very close friend. I'm probably the nearest she has to a next of kin.'

'Right. All I can tell you is that a young lady was brought in today. We have no ID as yet, so I can only suggest you contact your local police and speak with them. I can't give any further information or details over the phone.'

Carly's heart raced with both fear and joy. 'I understand. I'll ring them now.'

Shaking, she rang the number and held her breath as she waited for someone to answer.

'Swinton Police.'

'It's me again, Carly. We were in earlier about my friend, Dolores Walsh.'

'Yes, I remember. Look, it's still less than twenty-four hours –'

But before he could finish, Carly cut in, 'Yes, I know, but a girl has been admitted to Hope, no ID. Can you chase it, please? They can't give me any more details.'

'I can hear how distressed you are, Carly, so I'll do that for you. Can I get back to you on this number?'

'Yes, you can. Thank you. Thank you very much.'

Carly and her mum waited an eternity before the phone rang.

'Hello, this is Carly Barton.'

'Hello Carly, it's PC Davis from Swinton Police.'

Just those words made Carly fearful. 'Is there anything you can tell me?'

'That's why I'm ringing. There is a young lady who fits Dolores' description currently in ICU at Hope Hospital. It would be a help if you could tell me who her nearest relative is, so I can notify them, and they can identify her.'

'Identify her? She's not – ?'

'No love, but she's in a bad way, and they need to find her next of kin.'

Carly gave the name and address of Patricia, Dolores' almost-step-mum, although she and

James had never married. After waiting an agonising five minutes, Carly rang Patricia herself.

'Hi Patricia, it's Carly, Dolores' friend.'

'Carly? Blimey! How are you love?'

'I'm fine, but Dolores may not be. She went missing and a girl has been found and brought in to Hope. It may be her. The police will ring soon, but I wondered if I could meet you at the hospital?'

'Why didn't you let me know she was missing?'

'I'm really sorry. We didn't know for sure she *was* missing until now. I didn't want to worry you.'

'Well, we've not got time to talk now. I'll meet you there. I'm leaving right now.'

'I can't thank you enough, Patricia. I'll see you there.'

Carly called a taxi. It was quite a way to go, and she could ill afford it, but this could be life or death. It would take over an hour on the bus and she couldn't cope with the stress.

She arrived at the hospital within half an hour and made her way up to the ICU. The receptionist told her Patricia had arrived, but she couldn't allow Carly through as it was 'next of kin only'. Carly was frantic, but she understood. The receptionist spoke to one of the nurses, who would let Patricia know Carly had arrived. Carly took a seat and waited for her to come out. When Patricia finally emerged, blowing her nose into a tissue, Carly sprang from her chair as if it was on fire.

'Is it...? Is she...?'

'Yes, it's her. She's bad.'

'Can I see her? Do you think they'd let me?'

'You wouldn't want to, love. It's too much.' Patricia blew into her hankie again and sat down.

'I'm so sorry,' said Carly.

'Me, too. I know how close you were – sorry – *are*. We'd drifted since her dad died, but I still thought of her as my own, always did.' Patricia sobbed, and Carly put an arm around her shoulder.

'She always speaks very fondly of you, Patricia. I know she felt guilty for the stress she put you through when she was younger.'

'None of that matters now. I just hope she pulls through.'

'Oh God, I've not even asked! Where was she? What's happened to her?' Carly was suddenly desperate to know.

'She was pulled from the canal by some dog walkers.'

'She fell in the canal?'

'Yes, but I don't think it's as simple as that. She's a mess. Her face is all cut, and she has broken bones. She's in a bad way.'

'Oh, please God, let her pull through.'

EPILOGUE

One Year Later.

The creature leaned into her, sneering. It smelt rancid, of something like stale alcohol or fish, perhaps a mix of the two. Dolores turned her head and tried to crawl away, but she was tethered to the ground like a dog. She pulled at the rope...

A muffled scream woke Joe. Dolores had tugged the covers over to her side of the bed. She was sobbing and thrashing, so he did what he always did – held her until she was calm.

'It's ok, Dee, you're safe.'

'Joe?'

'Who else?'

Dolores hugged him tightly and he stroked her back.

'It came for me again, Joe, the creature.'

'Your brain will soon catch up and realise the creature has gone. There's nothing to worry about now, Dee.'

'I think it – I mean *she* – is haunting me from

her grave, and why wouldn't she, Joe?'

'What do you mean, why wouldn't she?'

'I killed her. My own sister!'

'We've been over this a thousand times, Dee. She kidnapped you, put you through that terrible ordeal and was about to kill you.'

'I know, but I can't help thinking what might have been.' Dolores was sobbing.

'We can't think like that, Dee, you *know* this,' said Joe, rubbing her back.

'I can't help it. If only Mum had told me about her, she could still be alive now. They could both still be alive.'

'It's so, so sad, but there was nothing more you could have done. Your mum had her reasons for not telling you.'

'Reasons we'll never know, now. Her parents are dead, Frank's dead. We'll never know the full story, only what others in the family have said.'

'And they're only speculating. She hadn't told a soul she was pregnant. She never told anyone why she spent so long in Ireland. They only had Frank's story,' said Joe.

'It's just so bloody sad,' said Dolores. 'All those young lives ruined because of their parents' decisions.'

'I think you need to try and put Shauna to bed

now, Dee. So, it isn't easy, but you know in your heart you've done nothing wrong. You are the sweetest, most gentle person I've ever met.'

'I killed her, Joe.'

'In self-defence! What she did was terrible.'

'But she was troubled. I can't imagine how she must have felt, knowing she was the product of rape. To know she was given away and kept secret for all those years.'

'It was the only way, back then. Your mum was so young and vulnerable, she did as she was told.'

'Then she blocked it out. I wish I'd have known sooner.'

'If only?' asked Joe.

During therapy, Dolores had explored the secrets and shame that had been a theme in her family since her grandparents' time and, no doubt, for generations before. She had come to understand she had no control over what had gone before.

She had wasted too much time living in fear. The future was a new voyage, one she wanted to share with Joe. She took his hand and rested it on her stomach.

Right on cue, they felt the slightest kick.

ACKNOWLEDGEMENTS

A huge thank you to CJ Harter (cjharterbooks.co.uk) my kind, patient, and always professional editor. Without your help, this book would still be stored as a document on my pc.

Thank you to South Manchester Writers' Workshop who gave valuable feedback for my first drafts. Your successes as published authors are testament to your talents.

Made in the USA
Middletown, DE
25 April 2023